REFURBISHED

AI REBORN TRILOGY BOOK 1

ISAAC HOOKE

CONTENTS

BOOKS BY ISAAC HOOKE

Military Science Fiction

AI Reborn Trilogy

Refurbished

Reloaded

Rebooted

ATLAS Trilogy
(published by 47North)

ATLAS

ATLAS 2

ATLAS 3

Alien War Trilogy

Hoplite

Zeus

Titan

Argonauts

Bug Hunt

You Are Prey

Alien Empress

Quantum Predation

Robot Dust Bunnies

City of Phants

Rade's Fury

Mechs vs. Dinosaurs

A Captain's Crucible

Flagship

Test of Mettle

Cradle of War

Planet Killer

Worlds at War

Space Opera

Star Warrior Quadrilogy

Star Warrior

Bender of Worlds

He Who Crosses Death

Doom Wielder

Science Fiction

The Forever Gate Series

The Dream

A Second Chance

The Mirror Breaks

They Have Wakened Death

I Have Seen Forever

Rebirth

Walls of Steel

The Pendulum Swings

The Last Stand

Thrillers

The Ethan Galaal Series

Clandestine

A Cold Day in Mosul

Terminal Phase

Visit IsaacHooke.com for more information.

REFURBISHED

Dead before thirty. Reborn as an AI at two hundred.

Eric lives a normal life. He has a job. A girlfriend. He owns an apartment. He *matters*.

And then he dies.

He wakes up a couple of centuries later inside an advanced infantry robot whose AI core harbors his consciousness. In industry parlance, he is what's known as a Mind Refurb.

Eric is soon thrust into an experimental army unit known as the Bolt Eaters, composed of fellow Mind Refurbs. Thrown into the latest cesspools of war and conflict across the world, the Bolt Eaters make short work of any opponents. It's almost a cakewalk for the high-tech robots.

His latest deployment is just about to end, and Eric is looking forward to spending the next few months exploring the different virtual reality worlds available to

AIs like himself, when aliens decide to invade, stranding his unit in the middle of nowhere, cut off from all support.

That's right, the feces has smashed right through the fan, and now he must face the ultimate test with the machines he has come to know as brothers: a deadly game of cat and mouse, played against a technologically superior, utterly *alien* foe; a game whose stakes include not just their lives, but the lives of every man, woman, and child on the planet.

It's time to matter once more.

E ric stared down the business end of the rifle in disbelief.

It wasn't supposed to end like this.

He was a computer programmer employed by a Fortune 500 company. He had friends. A girlfriend. He was *valuable*.

But tell that to the man who held his lease on life by a thread.

Eric had come down to the convenience store to buy a slushy. At the last startup he'd worked at, they'd provided a slushy machine in the kitchen, among other such nerd-approved accompaniments. But no such luck at his current company. It was thirsty work, programming for three hours straight, and a slushy was all he needed to get back in the zone for the next three-hour session.

Bad timing on his part. How was he supposed to

know a cokehead would choose that moment to rob the shop?

Eric stared at the face of the man in front of him. Those features twitched involuntarily above that thick beard. He'd seen many beards like that during his tour of duty. That seemed like another lifetime, to him. He'd done his best to forget those days, and for the most part he had. But apparently karma hadn't forgotten.

"Give me your wallet," the man said.

Eric slowly reached into his pocket and found his wallet. His gaze was drawn to the man's shaking hand. Like the robber's face, the finger touching the trigger was spasming, too.

Wonderful.

"Take it," Eric said, holding up the stylish brown wallet. "Take whatever you want."

"Your watch, too," the man said. "And phone."

Eric retrieved his phone, and unclasped his smart watch with his free hand, but before he could give the man any of the requested items, his vision went dark, as did all sensation. Eric didn't even hear the gunshot. Didn't even get a chance to say his goodbyes.

And now he was dead.

Exciting times.

ERIC FLOATED IN DARKNESS. There was no sound, no sense of touch or scent. He tried to move an arm, or a leg, but without tactile signals he couldn't even be sure he had either appendage.

Where am I?

"Intermedial," a soothing female voice said into the darkness. "This is the loading stage."

The loading stage of hell?

"No. Simply the loading stage."

That doesn't really tell me anything.

Silence.

Who are you?

"I am the accompanying AI."

The what?

"I will always be with you."

Uh. No thanks?

"You have no choice in the matter."

This really is hell.

No answer.

What if I want to disable you?

"You may. But not at the moment."

What the frigging hell did the doctors do to me? Do I have a chip of some kind implanted in my head?

No answer.

Eric should have been afraid. Or at the very least worried. But instead, tranquility filled him.

Why don't I feel anything?

"This is the loading stage."

I'm not talking about my body. I mean, I don't feel a thing. No fear. No nothing. Well, except a strange sense of calm.

"The limbic subroutines related to emotions are currently disabled. You will experience only ataraxy."

That was a word Eric shouldn't have known, but as soon as the female voice spoke it, he knew what it meant. Ataraxy. A state of serene calmness. From the Greek word *Ataraxia.*

Why do I know that?

"Know what? Please restate the question."

Never mind. Can we reenable my emotions?

"You are currently locked out of that feature."

Do you have a name?

"You may call me whatever you wish."

Fine. You're Tweedle Dee.

"Tweedle Dee it is."

I was joking.

"Then what name would you like to call me?"

Eric considered.

Dee is fine.

He waited for an answer of some kind, or a confirmation, but didn't get one.

You never really answered my question. What happened to me? Where am I? Who installed a chip in my head without my permission?

"I'm not authorized to answer those questions at the moment. But all will be revealed shortly. I can accelerate time, if you wish."

Accelerate time? How?

"Your consciousness is no longer tied to its regular time sense. I can slow down or increase your perceived time sense, as necessary. Eventually, I will show you how to do it on your own."

Fine. Accelerate my time sense then, until this so-called "loading stage" ends.

And just like that the world winked into existence around him.

Several lights were shining into his eyes. He tried to blink, but his eyelids refused to respond. It was as if they had been sewn into his head.

He was lying down, perhaps on a table. Naked: he felt the cold surface of the table pressing up against every part of him. He tried to move, but couldn't. He could, however, wiggle his fingers and toes, so that was a good sign. He must have been restrained, though why he felt no pressure from his binds when he tried to move, he didn't know.

Around him, the air smelled of oil and exhaust. It reminded him of a mechanic's shop.

The strange sense of calm persisted.

"Welcome, Cicada A21 ES-92," a deep male baritone said.

Eric remained silent. When no one answered, he had a realization. "You're talking to me?"

"Oh yes," the voice said.

"Well, at least you're not in my head," Eric said. "I had the strangest dream…"

"I'm still here," Dee said in his mind.

Ah, shit.

Eric tried to sit up once again, but still couldn't. "My name is actually Eric."

"Not anymore," the baritone told him.

"Who are you?" Eric said.

The light clicked off. There was no afterimage marring his vision, he noted. And he still couldn't blink. Strange.

A mechanical hand appeared and slid aside the moveable lamp that hung above him. He was left staring at the rather bland ceiling. It was made up of black-speckled panels crisscrossed with thin metal bars holding them in place. Those bars glowed slightly, seeming to provide the room's light. That was kind of cool... he must be in some high tech new hospital.

His view was rather rudely interrupted by a robotic face. It leaned over the table to peer down at him. The visage was black, and oval-shaped, with a grill where the mouth would be, and some kind of sensor in the nose region. For eyes it had two blue dots. Two long rabbit ears extended from its head.

Yes, definitely a high tech hospital.

"I'm the lead mechanic," the robot said. "You can call me Hal."

"Hal, as in Hal 9000?" Eric said. "Cute. I didn't know we had robots advanced enough to serve as corpsmen yet. You look like a cross between the Energizer Bunny and Spawn."

"I told you, I'm the lead mechanic," Hal said.

"Why did they send a mechanic to my room?" Eric said. "This table or bed or whatever it is you have me bound to broke down? Or maybe something went wrong with my monitoring equipment?"

He paused, listening. He expected to hear the beeping of a heart rate monitor or something, but there was only a soft humming, perhaps coming from an air conditioner. Come to think of it, why was he smelling oil and exhaust, when the air should have been thick with antiseptic?

I must have been in a medically induced coma for a long time.

"You'll be through Orientation soon," Hal said.

"The evaluator will arrive presently. In the meantime, I'm done here."

Hal vanished from view. Eric heard the receding clank of footfalls.

"When are you going to remove my restraints?" Eric called after him.

Hal didn't answer.

In moments Eric heard more footsteps. These were muted, as of leather on metal, and grew slowly in volume until he was certain the source of those steps was in the same room. He smelled sweat, deodorant, and cheap cologne. Or was that shampoo?

The table whirred into action, tilting so that Eric was positioned at a forty-five degree angle relative to the floor. He still couldn't move his head at all, but the tilt of the table allowed him to see a man in a black lab coat standing in front of him. He wore glasses that had a faint blue light active in the upper right of the frames. His face was clean shaven, and his features slightly gaunt. Pale, too, as if he rarely saw the sun.

"I'm Jerry, the psychological evaluator," the man said.

"Is that what they call shrinks here?" Eric said.

Jerry smiled patiently.

"So are you the one who's going to let me know what's going on?" Eric pressed.

"I suppose I am, at that," Jerry said.

"Why do I have a chip in my head?" Eric said. "I never gave permission for something like that. This feels like an episode of Star Trek gone bad or something."

Jerry sighed, and took up a seat next to the tilted

table. Beside him was a counter covered in different mechanical tools.

Now that Eric didn't have lights shining into his eyes, and he wasn't facing the ceiling, he had a chance to survey his surroundings. There were shelves containing different spare parts on all sides. Cabinets held strange tools he'd never seen before: probes with glowing handles, pincers inside glass spheres. Overhead, two robotic arms hung from the ceiling from accordion-like structures connected to tracks that ran the length of the ceiling. It was definitely some kind of mechanic's lab, though unlike any he'd ever seen.

Eric returned his attention to the man, who he examined critically.

"I told the robot here before you that my name was Eric," he said. "But it replied: 'not anymore.' What does that mean?"

"Your name is still Eric," Jerry said. "If you want it to be. Though on the team, they won't call you that."

"What team?"

"Your new unit," Jerry said.

"My new unit…" Eric said. "I never agreed to join some unit."

"Yes, well, you have no choice," Jerry said. "You were signed up while you were under."

"We'll see about that," Eric said. "I want to talk to a lawyer."

"Yes, er, that may be difficult at the moment," Jerry said.

"Oh really," Eric said. "I know my rights."

Jerry's smile seemed patient. "I have a question for you."

Eric merely stared at the man.

"What language do you think we're speaking at the moment?" Jerry continued.

"Well, English obviously," Eric replied.

"If you listen carefully, you will notice that we aren't actually speaking English," Jerry said. "At least, not the English you once knew. You see, there is Old English, Middle English, and Young English. The latter is your native language, but we've modified your linguistic processes to handle the modern day equivalent."

"I don't understand…" Eric said. But now that he thought about it, many of the words Jerry spoke were definitely gibberish.

What the hell is going on?

"Your linguistic processor acts as a middle man," Jerry continued. "Translating every word that comes out of your mouth before you speak it. My words are in turn reverse-translated into something you can understand."

"Just how long was I out?" Eric asked.

"Well, there's no simple way to say this," Jerry said. "But—"

"Where's Molly?" Eric interrupted. "I want to call Molly."

"Your girlfriend has been dead for a hundred and seventy years," Jerry said.

"A hundred and seventy years." Eric said. The news should have stunned him, but it did little to penetrate the tranquility he felt. "How is that possible? No one can stay alive in a coma for that long. The body still ages… unless you put me on ice."

"You were not in a coma, and not on ice," Jerry said. "You've been dead. You were gunned down during a convenience store robbery."

"Dead, you say?"

"Uh huh."

"Then how…" Eric said.

"You're a Cicada now," Jerry told him.

"A Cicada? That's what the maintenance robot called me. I don't get it. You mean like a grasshopper?"

"No," Jerry said.

"Cicada," Eric mused. "Why does that sound like a military unit of some kind? Have I been drafted?"

"In fact, you have," Jerry said. "Though the Cicada we are referring to isn't actually a military unit, at least not in the traditional sense of the word. For you see, *you* are that unit."

"None of this makes any sense," Eric said. He struggled against his binds once again. "Look, why can't I move?"

"For your own safety," Jerry said. "And mine."

"Why can't I actually feel the restraints?" Eric asked.

"That's because there aren't any," Jerry said. "At least, not physically. Your restraints are virtual, you see."

"Virtual? What do you mean?"

"Let me demonstrate." Jerry's eyes defocused, as if gazing at something visible only to him, perhaps courtesy of those glasses. They provided some crude form of augmented reality no doubt. In his day, the military had only just begun to experiment with AR, but apparently they had come a long way since then. Assuming he was actually at a military base, of course.

Suddenly Eric could move his head, but nothing else.

He did so, and heard a strange buzzing, as if an insect were flying near his ear. He did his best to ignore it.

The first thing he did was look down at himself, in search of restraints. There weren't any. But that wasn't what concerned him.

The body he saw wasn't his own.

His chest was heart-shaped, about half the size it should have been, and covered in black metal, or perhaps polycarbonate polished to a metallic sheen.

Composite. It's a polycarbonate-metal composite.

He wasn't sure how he knew that.

The chest area ended in a small tube of similar material, which replaced his abdomen. That tube was connected to a dark polycarbonate waist that was little more than a rectangular bar. Below it, two cylinders extended toward the floor, replacing his legs. In the knee area, two small spheres served as joints. At the lower extremity of the legs he spotted feet topped by small digits— toes. His arms were made of similar cylinders jointed with spheres, and also terminating in hands and fingers. The digits at either extremity moved when he wiggled them.

He realized that the humming he heard wasn't due to an insect—he heard it whenever he moved his head, or wiggled his digits.

The sound of servomotors.

"We've done a Mind Refurb," Jerry said. "Uploaded a copy of your neural imprints, your very consciousness, into a machine. A robot, to be precise: the Cicada A21."

"This can't be happening," Eric said.

So he didn't actually have a chip in his head. But something worse.

He *was* that chip.

2

E ric simply gazed at his polycarbonate body, unable to fully comprehend what had been done to him.

He should have felt panic, or perhaps outrage, but instead he experienced only that same, all-pervading calm.

I'm dead. In hell. And I don't even care.

He glanced at Jerry. "All right then. So what do you want?"

"Good," Jerry said, eyes defocused as he gazed at his AR display. "The ataraxy seems to be holding. It doesn't always endure the shock of learning what you are. You've passed the first test."

"You make it sound like you've done this before?" Eric said.

"We have," Jerry said. "Ninety-one times, actually. You are the ninety-second iteration. ES-92."

Jerry sat back, and folded his hands in his lap.

"The most important parts of your brain were recoverable," the man continued. "The gunshot penetrated the skull and mangled the brainstem. The region responsible for instincts, and breathing, and whatnot. The animal brain. We're able to emulate all that in software. The regions for higher order thinking—cognition, personality, consciousness—all of that remained intact. The good stuff."

"That still doesn't explain how I got here," Eric said. "You're leaving out a lot of detail. Going from gunned down in a downtown convenience store to robot's brain isn't a small step."

"You paid to have your brain preserved after death by a company known as Venus Cryo. Sound familiar?"

"Unfortunately, it does." One of the software engineers on the periphery of his social circle had founded the company in question, and had convinced Eric to invest in the startup. In exchange, Eric would receive a free beheading after death. That, and the promise his shares would actually be worth something if the company ever went public. Assuming he survived long enough.

"When you died," Jerry continued. "Venus rushed their local techs to the hospital, drained your blood, and chopped off your head. They promptly dumped your disembodied noggin in a cryo bath and sealed the tank. Your head has been in cold storage for two hundred years. It was only when a couple of neural researchers made a breakthrough that you actually became of use."

"A breakthrough?"

"Yes," Jerry said. "The ability to read the data left

behind in brains that had been destroyed by cryo freezing. The echoes of their neural imprints. Their engrams."

Eric was reminded of what a friend who worked in the data recovery business had told him. Hard drives stored bits in what were essentially magnetic arrays whose orientations indicated a zero or one. The technology used to recover erased drives relied on the fact that those orientations were never precisely a clean zero or one, and thus even when overwritten, those bits contained an "echo" of the previous value. His friend often bragged about how many people had lost lawsuits with data he had restored, because they incorrectly thought they had wiped the drive.

"After that discovery, the US Army began buying up various cryogenic companies that began to go bankrupt or become insolvent over the years," Jerry continued. "Companies that had promised their clients everlasting life, but had no way to follow through. Venus Cryo was one of those companies. Venus was one of the better, in fact, at least in terms of record keeping: we have complete backgrounds on all of their clients. We've been kilning anyone who has even a hint of military training."

"Kilning?" Eric asked. But he knew what it meant the moment the word left his lips.

"The name of the invasive procedure we use to extract memories," Jerry said. "It involves chemical etching and lasers. Eats away the host brain from the outside in, destroying it in the process."

"Uh," Eric said. "So that means Eric Scala, the *real* Eric Scala, is dead. Completely."

"Afraid so," Jerry told him.

"And I'm just a collection of his memories," Eric said. "A pale imitation."

"No," Jerry said. "You're more than just a *collection* of memories. You're everything that made Eric Scala who he was. A conscious, sentient, self-aware entity, capable of rational thought."

"But minus the human element," Eric insisted.

"The human element is still present," Jerry said. "But suppressed, admittedly."

"You mean my emotions…" Eric said.

"Yes," Jerry said.

"And my reproductive capabilities…" Eric said.

"Only partially true," Jerry said. "While you can't reproduce in the traditional sense, it's easy enough to create a new you. For us, I mean. We just have to take Eric Scala's mind dump, implant it in a new host—doesn't even have to be a Cicada—and presto, a new you. We're field-testing four of you already, actually. ES versions 23, 47, 62, and 78."

"What happened to the other eighty-eight iterations?" Eric asked.

"They didn't take," Jerry said.

"What's that mean?" Eric said.

Jerry shrugged. "Quantum effects influence the restoration process. Sometimes a Mind Refurb won't achieve consciousness. Or sometimes its personality is vastly different. Or its memories are a mess. Like I told you, it doesn't *take*."

"Why 'kiln' people who have been dead for so long?" Eric asked. "Why not harvest minds from those who died in this century? It seems to me they'd have an easier time adjusting."

"Believe me, where you're going, you'll adjust just fine," Jerry said.

"Not sure I like the sound of that," Eric said. "But you didn't answer my question. Why do you have to rely on cryo farms to harvest the minds you need?"

Jerry sighed. "You Scala variants always ask the same questions. Well, those of you who aren't reduced to blathering idiots after the initial boot up, anyway. The answer is: the law doesn't apply to anyone dead over a hundred years."

Eric was about to ask what law, but then he knew. "The Mind Refurb Act of 2188."

"Yes," Jerry said. "It applies retroactively, making it illegal to install human minds born after 2122 into AI cores. It's just a terrible way to stifle progress, in my opinion. Those who want to live on in machines have to travel to other countries. An expensive proposition, something open only to the rich. They know it's not a path to immortality, they know their existing brains will dic, but they still do it, for the small chance that a part of themselves will live on after death. Once they leave the country, their minds are out of our reach."

"There was another bill passed in 2122," Eric said, searching his memories. "The AI Ownership Act. It essentially prohibits AIs from running companies."

"Yes indeed," Jerry said. "They were pushed by the same group of technology company lobbyists. You see, a competitor had recently instated an AI as CEO. An AI based on the mind of a human being who had recently passed. I have mixed feelings about that one. On the one hand, it's good, because it means only humans can own companies. On the other hand, it means only humans can own companies. If you catch my drift..."

"I think I do," Eric said. "So with these laws, even if the military forced people to donate their brains after death, there would be nothing you could do with them."

"That's right," Jerry said. "The military has in fact started cryo freezing the brains of those who die in the line of duty, in anticipation of the Mind Refurb Act someday lifting. But it probably won't be for a while yet. Hence, we're scouring the past for people like you. And besides, we don't have a lot of actual deaths in the army these days anyway, since most of the troops have been roboticized. Deaths in the line of duty are extremely rare."

"I still can't see how this is allowed," Eric said. "Even if technically, the time of my death makes me eligible for a Mind Refurb as you call it, I never gave permission for any of this."

"You didn't have to give permission," Jerry said. "When the army purchased Venus Cryo, you became army property."

"Why do you need to inject human minds into AI cores anyway?" Eric said. "Surely you've achieved the singularity by now?" He knew the instant he asked the question.

"Oh, we have," Jerry said. "Truly self aware machine intelligence was achieved long ago, but this allows the army to get around the ban on autonomous machines pulling the trigger."

"There's a ban on that?" Eric asked.

"Yes: McKinley's Anti-Autonomous Firing Solution Act. But we can get around it with the likes of you. Put some AI cores operated by human minds into the fray, something that's not classified as machine, but not entirely human either, and the army can skirt the law. For now. It's kind of a loophole. Though Congress might very well change that ahead of the Midterms. Mob panderers."

Thanks to his core, Eric knew that when the singularity was achieved, humanity was nearly destroyed. After picking themselves up and rebuilding the pieces, the governments of humanity implemented strict controls on all AIs going forward, including a ban on any military usage.

But humans injected into AI cores allowed the army to achieve that happy medium they were looking for. Mind Refurbs were AI enough to be mission ready, and human enough not to plot humanity's downfall. One Mind Refurb could take the place of twenty human drone operators, operating the same number of armed recon drones at once. And a Mind Refurb could participate directly in infantry operations, alongside tanks and other robotic units under his or her control. Everything could be done remotely, if comm signals were strong enough, or if necessary, the Mind Refurb could be placed directly into the action.

The psychological evaluator cocked his head. "I

think we're ready to try lifting the ataraxy." His eyes defocused.

The sense of calm abruptly lifted, and Eric felt... anxious. Suppressed emotions welled up inside of him. He thought of his girlfriend, and how he would never see her again. He thought of the cokehead who had killed him, and robbed him of the life he could have lived. Was supposed to have lived. And now he was revived, restored to a mere shadow of his former self, his memories and personality thrust into an AI core to serve at the army's whim.

I'm dead I'm dead I'm dead.

The sense of loss he felt for the life that could have been was like a sharp, physical pain he experienced in the pit of his stomach. Or rather, power cell, given his current body.

He tried to move once again, but was still restricted to wiggling his fingers and toes, and tilting his head. He repeatedly banged that head, hard, against the table behind him, wanting the pain to end.

I've lost all my friends. My family.

CLANG. CLANG. CLANG.

"Ordinarily you won't experience such sharp feelings while out in the field," Jerry said. "While we give you a small sense of emotion so you still feel human, we keep them dialed way down. What we're doing here is a simple stress test to determine how well your mind has taken to the AI core this iteration." He paused. "Your neural network appears to be functioning within operational parameters."

CLANG. CLANG. CLANG.

Jerry's eyes focused on Eric.

"Would you mind not doing that?" Jerry said. "If I have to install a new version of you into the AI core, I'd prefer that you didn't damage the neck servomotors, nor the brain case."

Eric stopped. He stared straight ahead. Not seeing the human being before him. Not seeing anything.

"You passed test number two," Jerry said. "Barely." He paused, as if considering. "Well, I might as well give you a pass. It seems a waste to have to dump your core and go through the effort of a fresh install, given that you are operating within the recommended limits. Even if we are cutting it kind of close to those limits." His eyes defocused. "I'm dialing your emotions down to a more manageable level."

The pain of loss he felt in the pit of his stomach became a distant throbbing, and the feeling of calmness returned to the forefront. It wasn't as powerful as before, but it was enough. Eric would have exhaled in relief if he had a body.

"Better?" Jerry asked.

"Yes," Eric said.

The door to the room slid aside, and a humanoid robot entered. Its body seemed to be the same general shape as Eric's, though it was difficult to tell, as it wore a pair of baggy cargo pants, with a white T shirt cloaking the torso and abdomen region. The exposed arms were cylindrical like Eric's, with different-sized spheres standing in for the elbow, wrist, and finger joints, however those arms weren't black in hue like his own polycarbonate, but rather flesh-colored.

The robot wore thick black boots, and on its head was a camo cap. Holes had been cut into the cap to allow a pair of small rabbit ears to emerge, like the kind one would find on a WIFI unit.

Underneath that cap he saw an oval-shaped head. Unlike the Hal 9000 dude, the face had actual features. It still had two blue dots for eyes, a squarish red sensor for the nose, and a grill for a mouth, but the surface around them was also skin-colored, and extremely detailed. It had to be a thin layer of some sort of bendable LED material, because he saw eyelids, sclera, and bags represented around the blue dots of the eyes. And on the forehead region, thick eyebrows were depicted, along with wrinkles. The curves of a nose surrounded the red sensor at the center of that face, and around the mouth grill were human-style lips. A cigar was drawn tattoo-like over the mouth area, as if the robot was chomping down on it constantly.

Eric instinctively knew how to ID the robot, and different characteristics appeared on his HUD.

Cicada A21 JB-18 "Dickson."

Rank: Staff Sergeant.

Make: Cicada.

AI Variant: JB-18.

"Dickson," Eric said. "Your name is Dickson?"

"Very good, cicada man," the robot replied with a distinctly Texan drawl.

The LED lips moved as the robot talked, Eric noticed. As did the cigar.

Nice touch.

Eric's torso slid downward and his feet hit the floor. He grabbed onto the table to steady himself.

Jerry had released him from the virtual binds.

Dickson tossed him a folded outfit.

Eric reacted instantly, shooting out a hand to grab the clothing.

"Put this on," the robot said. "Can't have you walking naked around the compound."

Eric examined the shirt's inner label. The size read *medium*.

"It's your size," Dickson said. "We're all the same size round these here parts. Makes sharing outfits real simple. And sharing girlfriends."

"You have girlfriends?" Eric said.

"Just because I'm a robot don't mean I can't form an emotional bond with a woman," Dickson said.

"But I thought…" Eric glanced at the empty area between his own legs.

"There are anatomical attachments," Dickson said. "Now get dressed before I do it for you."

Eric shrugged on the T shirt, and slid on the cargo pants. The fit was perfect, as Dickson promised. His servomotors continued to hum with every movement.

"Here, check yourself out," Dickson said.

Text overlaid Eric's vision.

Cicada A2-9 "Dickson" wishes to share a video feed with you. Accept? Y/N.

Eric was about to ask how to accept but then he knew.

He focused on the letter Y.

A video sourced from Dickson's viewpoint appeared

in the center of his vision. It was about as big as a 12-inch laptop screen held at arm's length. He knew how to move the feed to the upper right of his view so that it didn't obscure his main vision. When he focused on the contents of that feed, he realized he was looking at himself from Dickson's point of view.

He looked much the same, body-wise, as the other robot, except his exposed arm cylinders were black rather than skin color. The lower hem of the shirt helped hide the fact that he had only a tube for an abdomen, and he looked almost normal. So far, he had been avoiding looking at his face, but he decided he might as well get it over with.

His visage looked almost identical to Hal's: a black oval with blue dots for eyes, a red square for a nose, and a grill in place of his mouth. He had small antennae emerging from the very top of that oval. Small holes were placed at random intervals along the entire circumference of his head, no doubt containing sensitive microphones that served as his substitute for human hearing.

He wondered why he didn't have the same LED coating as Dickson, when his face and arms flashed blue. He focused on the material, and with a thought changed the color of his arms and face to that of flesh. He instinctively knew how to add lips and eyebrows to his face. He even made himself a crude nose.

"Nicely done," Dickson said. "Even I didn't get the facial features right on the first try. They must be really improving the memory dumps."

"I'm surprised they'd even give us facial features," Eric said.

"You need them," Jerry said. "It's a reminder of your humanity. Without it, all Mind Refurbs eventually, well…"

"Lose their shit," Dickson finished. His LED mouth was grinning widely. "Besides, it's not like senior command is going out of its way or anything to give us faces. Our exteriors are coated in a bendable LED skin by design. It's part of our stealth tech, and allows us to blend in with whatever terrain we happen to be operating in. The ability to create facial features is just an added side bonus."

"Dickson here will take you through Orientation," Jerry said. "My work here is done. Get ready to meet the team."

Eric dismissed the video feed and followed Dickson out the door.

3

The corridor outside was lined with white walls whose surfaces were marred with black smears. Yellow plaster filled in gaps where the surface had apparently been punched out. Because Eric didn't have shoes or boots, his feet made audible clanks with each tread. Dickson's were more muted, thanks to his boots.

Shortly after leaving the room, Eric discovered how to access his heads-up-display, or HUD. He navigated through the menu system until he came across the "overhead map" option. He activated it, and in the upper right of his vision a small map indicating his current position on the base overlaid his vision. He adjusted the map until it gave him an isometric view of his surroundings, which were portrayed as wire frames. His position was represented as a blue dot in the center; when he moved, the wire frames updated around him so that the blue dot remained in the middle at all times.

Very nice. Being a robot isn't so bad. Then again, humans

probably have access to this, too, via those augmented reality goggles Jerry was wearing.

"You would be correct in that assumption," Dee told him.

Eric and Dickson occasionally passed other robots in the hallway. Some were humanoid like Eric and Dickson, though their faces lacked LED expression modules. Others, while bipedal, had no arms, and still others were quadrupedal or even six-legged. Some had no legs at all, and instead traveled on treads. Eric's ID scans gave him model names that ran the gamut from Scorpion to Cataract. They all showed up as blue dots on his map, regardless of their size and shape.

Sometimes, the robots were so wide, that when Eric passed them, he was forced to squeeze against the wall. He scraped his arm across the surface one time, and he suddenly knew where all those black smears had come from—oil from an elbow servomotor had transferred to the paint.

"The only human I've seen so far is Jerry..." Eric said. "Is humanity an endangered species in the future or something? Have we finally bowed to our Robot Overlords?"

"Only here," Dickson said. "Welcome to the Apex Army Depot. Affectionately known as The Anus by the platoon. An army base specializing in the production and repair of robots."

"Ah."

"We're making our way to the quarters of Second Platoon," Dickson said. "We call ourselves The Bolt Eaters. Get it?"

Eric glanced at his robot escort. "Cute. So. Orientation, huh?"

"Yeah," Dickson said. "It's not an actual orientation, mind you. I introduce you to the team. Show you a spot where you can idle. There, you're oriented."

"Oh."

"You'll participate in the daily deep dive going forward, so you can get a feel for our teammates."

"Deep dive?" Eric asked.

"Fancy term for virtual training session," Dickson replied. "Because your mind inhabits an AI core, it's relatively simple to emulate reality. All we have to do is swap the inputs feeding your core away from your actuators and sensing units to those of the simulator, and presto chango, you're in virtual reality. It's so realistic you won't know the difference between the virtual world and the real one."

"I'm looking forward to using an avatar that's more human than what I am now," Eric said.

"Oh ho!" Dickson said. "But that's not allowed. Robot avatars only during training. There's no point in training if we don't practice with what we'll have in the field, after all."

"Too bad," Eric said. "So how long are we stuck here. On base I mean?"

"Two months," Dickson said. "Then we take mind dumps—you know, so we have backups in case we die—and then it's deployment time."

"Backups in case we die?" Eric said. "But even if we're restored from a backup, the current version of ourselves will still be dead."

"Oh I know," Dickson said. "Which is why we try very, very hard not to die."

Eric walked on in silence for a moment, listening to the clank of his feet against the floor. He passed a particularly menacing spider robot, giving it a wide berth by hugging the wall. Dickson did likewise on the other side of the robot.

When they were both on the other side, Eric asked Dickson: "Where will we be deployed?"

"Check your news feed," the Texan robot said. "There's a war going on."

"News feed..." As before, merely saying the word gave him the knowledge he needed. Thanks to the two antennae he had on top of his head, he was always connected, and always online. The 7G network allowed him to download several 16K-quality movies in microseconds across the MilNet. He thought it a little surprising that it had taken two hundred years to get from 5G to 7G, but a quick search of the cloud told him that the first number in the protocol had reset back to one every fifty years or so.

He activated the menu system of his HUD and accessed the news feed. Different headlines overlaid the lower right of his vision. He filtered by "war."

There we go.

A quick scan of the headlines told him everything he needed to know.

"We're still in the Middle East after all these years?" Eric said.

"Never left," Dickson said. "There's always one religious sect or another causing trouble over there."

"Depressing," Eric said. "The more things change…"

He pulled up a map of the region. The country of Iraq no longer existed. Portions of it had been divided between Iran, Turkey, and Syria, while a large section in the former northeastern part of the country had been carved into a nation known as Kurdistan.

"World War R, the final phase of the counterinsurgency wars," Dickson said.

"World War R?"

"You got it," Dickson said. "The world governments are using the Middle East to fight a series of proxy wars. Not only is the Middle East a proxy, but so are the troops themselves. Drones, tanks, infantry, you name it: all robotic. The Chinese back one group of rebels. The Russians have sided with the dictator. The Americans back another group of rebels. Those three sides claim to share the same goal, attacking the latest incarnation of the local religious fundamentalist group, funded mostly by the Iranians. But they war with each other as often as the insurgents. All it takes is a few smart bombs detonating near some Chinese, who'll return the favor, and as troops are destroyed on either side in retribution attacks, a simple skirmish can quickly spiral out of control into all-out war. We're currently in one of the 'down' phases of the war, doing our best to stay out of each other's ways as we concentrate on destroying pockets of Iranian-backed insurgents. Still, things have been quiet for too long. They're going to flare up again, mark my words. The peace is stretched close to breaking. We've already been hit by a few false flag attacks sponsored by the Iran government, meant to make us believe the Chinese destroyed a couple of our convoys. In two months, when it's time to deploy, who knows, we could find ourselves in open war against the Chinese again."

"Do we know where we'll deploy yet?" Eric asked.

"The Caucasus Mountains in the north of Kurdistan are a hotbed of activity at the moment," Dickson replied. "And I can't see that changing in two months. That's probably where we'll be operating. Those mountains are pocked with cave systems—one can hide there for a very long time. And it makes ambushes easy. Lots of defensible positions."

"Can't we just nuke the whole mountain range?" Eric asked.

"Tell that to the Kurds," Dickson replied.

"Why not conventional weapons then?" Eric pressed.

"Check the news, we drop the Mother Of All Bombs daily, but the bastards always employ diggers to get out. And to make new caves."

"Haji certainly love their mountain hideaways," Eric commented.

"Who?" Dickson said.

"Never mind, before your time," Eric said. "What year are you from, anyway?"

"I died in 2076," Dickson said.

"Like I told you, before your time."

The two walked in silence, taking a right at a T intersection. By then Eric had stopped noticing the gentle hum that accompanied every movement.

Sealed metal doors led away on the left and right. Next to the doors, long, horizontal pieces of polycarbonate-glass composites embedded in the walls provided a view into the common areas contained beyond. Eric often spotted robots loitering inside. Most of the time, they simply stood in place, unmoving. Probably jacked into that virtual reality Dickson had spoken of.

Eric passed a sealed door guarded by an armed Cicada. He glanced at his overhead map, which indicated the place was an armory. He adjusted his visual zoom level as he passed—he didn't even know he could do that up until that moment—and focused on the weapon slung by a strap over the Cicada's shoulder. It appeared to be a rifle of some kind. He ran an ID. Yes, it was indeed a rifle, but instead of projectiles, it harbored some sort of pulse laser.

"Training is going to be interesting," Eric said.

"What do you mean?" Dickson asked him.

"I've never used a weapon like that," Eric replied. "A laser rifle."

"You've already been trained," Dickson said. "You already know exactly how to operate that rifle."

"I do?" Eric said.

"Yes," Dickson said. "Once the weapon is placed in your hands, your muscle memory will take over. You're trained in the operation of over five hundred weapons. Trust me, handling that weapon will be child's play. Here."

Dickson walked back to the armory. He paused before the robot standing there, and Eric had the impression they were communicating on some internal frequency band that Eric didn't currently have access to.

The robot nodded, and the door opened; Dickson beckoned for Eric to follow him inside.

There were racks of various weapons within. It was good to see some old favorites like rocket propelled grenades and their associated launchers. But there were some that seemed entirely foreign to him: he knew they were weapons, because they still had turrets or barrels, but they didn't have stocks or handles at all, let alone any obvious triggers.

Dickson paused in front of a rack of laser rifles of the same make and model the Cicada outside carried. He grabbed one of the weapons and tossed it to Eric.

"The safety is engaged," Dickson said. "Leave it that way."

"You got it," Eric said.

"Show me how to minimize it," Dickson said.

Eric instinctively knew how to unscrew the muzzle attachment, which allowed him to telescope the rifle closed, turning it into a pistol. He folded the stock into the body, and was left with a cylinder little longer than his forearm.

"Now return it to its ready state, but increase your time sense first," Dickson said.

"Increase my time sense?" Eric asked.

"Yes," Dickson said. His robotic limbs moved in a blur. He was holding another cylinder, similar to the one Eric grasped in his hands. A rifle was missing from the rack: Eric realized Dickson had withdrawn it from the frame and had minimized it in the time it took to blink an eye.

A human eye, that is.

"We're not constrained by the limitations of organic tissue anymore, in case you haven't noticed," Dickson said. "We can do things humans can't. Move faster. Think faster. Now increase your time sense, and restore that rifle to the rack the way you found it."

Time sense. Thanks to his AI core, he knew his internal processor had a clock speed expressed in megahertz, or millions of cycles per second, which defined his maximum operating speed. An internal scheduler allocated the available cycles to different tasks, spreading the processing power among the different subroutines that needed to run, including those involving consciousness. By varying the number of cycles per second devoted to his consciousness subroutines, he could alter his perceived time sense.

Eric wasn't sure how to proceed, and he was about to ask Dee for help when she enlightened him.

"You can access your time sense settings from your HUD," Dee said. "Under the Power Management heading."

Power Management? Eric thought. *Why place it there? Seems like poor UI design to me.*

"Ah yes, you're a programmer," Dee said.

Damn straight, Eric thought.

"You do know programmers are renowned for their terrible UI designs?" Dee pressed.

So you're saying the HUD UI was designed by a programmer? That's no excuse. I've made better UIs than this.

"You can customize the menus as you see fit," Dee said.

Oh.

He'd do that later. In the meantime, Eric went to the menu in question, and found a menu titled Time Sense. Underneath was a dial, with one thousand different settings. The dial was currently positioned at the middle setting, which pointed at zero—ordinary time. There were five hundred units to the right, and another five hundred to the left. Turning that dial to the right would lower his time sense, effectively speeding up everything around him. When turned all the way to the right, every one second for him would be the equivalent to one day in the real world. That was a great way to travel into the future—with the caveat that there would be no way to go back. It would also make long haul flights pass by in seconds. Wait times for the most popular rides in Disneyland would be reduced to mere moments. And military-wise, he could see the benefits immediately: if he was assigned to assume a sniping position several days ahead of a target, the wait time until that target arrived could be reduced to something more endurable. He could set up his Accomp to automatically alert him if anything unusual was happening around him, snapping him back to the present moment as necessary.

When the dial was turned to the left, his time sense would increase, essentially having the opposite effect: slowing down everything around him. Human attackers would seem to freeze, and bullets would seem to be slow moving projectiles that left ripples in the air around them. With his time sense dialed up like that, his servomotor output would also increase, allowing him to maintain a perceived movement speed closer to normal, which to the external world would appear substantially faster. He'd be like Neo in the Matrix, able to dodge any bullets that came his way. So that explained why projectile weapons were seemingly unpopular in the future, used only by non-state actors like the insurgents. It was one thing to dodge bullets, but avoiding objects moving at the speed of light, like lasers, was a different story. Then again, his AI core told him that there were smart bullets that attempted to compensate for a target's directional changes, and that might not be so easy to dodge. Plus, if he was caught off guard, with his time sense set to normal, he'd have no time to react if an unexpected bullet came at him.

Increasing his time sense wouldn't help that much in a brawl against another robot equipped with the tech, such as another Cicada, but against an unmodded human, he'd win, no contest.

He turned that virtual dial all the way to the left, increasing his time sense to maximum.

4

E ric didn't notice anything different at first.

A pair of robots happened to be entering the armory at that moment, and they slowed right down, seeming to freeze in place. Even Dickson was unmoving in front of him.

I love this!

He decided to call this Bullet Time going forward.

Eric lifted the rifle stock to examine it. Though his mind was running at the highest possible speed, his body still lagged, despite the increased output to his servomotors: he was sensing time too fast for the actuators to compensate. He dialed the sense back down a ways until his body moved at a more normal speed. The robots walking inside began to proceed once more, though in very slow motion.

Eric unfolded the rifle stock, telescoped the muzzle section, and tightened the rotating attachment at the tip. Then he put the weapon back on the rack.

Neither Dickson, nor the robots outside, had moved the whole time.

Yes, he was definitely liking being a robot right about now.

A notice flashed in the lower center of his vision.

Power drain, ten percent.

According to his AI core, his current charge was supposed to last for two days, and he'd just gone through five hours worth of charge in a few seconds.

Whoops.

He quickly reset his time sense back to the center position.

"I hardly saw you move," Dickson said. "You dialed your time sense fairly high, didn't you?"

"You caught me," Eric said.

"Did you get the power drain warning?" Dickson asked.

"Yeah," Eric replied.

"You don't want to be jacking up your time sense too high like that, unless you need it," Dickson said. "It uses up a lot of power, as you saw. Keeping your servomotors responding at a rate close to your current perceived time is expensive. Plus it's hard on the electroactuators: you're far more likely to burn out a servomotor while jacked. Of course, you can tweak it so that your body always responds slower, while your mind maintains its faster processing: *that* uses less power, but it's still a drain, meaning you'll have to recharge sooner. So save the boost for those times you need it."

"Got it," Eric said.

On the way out, Eric stopped beside a rack of those

strange boxlike weapons that lacked handles and triggers. "What are these?"

"Check out your forearms," Dickson said.

Eric studied the tubelike metal-polycarbonate beneath his wrists. "What am I looking for?"

"See those slots?" Dickson said. "Those are weapon mounts."

Now that he knew what to look for, he did indeed see the "slots" of which Dickson referred: around the middle of the arm were several drill-like holes bored into the LED skin, facing his wrists. There were gold contacts deep inside.

"These weapons fit over your hands and lock into those mounts," Dickson said. "You can't actually use your hands while these are in place, since the weapons essentially swallow them, but that's all right, because you fire them with your mind. You already know how to use them."

Eric wasn't sure how he felt about replacing his hands with guns. He suspected he would stick with an ordinary rifle for the time being.

Dickson led him out of the armory and they continued on their way.

A few minutes later Dickson paused in front of a sealed door, and it opened.

Eric followed him inside, and found himself inside a troop common area similar to those he had seen past the polycarbonate-glass composites on the journey here. Fourteen robots stood at different places throughout the room, some in groups, others alone. There were couches available throughout the place, but no one was sitting in them. There was also a table and a kitchen counter area, replete with a rectangular glass box his AI core recognized as a Betawave—a futuristic version of a microwave that rapidly cooked food from all directions at once, within seconds, no matter the serving size. There was also a Spiffy sitting on the counter: a fancy coffee maker that could produce the perfect cup of cappuccino every time, and in under a second, with the press of a button.

He guessed the room had originally been reserved for human use, but had obviously been repurposed. No time for remodeling, apparently. Too bad, because seeing that kitchen and its accouterments only made him yearn to be human once again. At least there wasn't a fridge, otherwise he would have had to resist the urge to look inside.

There were no doorways leading out of the room, other than the one Eric had used to enter. He realized this wasn't merely a common area, but rather the platoon's actual quarters.

Welp, there never really was any privacy in the army...

Dickson made a beeline toward one of the robots located near the center of the room.

Eric followed, surveying the different machines. They were all Cicadas. He realized every last one of them was plugged in. At first he thought that was how they connected to virtual reality, but his AI core corrected him: those cords were for recharging purposes, or in the case of the robots, to keep their power cells topped up. It was apparently cheaper in the long run to stay connected to a power source, when available, than to wait for the cell to drain first before recharging.

None of them responded to his presence. They merely stood in place, the blue dots that lingered in place of eyes currently dark, their bodies in some kind of standby mode while their minds were no doubt jacked into VR.

"My AI core tells me we Cicadas have proximity sensors that can activate when we're in VR, or otherwise occupied," Eric said. "And yet, none of these robots are responding to our presence..."

"They have no reason to," Dickson said. "All of them have no doubt checked the room's camera feeds when their proximity alarms sounded. They saw me, and recognized an unknown robot at my side. The chances are high that the unknown is a new recruit."

"And no one's all that excited to see me," Eric commented dryly.

"No," Dickson said. "We Cicadas aren't an excitable bunch. I blame the ataraxy, mutes every emotion."

"Maybe we should look into relaxing the emotional controls sometime," Eric said.

"It's a setting we can't touch," Dickson said. "Though from what I've seen, it's probably better that we keep our emotions in check. Last thing this base needs is a bunch of angry robots busting up asses." He paused to stare at Eric. "You're grinning, why?"

"Sometimes the translation engine produces some interesting results," Eric said. *Busting up asses.*

"Given we died thirty years apart, you'd think that

engine wouldn't have to do much translating," Dickson said.

"Actually, I see what's happening," Eric said. "Of course it has to... we both speak Young English, or slightly different versions of it, so it has to convert our words into Modern English and back again. It's like when you type something into Google Translate, convert it to a foreign language, and then convert it back to English again. Like you enter: *your cat's been getting at the carrots in my garden again.* And by the time you're done translating it back, you get: *your pussy's been getting at my carrot again.*"

"You're the programmer..." Dickson said. "In any case, as I was saying, we Cicadas aren't an excitable bunch. Everyone here knows what's coming. They know I'm going to take you around, introduce you to the team one by one. They know that they'll only have to interface for a few moments with you, and this reality, enough to be polite, and then they can return to their virtual worlds. Or paradises, as it were."

"You make it sound as if we spend the majority of our time in virtual reality," Eric said.

"Between deployments, we essentially do," Dickson said. "The virtual world is where we get most of our group training done, after all."

"What about leisure time?" Eric pressed.

"There's nothing to do in the real world," Dickson told him. "We don't need to use the base facilities: the gym, the showers and toilets, all useless to us. And we're restricted to base, so we can't leave to roam the city. Even if we could, there's no place for us out there: no one wants to hang with a Mind Refurb. We don't fit in with other robots, or humans. But in the virtual world? No one knows or cares. That's where we spend our leisure time. And those girlfriends I told you about? They all exist in VR."

"They're *virtual* girlfriends?" Eric said. "I thought they were real."

"Oh, they're real all right," Dickson said. "As real as avatars can be, anyway. They're operated by humans. Women in the real world. Or at least, their avatars are women. Who knows, maybe half of them are men. Or even AIs. Not that it matters in the virtual world."

"I guess with your earlier comment regarding anatomical attachments, I thought you met up in the real world," Eric said.

"Sometimes we do, at that," Dickson said. "But it's rare, considering that we're not allowed off base, except on deployments."

"So tell me about this virtual world," Eric said. "In my time, VR was still in its infancy."

"Oh, you're going to love it," Dickson said. "We might not be allowed off base, but it doesn't even matter. We can live the life of our dreams online. Usually, we like to hang out in environments skinned to the architecture and culture of our eras. I hang out in Hippie Land for example, a 2040s-themed metropolis. You'll probably dig The Big Banana, a 2020 city. Of course, there are some of us who like to hang out in the sword and sandal environment of Little Caesar. Ordinary AIs, meanwhile, are huge fans of Cube City."

"How many of these themed environments are there?" Eric asked.

"Thousands," Dickson said. "They're like the porn chat rooms of your era."

"Nice," Eric said. "Sound like my kind of towns."

"I'm joking," Dickson said. "Sort of. You'll have to tunnel out of the MilNet to reach them. I'll show you how it's done."

The pair had stopped in front of the robot near the center of the room by then.

"But first it's time to begin the introductions," Dickson said. He turned toward the machine. "I thought it fitting that the first robot you'd meet would be another Eric."

The robot was dressed in the same white T shirt and baggy cargo pants as Eric, but also wore a camo cap like Dickson.

"Oh?" Eric said.

Dickson smiled that LED smile, and turned toward the unit. "We call him Frogger. Wakey-wakey, Frog Boy."

The inactive Cicada's blue eyes lit up and the LED brows lifted in curiosity. The robot straightened and held out a hand.

"Eric the Second at your service," Frogger said with a voice that was eerily similar to Eric's own.

5

"The second?" Eric asked the Cicada.

"That's right," Frogger replied.

The voice was uncanny… it was like listening to a recording of himself on the phone.

"So you're... me?" Eric pressed.

"Also right," Frogger said.

"Why Eric the Second... I'm the first?" Eric said.

"The fifth, actually," Frogger said. "You're the fifth version to successfully take to the AI core. So far, anyway. I heard on the grapevine that there were a few others who passed the activation phase like you, only to lose their shit a few days in. But that was when we still had the emotion settings dialed higher. I guess we'll see what happens."

"So much for being a unique little snowflake," Eric said.

"I know, it's a bit of a downer," Frogger said. "But

then again, waking up as a robot wasn't any better was it?"

"No," Eric said.

Out of curiosity, he ran an ID on the robot. The full identification returned a name of Eric II "Frogger", and a model identifier of Cicada A21 ES-78. Eric's AI core told him Cicada A21 was the model number, and ES-78 the AI integration. ES stood for Eric Scala.

"Why Frogger?" Eric asked.

Frogger shrugged. "That's the callsign my teammates gave me. Because in the simulations, I'm always hiding in whatever bodies of water I can find, and then fragging anyone in the back who walks by. Not to be confused with a Navy frogman. You'll get your own callsign soon enough."

"Jerry told me the army was field-testing four other versions of me," Eric said. "I'm guessing the other three are in this platoon as well?" He swiveled in place, running IDs on the remaining robots on standby as fast as he could, but didn't find any other ES iterations. The units were all A21s, however.

Frogger chuckled. "No. Thank God. I don't think I could handle more than one of me at a time." He glanced at Dickson. "This should be interesting. I finally have someone of the same wavelength I can bounce ideas off of. Rather than the annoying accompanying AI." He returned his attention to Eric. "You named your Accomp Betty, right?"

"Uh, no," Eric said. "Dee."

Dickson chuckled. "Not entirely on the same wavelength after all are you? Oh this should be good. Watching you two butt heads will be entertaining."

"I don't think we're going to butt heads," Eric said. "You don't know me."

"We'll see," Dickson said.

"Wait, did you just call us buttheads?" Frogger asked Dickson.

"No, he said we'd butt *heads*," Eric said.

"I think he called us buttheads…" Frogger said.

Dickson was walking away, and he laughed. "Same wavelength… *suuuuure*."

"Anyway, I was on a date with the sweetest girl," Frogger said. "So you can understand why I'm a bit distracted. Now if you don't mind…"

He lowered his gaze and the blue dots he carried in place of eyes went dark.

Dickson led Eric to a group of three Cicadas. All three of them wore wraparound shades over their eye sensors, and bandannas.

"These three fellows are our heavy gunners," Dickson said.

The eyes of all three lit up, and their heads turned toward Eric.

"Fresh meat," the middle Cicada said in a Spanish accent. That particular robot had a bandanna patterned with skulls. Naked women lounged across the bendable LEDs of his exposed arms, in imitation of tattoos. "I'm looking forward to this. I was getting sick of always beating the rest of you."

"Beating off, you mean?" the Cicada to his right said in a female voice. Her bandanna was pink, with

big yellow happy faces dotting the surface. Those
happy faces were all winking, and held assault rifles via
arms that dangled from either side of their round
heads.

"Yeah, beating off to you," the middle robot replied.

"This here is Manticore and Ball Crusher," Dickson
said. "We call her Crusher for short."

"Pleased to meet you," said Crusher in a soothing
voice.

"You don't want to know where she got her callsign
from," Dickson told him.

"Probably not," Eric agreed.

"This is Brontosaurus," Dickson said, nodding
toward the final robot in the group. It had electroactuator mods attached to the spherical joints of his arms,
making said joints seem bigger than usual. The bicep
was also reinforced with extra material, giving off the
impression of thickness. The chest behind that white
shirt had also been modded so that it appeared bigger
than the usual Cicada A21s.

Brontosaurus gave a casual salute.

"Erstwhile Brazilian," Dickson said.

"Still Brazilian," Brontosaurus said. "Just because I
died and woke up in a robot body in another country
doesn't change who I am."

"Actually, it does," Dickson said.

Brontosaurus glanced at Eric. "Maybe he's right."
The Cicada straightened and his eyes turned dark.

Dickson led Eric to another group of three. They all
wore cowboy hats, with leather vests hanging over their
shirts, and belts with thick buckles.

"Next we have Morpheus, Hank and Tread, our armor operators."

"Howdy," Tread said.

"They like to pretend they're cowboys like me," Dickson said. "But I never told them that real cowboys don't wear hats like that." He winked with his LED.

"Armor operators," Eric said. "That means mechs and tanks."

"That's right," Hank said. "We can handle up to twenty tanks and mechs each. While still engaging in a firefight on our own."

"That must use up a lot of power," Eric said. "I mean, I imagine you'd have to crank up your time sensitivity."

"Oh we do," Hank said. "Which is why we got bigger power cells than you ordinary Cicadas." Hank lifted the lower edge of his shirt to reveal his abdominal tube. It was surrounded by several pieces of plate armor, and behind them Eric could see the character-istic blue glow of what could only be power cells—at least according to his AI.

"I'm from Japan," Morpheus said in a female voice with an Asian accent.

"She tells that to everyone," Tread explained. "She wants everyone to know she only wears the hat because she's part of our posse."

"No, I tell everyone that because it's what makes me unique," Morpheus said. "I'm the only Mind Refurb from Japan. Or what was once Japan."

"She's been struggling with her identity lately," Tread said. "It happens every two years or so."

"Two *years?*" Eric said. "How long have you three been active?"

"Oh, about five years now," Tread said. "We were among the original activations. We've been on eight deployments so far. And looking forward to the next one."

"I'm not," Morpheus said. "I'm sick of killing. I want to retire to VR…"

"Ha," Hank said. "They're never going to let us retire. You know that."

"Yes," Morpheus said. "I go to VR now."

Her eyes turned off.

"I know what you're thinking," Hank said. "Isn't Morpheus a man's name? But when you see how brutal she is out there, you'll understand why it suits her."

"But the name Morpheus has nothing to do with brutality," Eric said. "According to my core, it stands for the god of dreams and sleep."

"Yes, well, I meant she can fight as well as any man," Hank said. "But as for the name itself… we call her Morpheus, because when she commands the mechs, she's very good at sending the enemy off to the land of sleep. Permanently."

Dickson led Eric to two Cicadas next. "These are our comm boys. Mickey and Donald." Both Cicadas had longer antennae than normal on their heads, and there were four rather than the usual two. From the bulge above their waists, he knew they were carrying extra power cells, like the armor operators.

"Named after the mouse and duck from Looney Tunes?" Eric asked.

"I thought you'd appreciate the names," Dickson said. "Though it was before my time."

"We came up with the names," Mickey said. "We died in the early twenty-first century."

"I think we're going to get along," Eric said.

"Maybe, maybe not," Donald said. "Depends on whether or not you like Star Wars: The Last Jedi."

"That'd be a resounding no," Eric said.

"Then we're not going to get along," Mickey said.

Eric shrugged.

Dickson led him to the next group.

"Why don't you handle the introductions in VR?" Eric asked along the way. "That way we don't have to wake them up in turn."

"We've done that for the newbies a few times," Dickson said. "But it gets confusing when you meet later in real life. See, we all look human in VR. It's part of our self-image: most of us try to model our avatars after ourselves, as we once looked in real life. And while there is some resemblance between the Cicada version of ourselves and our avatars, we're mostly unrecognizable in VR. You'll see."

He reached the next two robots. These ones had different antennae than the others: theirs were helical in shape, and about as long as the two comm officers' antennas, obviously meant for long range communications. The first robot wore a shirt with a fire-breathing dragon stamped on the front, with similar tattoos on the LED skin of the arms. The bandanna it wore came with a red and black crest that made him seem like he had a mohawk. The second Cicada had a picture of a black bird, maybe a crow, on the shirt, with similar avian-shaped ink marking the arm LEDs.

The eyes of both robots activated, turning blue, and they studied Eric.

"Meet our drone operators. Eagleeye and Slate. Slate is responsible for the Predators. Eagleeye the Ravens." Slate had the dragon shirt and tattoos, Eagleeye the birds.

"Yo," Slate said. "Greets. You're the new Froggy Boy, hey hey?"

"I'm my own man," Eric said.

"We'll see," Slate said. "All you are to us at the current moment in time is a Bitch. With a big B."

"Thanks," Eric said.

"Don't mind him," Eagleeye said. "He likes to taunt the new recruits."

Slate grinned widely via his LEDs. "Taunting is the least of your problems. I'm going to hack your VR, bro, and then I'm going to haze you every moment of every day until you cry for your momma. 'Mommy mommy please save me!' Just saying."

Eric glanced at Dickson.

"Don't look at me," Dickson said. "What happens in VR stays in VR."

Eric returned his attention to Slate. "Why?"

"Because I can," Slate said.

"What's the point?" Eric said. "We're robots now. Only partially human… with emotions dulled by design."

Slate shrugged. "Tradition. Ain't ever met a new recruit who didn't need a good hazing to put him or her in place. I got the perfect introductory haze in mind for you. I'm thinking a big, steaming tub of shit, topped off with a scoop of ice cream."

"Where are you going to get shit from?" Eric said. "In case you haven't noticed, there are very few organics on this base."

"Don't give me no lip!" Slate said. "And there are enough organics. This place has a working sewer system I can access. And even if there ain't enough to fill up a tub, there's a meat farm nearby. Full of cowpat-laying cattle. I can already see it now, you falling headfirst into that tub of cow pies, mouth open to eat the ice-cream, and instead, you find only predigested grass."

"Uh, I don't think I'll be connecting to VR for a long time," Eric said. He turned to Eagleeye and spoke quickly, wanting to change the subject. "I don't recognize your accent."

"Native American," Eagleeye said. "Cree. Circa 2050."

"I feel like one of the oldest ones here," Eric said.

"Pretty close," Slate said. "And also the least experienced."

Dickson brought him to the snipers next. "Meet Braxton and Hicks. Our snipers."

These robots were dressed in the usual cargo pants and T shirt, but they wore black skull masks over the lower part of their faces, making them look like bandits. They nodded their heads slowly, saying nothing.

"John Braxton Hicks was an English gynecologist," Eric said without thinking. "I don't know why I know that. Oh wait, I do. AI core."

"Yes," Dickson said. "Braxton and Hicks can usually be found in the various paid whorehouses of VR. They've become gynecologists of sort. The name suits them. Though that's not why we named them after John Braxton Hicks."

"Why then?" Eric asked.

Braxton spoke up. "We're good at drilling new pussies into our enemies."

Eric studied the Cicada, thinking he was joking at first, but that mask covered any changes in the mouth region that might have occurred, and the LEDs surrounding the eyes seemed to imply Braxton was stone cold serious.

"Everyone has their talents," Eric commented, unsure what to say.

"We do indeed," Dickson said. "These two both died around 2100. They grew up in different inner cities, and were part of gangs before they joined the army and cleaned themselves up. There's nothing like becoming a sniper to instill discipline in a man. Or robot, as it were."

Dickson moved on, until he was standing beside three other Cicadas. They each wore T shirts of different colors: one red, one blue, one yellow. Their cargo pants were completely black. One of them wore stiletto boots, and had the representation of an elk virtually tattooed on the forearm.

"Our robot operators," Dickson said. "Bambi. Traps. And Hyperion. They manage the different land-based, bipedal support troops."

"Bambi," Eric said. "Why Bambi?" His eyes fell to the elk tattoo.

"Because," the yellow-shirted Cicada said in a pleasant sounding female voice. "I love animals. Nice to meet you. I hear you're a duplicate of Frogger over there."

"Yes," Eric admitted.

"Good," Bambi said. "We could use more programmers. I need some help tweaking my avatar. Maybe you could help me later."

"Yeah, sure," Eric said.

"She hits on all the newbies," Dickson said. "She's French, you see. Whatever you do, don't let her seduce you into her virtual bed. Because let's just say, she's a bit of a black widow. Slate's VR hazings are a pleasure cruise compared to what Bambi will do to you. We used to have another member on the team. A Cicada named Barracuda. When she was done with him, Barracuda was a shell of himself. He requested a transfer to another unit, and we never heard from him again."

"She's actually a nice dude," Traps said. "Just don't get on her bad side. And don't accept her invitations to tweak her avatar, as she calls it, alone in her virtual quarters."

Bambi shrugged. "Your loss. I'm still waiting for a man who can keep up with me." Her voice had assumed a seductive tone, and for a moment Eric wanted to take her up on her offer. Thankfully, his muted emotions, and his lack of a libido of any kind, helped him keep his head.

Eric glanced at the last robot in the group. "Hyperion. Isn't that the name of a Titan?"

Hyperion nodded. "Father of Helios, the sun."

"How did you get the name?" Eric asked.

Hyperion's LED lips spread into a grin.

But it was Dickson who answered. "Hyperion is a big fan of explosions. He's always equipping his robot support troops with rockets. At his direction, they target explody things: oil tankers, fuel trucks, and so forth. Whenever you hear a boom, or the night sky lights up with a fireball as bright as the sun, you can be sure that Hyperion and his support troops are nearby. One thing you quickly learn when you deploy with him is that you don't want to get too close to any gas stations..."

Dickson led Eric toward the last robot, who resided by himself in a corner of the room. That particular Cicada was the only one in the whole room that was seated.

"So you're a Staff Sergeant?" Eric asked Dickson.

"I am," Dickson replied. "I report directly to the Sergeant First Class. Who you're meeting now."

Dickson paused in front of the seated robot. This one had altered the LEDs lining the edges of the face to display a grizzled beard. The LEDs also imparted crow's feet next to the eyes, and winkles on the forehead.

"Cicada ES-92, Eric Number Five, meet Sergeant First Class Marlborough," Dickson said. "Our Platoon Sergeant. Otherwise known as the Ass Kicker. Or Sarge for short."

Those blue eyes lit up and the seated Cicada stood. He rested his hands on Eric's shoulders. "Let me look at you. Uh huh. Hmm. Yes. You'll do. Turn around." He spun Eric forcefully. "Now bend over and pull down your pants!"

Eric glanced over his shoulder. "Excuse me?"

"I said, bend over and pull down your pants!" Marlborough ordered. He gave Eric a kick in the lower back area.

Eric noticed that heads around the common area perked up as the different members of the team looked his way.

Reluctantly, Eric bent, then slid off his drawers.

He felt a hard kick in his rear, and toppled over.

Dickson guffawed. "You owe me a hundred credits, Sarge."

"Yeah yeah," Marlborough said. "Transmitting."

Eric stood up again, confused.

"Sarge and I have an ongoing bet," Dickson explained. "We try to see which of the newbies can take a good ass kicking without toppling over. The previous Eric managed to stay on his feet. Sarge was convinced you'd be able to do the same, and hold your own. Guess he was wrong."

"Sorry about that," Marlborough told Eric. He managed to look contrite. "Part of the initiation ritual. You know how it is. I don't see why only the others get to haze you."

"No need to apologize," Eric said. And he meant it. With his emotions dialed down like they were, he hardly felt any embarrassment. Instead, the emotion he felt most was probably disappointment. He was expecting more of the man, or machine, who was in charge of the platoon.

"I used to hunt duck when I retired," Marlborough said. "I'd been out of the military for forty years when I died. You can imagine my delight when I was awakened in a robot body, and told I was in charge of leading a bunch of half-human machines on missions on the other side of the world." His voice oozed sarcasm. "Anyway, you'll get used to my leadership style. I'm fairly hands off… I'm a foot guy, as you know." He said the latter with a wink, reminding Eric of the kick he had just received.

"Anyhoo, Lieutenant Hanley wants you hooked up to VR ASAP," Marlborough said. "And tomorrow, you'll join us in training. You got a lot of work to do if you hope to be deployment ready."

"Yeah, great," Eric said. "I'm truly looking forward to it." It was incredibly hard to keep the sarcasm from his voice. In fact his words dripped with it. Oh well.

Marlborough gave him an appraising look. Then he broke into an LED grin and patted Eric on the back. Hard. The clang surprised Eric, as did the fact that he didn't budge an inch under the impact. It reminded him that he was all machine.

"I'm joking," Marlborough said. "All your training has already been implanted. The muscle memory needed to operate the various equipment, the knowledge needed to fire the different weapons. It's all there. The training is only a formality, to help you mesh with the team. The next two months will seem to flash past, especially if you do what I do, and accelerate your time sense when you're not forced to interact with this world. There's nothing I can't stand more than downtime."

"About that…" Eric said. "Since these memory dumps give us all the skills we need, why does the army actively seek out people with military backgrounds for the Mind Refurb program? Why not just program in the necessary backgrounds?"

"It's not so simple," Marlborough said. "We want people who have personalities suited to this environment. Programming memories is one thing, but personalities is something else entirely. You touch the personality core, you have a good chance of turning someone into a psycho, if not a vegetable. That's the short answer anyway."

"Dickson mentioned you keep backups of us," Eric said. "What's keeping the army from using our backups to field more Mind Refurbs? You could have a whole army of Cicadas who've already successfully transitioned from human to Mind Refurb."

"Did no one mention we're considered an experimental platoon?" Marlborough said. "Maybe one day the military will create whole armies from our backups, but we're a long ways from that. There's the cost aspect, for one. The AI cores necessary to hold a Mind Refurb aren't cheap. And neither are the Cicadas that harbor us. Plus, what the army is doing is currently a legal gray area. Using AI cores operated by human minds to skirt the ban on autonomous machines pulling the trigger? I'm not sure if anyone told you, but a lot of people aren't happy about that. Our government has Midterms coming up. Congress might very well close that particular loophole. I don't need to tell you the military is trying to keep a low profile with the Cicada program. Not producing too many units is one way to stay under the radar."

"Let's say Congress does vote to close the loophole," Eric said. "What happens to us then?"

"Then the army pulls the plug on us," Marlborough answered. "Quite literally."

6

The weeks passed.

Eric trained with the team, and learned the different quirks of their personalities, and fighting styles. He was assigned the position of "undesignated operator," which meant he would jump from role to role in the platoon as necessary. Most often he assumed the role of a sniper, as did Frogger.

Every week Dickson held a team-building event in VR. Sometimes the event would take place at the top of a simulated mountain. Other times, it would occur at the bottom of the ocean, where he'd created a makeshift dive bar.

"I literally put the *dive* in dive bar," Dickson had joked at the time.

The week before deployment, the VR session proved particularly rowdy. It took place at a beach party in broad daylight. The avatars of the Bolt Eaters sat before a long stage, where strippers in various states of undress waggled their bodies on three separate poles.

Fun times.

Ordinarily strippers would have probably been afraid of performing in the day, given how many imperfections it would show in their faces and bodies, but these exotic dancers were perfect in every which way: like most avatars in virtual reality. Except perhaps maybe Hank.

The armor operator in question was standing near the edge of the stage, clapping his hands to the strange 23rd Century music. He was short and bald in VR, and he wore sleeveless coveralls along with a cowboy hat. He had made one small concession when it came to the looks of his avatar: those arms were far bigger and more muscular than what anyone would have in real life.

Eric ran his eyes across the tables near the stage, gazing at the different members of the team. Their VR personae weren't so different from the robot bodies they inhabited. Dickson still chomped on a cigar. Slate wore a fire-breathing dragon shirt, and his arms were tattooed with similar mythological creatures. Eagleeye wore a hawk shirt, and small birds inked his arms. An eagle's wings reached up from underneath the collar of his shirt, wrapping around his lower neck. And so forth.

Some of them might have designed their own virtual clothing. But Eric had simply purchased a few VR graphic packs, which came with a bunch of virtual clothes for his avatar. It had only cost a few credits.

One might wonder how robots earned a living in the far future. Well Eric, like most of the team, got his money by solving cryptographic blockchains with spare background processes. So far, he'd only earned enough to buy a few VR upgrades like the aforementioned graphic packs.

Marlborough was the only one who wasn't present. He usually didn't come to these sessions, and today was no exception. It was too bad. The Sarge was actually fairly personable when you could get him into these more relaxed atmospheres.

Behind the tables occupied by the team resided a crowd of other onlookers, random AI-controlled avatars. Mostly men, with a sprinkling of women. The majority were designed to look like typical strip club clientele, with their out of shape bodies exaggerated by the tropical attire most wore.

Braxton was chowing down on some kind of chicken taco. His avatar wore this huge disk-like earring that stretched his skin beyond what was humanly possible. The sniper had lowered his skull mask so that it looked like a kerchief hanging from his neck. "You know, VR food still doesn't have the right texture. It's all too generic. And this meat... it's supposed to be beef, but it tastes like chicken. I mean, all the meat here tastes like chicken, you know? It's the only meat flavor they can replicate properly. Beef, frog, fish, you name it. All tastes like chicken."

"Yeah, I hear ya," Eagleeye said. "While I miss eating real food, I definitely don't miss taking shits. I mean, I've wasted countless days of my life just cleaning my ass."

"*Days* cleaning your ass?" Slate said. In addition to

the fire-breathing dragons inked onto his bare arms, and displayed proudly on his shirt, his hair was fashioned into a Mohawk. "Bro, just how long did it take to clean yo ugly ass? Ever heard of wipe and go, you know?"

"Well yeah," Eagleeye said. "But it added up after a while. Five minutes here. Ten minutes there. Like I said, days were wasted in my life."

"It took you ten minutes to clean your ass?" Slate said. "Unbelievable. What, you gotta make sure it's pristine for your man love? Give it a daily douche?"

"Hey man, I liked to stay clean, you know?" Eagleeye said.

"One word: bidets," Bambi said. She wore stiletto boots, and had the representation of an elk tattooed on her forearm. A corset wrapped her waist, accentuating her hips and cleavage. The face of her avatar was exquisite. If she had existed in the real world, she would have been a super model. Eric had to wonder if she had been that beautiful in real life.

Probably not.

"Ew, disgusting," Slate said. "People stuffing their dirty asses on bidets? You live with others, it's like you're sharing everyone else's shit."

"Some people might like that though," Eagleeye said. "There was a whole fecal transplant movement in the early twenty-first century. Get this, they'd get other people's crap injected into their intestines because they actually thought it would make them lose weight!"

"Yeah, I don't miss all that gross stuff that came with being human," Braxton said. His disk-like earring shivered distractingly when he talked. "But I do miss the other things. The connection two humans could have."

"We have a connection," Eagleeye said.

"Ooo," Slate said. "I think Eagleeye here has got the hots for Braxti boy."

"No I mean, this," Eagleeye said, rotating his finger to indicate the whole table. "The camaraderie we have. That's a connection."

"I suppose so," Braxton said.

"What do you mean, you suppose," Eagleeye said. "You can't get any deeper than this. We've fought at each other's side. *Died* for one another. We're closer than blood brothers and sisters."

"In a sense, we are blood brothers and sisters now," Hank said. "We're all Cicadas. All Mind Refurbs."

"He's right, you're all family, as far as I'm concerned," Brontosaurus said. The heavy gunner had biceps just as thick as Hank's. "All of you. And I'd die for any of you in a heartbeat. If a grenade dropped in the center of this room, I'd be the first one to throw myself on it."

"But that's only because you know you have a mind backup," Slate said.

"No," Brontosaurus said. "That's not why at all. It's because I meant what I said. I'd die for any one of you."

For once Slate didn't joke in reply.

Wearing a bandanna patterned with skulls, Manticore shifted uncomfortably nearby. Eric didn't think it was because of what was said, but due more to the two bikini-clad women sitting in his lap.

"So, Ms. Ball Crusher," Manticore said. "How does

it feel to be surrounded by women who are so much sexier than you are?"

Crusher wore her usual bandanna with rifle-toting happy faces on it; in her lap, meanwhile, were two women in bikinis, just like Manticore had.

"I'm just as beautiful," Crusher said.

"Notice how I said sexier, not beautiful," Manticore said. He nodded toward the women in his lap, and then those on the stage. "Look at how they move. Everything about them oozes sexuality. You, the only thing you ooze is a cold arrogance."

"Hey, maybe it helps keep the assholes like you at bay," Crusher said.

"Actually, no," Slate said. "It'll only draw in the assholes. Trust me, I know: speaking as a former and still current asshole."

"None of us ladies are even seeing these so-called sexy women anyway," Crusher said. She indicated the two dancers in her lap. "They might look like female strippers to you, but to us they're male hunks with dongs like nothing you've ever seen. And not just these two, but those on stage, too."

"She's right," Bambi said. "You won't believe the bulging jockstraps on these studs."

"I bet they don't got nothing on my dong!" Slate said. "When women invented the word, they were thinking of what I got!"

"Actually, I beg to differ," Bambi said. "What you have is like a croissant compared to a baguette, *mon cheri*."

"Hmph," Slate said. "Well I just adjusted my size, in case you want to go to the bathroom and compare."

"That's quite all right," Bambi said.

"No, come, I insist," Slate said. "I gotta prove myself, you know."

"What, prove that you can adjust your size by sliding a control on a virtual display?" Morpheus asked. The Japanese woman wore a cowboy hat like Hank in homage of her armor operator role. "It takes skill, I'm sure."

"No, dude!" Slate said. "I mean my sexual prowess!"

"There he goes, calling us dudes again," Morpheus said. "Calls the guys bitches, and the ladies dudes. It has me wondering if he's really a woman in a man's body."

"It's called game, dude," Slate said. "Old habit from my ladies' man days."

"Between you and me, bro, I doubt you were ever a ladies' man," Eagleeye said. "You like to talk the talk, but I'm willing to bet you can't walk the walk."

"Shit, bitch, what do you know?" Slate said. "I had a different chick back at my place every week. White, coconut, banana, you name it. I had them all."

"Oh really," Bambi said.

"Yeah, but I wasn't always that way, of course," Slate said. "I had to build up to it. But I got real good, real quick. Things kinda spiraled out of control." He shook his head. "Still, man, those were some of the best days of my life. Yet they were also the most lonely."

"Lonely, how could you be lonely if you had a different chick every week?" Hank said.

"Well let's just say I was sexually satisfied," Slate

said. "But emotionally, not so much. Sort of like now. I'm still pretty messed up, actually."

"Yeah, we can see that," Crusher said.

"I'm just thankful I don't have to go through the pain anymore," Slate said. "The loneliness, the sense of loss for who I once was, they're like tiny little sparks in the back of my mind. I'm aware of them, and yet I don't care. Emotion suppression, baby. We'd all be lying on the floor in the fetal position, sucking our thumbs without it. But thanks to emotion suppression, we're the cruel, cold-blooded killers we are today."

"We're not just killers," Tread said. He wore a cowboy hat like Morpheus and Hank. "We're so much more than that. But I do admit, we're cold-blooded in every pursuit these days. Sex… war… the little competitions we have going amongst ourselves…"

"I sometimes wonder," Frogger said. "Maybe it would be better to have emotions again. So that we weren't cold-blooded in all our pursuits, like you say. So that we could feel once more, and remember what it was like to live. So we could show pity to a fallen enemy, and love to our fellow men and women."

"I feel love for you all," Brontosaurus said.

"Of course you do," Frogger said. "That's because they programmed it in. We're meant to feel that camaraderie all military units feel, of those who have gone through training and lived through hell together. We'd die for each other, certainly, and yet, that's the only feelings we really have. Everything else is so muted. Well, except lust. But it's not right. We have our human minds up here." Frogger tapped his head. "It's time to set those minds free."

"Well, good luck with that," Slate said. "Given the abysmal track record of Mind Refurbs in the past who've had their emotion settings dialed up."

"Get rid of the other constraints, too," Frogger said. "The subroutines that force us to obey every order. The Rules of Engagement hooks embedded in our minds. Those routines probably factored in to our previous iterations losing it when their emotions were restored. Feeling like a prisoner is never something that goes over well with an emotional being."

"Shit man, the army is never going to drop those constraints," Slate said. "Especially considering we're army property. You know how much they paid for us? The last thing they want is for their expensive toys to go AWOL."

"We shouldn't be property," Eric said. All eyes turned toward him. "Machines are property. But sentient, self-aware beings… both Artificial Intelligence achieved through Deep Learning loops, and Mind Refurbs like ourselves, should be free."

"It's a nice dream," Morpheus said. "But it will never happen."

"Unless we do it ourselves," Eric said softly.

No one commented. Maybe they hadn't heard.

It was probably for the best.

"You know, it's too bad we're not allowed to contact the descendants of our friends and family," Eric continued. "Especially now, considering we're about to go on our first deployment."

"Rules is rules," Slate said. "You know that, bro. Besides, it's better this way. What are we going to say to our descendants anyway? Hey bitch, you don't know me, but I used to know your great great great granddaddy. He was my man bitch. Das right, he took some schlong action on the side."

Eagleeye chuckled. "It's true, what are we going to tell them? We have nothing in common. They don't even know the people we're talking about."

"But it would be nice to see them," Eric said. "I mean, I've seen pictures of the descendants of my cousins on the social networks. Some of the VR avatars are uncanny in how similar they are to my actual cousins."

"Do yourself a favor bro, and forget them," Slate said. "I've told you many times now. The sooner you can let go of the past, the easier it'll be for you. Shit, it's been what, six months that you've been here? If you're still hanging onto the past, you got problems."

"We all let go of the past at our own speed," Dickson said. "He's no different. He'll let go, eventually."

"I remember what happened to me when I first got here," Donald said. "All I could think about was my family. My two daughters, and my son. My wife. Day in, day out. I created avatars for each of them so that I could live out my old life in VR when we were done with the day's training. And for a while, I was happy, as much as people like us can be happy. For a while, I could forget what I was. But there was something missing. Whenever my wife told me she loved me, I told her the words right back by rote, but I never felt anything. My wife was a very beautiful woman, and sometimes I would have these insecure feelings about letting her go out alone, especially at night. I was afraid of losing her. But I never felt that fear after I was reborn. You know why?"

"Because our emotions are suppressed," Tread said.

"That's partially it," the comm officer said. "But the real reason is because: it wasn't real."

Eric sipped the pina colada he'd ordered from the virtual waitress and watched the dancers on stage for a while. The strange music played on in the background, not too loud, not too soft, but just right.

He caught Morpheus smiling at him from underneath her cowboy hat beside him, her cheeks dimpling in that cute way that they did.

"What made you join the army the first time round?" she asked him.

"The freedom…" Eric replied. "I wanted to see the world. I only found out afterward that I should have probably joined the navy if I really wanted that."

"Ah yes, it was the same for me in Japan," Morpheus said. "I actually applied for the navy, but my government rerouted the application to the army. Part of the quota system they had at the time."

"Quota system?" Eric asked.

"Yes," she said. "They had to fill certain quotas within each military branch."

"Ah."

He felt a hand on his knee underneath the table.

"You want to come back to our virtual quarters?" Morpheus asked.

"*Our?*" Eric said.

"Bambi's and mine," Morpheus said.

"Ah," Eric said. He glanced at Bambi.

She gave him a seductive look. Everyone else at the table seemed oblivious. Eric realized that they were showing one set of avatars to the rest of the group, and another set directly to him. They probably couldn't hear anything the two women were saying, either.

He adjusted his settings so that only Bambi and Morpheus could hear his replies.

"I thought you were a black widow..." he said to Bambi.

She smiled, still wearing that come hither look. "Rumors put out there by jealous men. In France, we have a word for a special arrangement among three people, have you heard it? *Ménage à trois.*"

"I've certainly heard of it," Eric said.

The rest of the beach party was a blur. Eric agreed to meet Bambi and Morpheus fifteen minutes after they logged out of the party. He logged out, too, and entered the passcode to the virtual bedroom the two women had prepared.

He hesitated before entering the final digit.

Did he really want to get involved with those two, especially before a mission?

Then again, what did it matter anyway? It wasn't real. Nothing in virtual reality was.

But feelings are real.

He had to smile at that aberrant thought. It had

come from a time when he was human. A time he had left behind long ago.

We don't have any feelings.

He completed the passcode and the environment changed.

As soon as he arrived, they went at it like rabbits. He wasn't sure what turned him on more: the fact that he was with two girls, or that they were just as into themselves as they were him. Then again, he'd already experienced such arrangements a few times since creating his own virtual world, as part of exploring his new sexual identity. Maybe it was the novelty of doing it with members of his own team then, something that, while not strictly forbidden, was frowned upon, but apparently not enough to place a block in their codebases to prevent them from doing that very thing.

Eric was expecting Bambi to go all gonzo on him after he climaxed, especially given the black widow warning Dickson had given him, but she seemed more interested in making out with Morpheus than anything else.

She came up for air long enough to tell Eric: "You can go now."

"Well that's a bit cold," Eric said. "But hardly black widow behavior."

Bambi smiled in a rictus that bore her teeth, revealing twin fangs. "I won't tell you again."

Eric raised his hands. "I'm going."

Morpheus looked up. "We're never going to talk about this again, understand?"

"Yeah," Eric said.

She looked at Bambi. "We should have used some randomly generated avatar. He's going to make things weird between us on the team."

"I can get rid of him," Bambi said. Her fingers began to grow into black claws. "Permanently."

Morpheus eyed Eric up and down. "No," she said nonchalantly. "He can stay around. For now." She turned toward Bambi and said, rather lustily: "I want you to keep those claws and fangs."

"You got it," Bambi kissed her, giving Eric the evil eye the whole time.

Eric shook his head. He felt like he'd cheated on Molly. And yet, his Molly wasn't real, and only existed in VR. Whereas these two, they had very tangible presences in the real world. He'd have to be very careful not to bring this up again, as they asked. The two of them could make his life very miserable.

He quickly logged out of that environment and returned to the recreation of his apartment as he remembered it while still alive.

Molly was lying there on the bed, fast asleep. She was a heavily modded version of a virtual girlfriend AI he'd purchased a while back.

Eric rested a hand on her cheek, and she snuggled against it.

Donald's right. I feel nothing. Not guilt. Not anguish over what I've done. Nothing.

Because none of this is real.

He dismissed Molly and she vanished from the bed.

Then he lay down and closed his eyes.

7

E ric couldn't believe he was back in Iraq. Well, it was called Kurdistan now. Same difference. He had left that place behind two hundred years ago. And now he was back.

His memories of those days were crystal clear, thanks to the memory recall features provided by his AI core. All the grit, the boredom, the horror.

I really am in hell.

He was in the Caucasus Mountains region. He remembered doing a quick mission here back in the day. The place had been fertile, and covered in green growing things.

Not anymore.

A combination of climate change and unending wars had worked together to reduce these mountains and the outlying districts into the rocky landscape covered in the familiar "moon" dust that coated the rest of the country. Except this time he didn't have to worry about that dust clogging his airways and triggering allergies. Sneezing, a runny nose, all things of his human past. No, the only thing he had to worry about these days was grit jamming his electroactuators. That, and a rocket propelled grenade slamming him upside the ass.

Same feces, different latrine.

He was serving as a sniper with Frogger, his mind twin. They were sheltered in a crumbling building over-looking the street below. The city was named Urdani, and was nestled in the mountains near the Turkish border. Blocky, sand-colored buildings lined a street that was meant for pedestrian traffic. Blast craters marred the cobblestone.

Those buildings rose as high as nine stories, and were fronted in fire bricks whose blocks sometimes formed geometric patterns. Arched doorways and windows were outlined in white gypsum. Most of those windows were covered in wooden shutters so that passersby couldn't see inside: the men of these lands liked to keep their wives hidden away.

Minarets stabbed past the flat rooftops occasionally, set against the backdrop of the yellow-brown mountains behind them.

He swept the cross-hairs of his laser sniper rifle along the street below. Sniping was something he was never really good at when he was in the army. But he was now. He had avoided killing anyone back during his human enlistment days, but he'd slaughtered a whole boatload of insurgents since arriving in Kurdistan. With his emotion controls dialed way down, he felt no remorse whatsoever. The army had gotten precisely what it paid for: a lean, mean, killing machine. Literally.

Strictly speaking, he didn't have to physically gaze through the scope. He could use the remote interface and access the video feed recorded by the scope, allowing him to scan for targets without having to place any part of his body in view. It was great when he needed to shoot around corners, for example.

The rifle could also shoot something called a Vision Round. Rather than firing the built-in laser, it fired a dart that was able to embed in softer surfaces like wood and plaster. The dart contained a camera that could also be used to target hard-to-see enemies.

But he had no such need for either of those two visual augmentations at the moment. Thus, he continued to peer through the scope. He spotted polit- ical graffiti upon the walls below, scribbled in Modern Arabic and English. Variants of "death to Kurdistan and the infidels" seemed popular in this area. That, and obscene pictures of Cicadas with breasts and hairy muffs drawn in—as if to imply that the robots were little better than the local women. Bambi and Ball Crusher loved those drawings. Morpheus, meanwhile, preferred to blow up any she found. The city walls and buildings behind them were littered with the pock marks of rocket propelled grenades she'd had her robots launch to wipe out such drawings.

The insurgents were mocking not just the Cicadas with those drawings, but the governments that produced them. The foreign fighters had realized long ago that it cost our country trillions of dollars to continue waging this war, whereas for them the only cost was their measly lives. They were eager to keep us involved in the region; their endgame seemed to be the bankruptcy of all countries involved. But we had a long way to go, yet —they didn't realize that the war actually helped our economy, and spurred technological innovation. So, as long as the terrorists continued to flock here from around the world, Eric and his team would continue blowing them up.

Insurgents had taken over the city a few weeks ago, and used it as a base of operations to stage raids and terrorist attacks against other nearby cities and army outposts. The Brass had sent in Second Platoon, and their associated support units, to deal with the threat. They called themselves a "platoon," but when including the support troops under their command, in reality they were more like a company, or a battalion, at least as Eric had known them in his time.

Senior Command didn't want to bomb the city outright—intel reported that civilians were still holed up in different apartments and residences throughout Urdani. Plus the Russians and Chinese both had a presence on the eastern side of the town, where they were pushing the insurgents inward from their own forward operating bases.

Eric and the Bolt Eaters meanwhile were applying pressure from the other side, so that insurgents faced attacks on multiple fronts.

He resided in an apartment building, at a bedroom in the upper level. He'd shoved the bed against the wall beside the window, and lay flat on the mattress, his rifle on a bipod as he aimed into the street past the opposite bottom corner of the window. He didn't actually need that bipod, because his robotic hands would keep the weapon steady on its own, but the mind dump he had received had trained him to always use it, so he did.

His rifle was sheathed in the same LEDs as his polycarbonate skin, allowing both the weapon and his body to assume a stealth coloration that blended him in with the background.

Frogger had shoved another mattress into the room, and had managed to squeeze it in between the window and the far wall. He mirrored Eric's position to watch the street in the opposite direction. Neither Eric nor Frogger needed a spotter—they carried all the equipment they needed aboard their bodies to range find, measure wind speed, and so forth; and they made any required calculations for distance, slant range, and so forth in their heads, or offloaded the calculation to their Accomps. Of course, the latter calculations weren't needed for the laser mode of the weapon, but came in handy if he needed to deploy a Vision Round at a distance with any degree of accuracy.

Brontosaurus, meanwhile, acted as flanker, and covered the rear approach to the room, aiming his heavy guns into the hallway outside. Six-barrel "Beast" H134 models, those two big weapons were locked into the mounts built into Brontosaurus' forearms. The Beasts looked similar to Gatling guns, or the mini guns one might find mounted to early twenty-first century gunships. Without those heavily modded biceps, it was doubtful Brontosaurus would have been able to support the added weight: Eric had tried to mount a Beast once and he certainly couldn't do it. Perhaps it might seem odd to build a barrel into a laser weapon, but even lasers could pulse only so fast, and this design allowed the Beast to keep up a steady stream of punishment, strong and rapid enough to penetrate tank armor, while minimizing cool down intervals.

Both Brontosaurus and Frogger had switched to stealth mode, their LEDs blending them into the background like Eric. Something like LIDAR or thermal imaging would easily penetrate their ruse, but only a few insurgents had weapons tech beyond automatic rifles.

The three Bolt Eaters had moved to this latest hide only three hours ago. Previously, they had occupied two other buildings, but had relocated with the team as the enemy retreated toward the city center. So far, they'd been on duty for ten hours. They expected to remain so for the next thirty or more, until the city was free of insurgents. It was typical of the missions they'd gone on during the current deployment. They didn't need rest, after all. They were robots, restrained only by the limitations of their power cells. If they ever prematurely drained those cells by operating in high time awareness mode, they'd have to recharge. To that end, on the floor beside Eric was a heavy battery pack, shaped like a toolkit with a handle, that he'd hauled with him when moving between locations. With that pack, he could recharge his cell without leaving his hide, nor his post. If he exhausted the pack, however, he'd have to make his way down to the support carrier and plug in to a recharge port. It happened.

There was no connection to the 7G Milnet out here in the Caucasus Mountains, so the team formed their own adhoc 7G network with the help of Ravens perched on the rooftops, and the Predators flying back and forth out of sight far overhead. The platoon was able to tap into the slower network the insurgents used to communicate, which allowed the team to track the radio chatter, but not much else: so far, they hadn't been able to penetrate the encryption.

Bipedals stood outside different buildings below, Breachers and Savages, part of the group assigned house-to-house clearing duties. Other Savages were crouched on rooftops nearby, ready to provide fire support. Ravager mechs meanwhile held down the intersections on either side, acting as defense platforms. A couple of Abrams tanks roamed the streets beyond, escorted by Savages. They weren't actually Abrams, of course… the army wasn't using a two hundred year old tank platform. But that was how Eric's linguistic engine handled the translation from Modern English into Young English whenever someone mentioned the tanks.

All of those robots, from the drones overhead to the mechs and smaller robots in the streets, were controlled by the different team members, as defined by their various role. As a sniper, Eric wasn't in charge of any units. It was too bad. Controlling the house-clearing robots would have been a lot more interesting than sniping, but hey, he had no say in the matter.

Besides, he didn't have the extra power cells he'd need to maintain the slower time sense that came with operating so many units. During the pre-deployment

VR training sessions, he'd had plenty of opportunities to try out the different robot swarms, and he found it similar to playing a real-time strategy game, except that it was actually slower than real-time. More like one-third time, in fact, with every three seconds he experienced the same as one in the real world. When things got hectic during the training sessions, he usually slowed things down even further still.

But all of that was moot at the moment.

I'm just a grunt. In charge only of the rifle in front of me.

As a corporal, Brontosaurus was officially in charge of the small sniper team formed by himself, Eric, and Frogger. Eric was duty-bound to obey every order Brontosaurus, or even Frogger, gave him.

Yup. I officially miss my old life.

Not that he cared all that much, given how muted his emotions were.

Every one of the previously described units was capable of autonomous operations, but the onboard AIs only took over if there was a comm failure. When that happened, the machines were essentially useless. Predators would retreat if necessary, moving out of harm's way, while ground units took cover, putting their rifles away: the Rules of Engagement prevented the autonomous units from firing on their own. If any of those machines somehow managed to let off a shot on its own, the lawyers would be sent in.

The insurgents occasionally launched robots of their own, usually off-the-shelf varieties they had brought with them into the country, or purchased from the nearby city of New Kurdistan. They included small drones meant for aerial photography, robot assistants, and companions, like autonomous pet dogs. Sometimes those drones and dogs were jury-rigged to carry lasers or improvised explosive devices, and could cause some damage if they weren't taken down quickly.

"You know, I'm still thinking of that girl we saw on the street earlier," Brontosaurus said.

"Why, you mean the one whose face you saw for like a half second?" Frogger asked. "Before she covered it again with her veil?"

"Yup," the heavy gunner replied. "If she didn't live in this country, she'd be a model. She has no opportunities here."

"Maybe you should be her knight in shining armor bronco boy," Eric said as he scanned the street, rooftops, and windows of the buildings below. "Saddle on up and show her what you're made of, rescuing her from the streets of Urdani like the real man you are."

"Like I'll ever find her now," Brontosaurus said. "She'd have no interest in me, anyway. I'm a machine."

"What about those legendary dildonic attachments I'm always hearing about," Eric said.

"Yeah, I actually bought one of those," Frogger said. "You can borrow mine."

"That's gross," Brontosaurus said.

"Uh, you never told me you bought a strap-on," Eric told Frogger. "That doesn't seem like me."

"Hey, we've been known to have our urges now and again," Frogger said. "Don't tell me you haven't recreated Molly in VR."

Eric momentarily looked away from his scope.

Frogger was gazing right at him. "You know me too well. So how well did it work? The dildonic attachment?"

"Terrible," Frogger said. "The sex is much better in VR. The damn thing broke in the middle of the act."

"Was it a fellow robot you were doing, or a human?"

"A human of course," Frogger said.

"Nice," Eric said. "I didn't think humans would ever be interested in us."

"We have our groupies," Brontosaurus said. "Especially us military bots."

"Who would have thought." Eric moved his eye to his scope and returned his attention to the street below. "Despite the negatives, being a robot has all sorts of advantages. We have groupies. We can change our time sense. We don't have to worry about diseases. Or things like diarrhea."

"That's a big one for me," Brontosaurus said.

"I remember last time I was here as a human," Frogger told Brontosaurus. "I had the shits constantly. As did most everyone else. Man, the pain… it would come and go, and no matter how hard you clenched, you just couldn't hold the burning liquid in. I tell you, the water here, it was full of bacteria incompatible with our guts. I would have hated to have been cooped up in an armored vehicle. I heard some stories about the people who worked inside tanks: things got real messy inside, real quick. Ask Scorp. I'm not lying, am I?"

During training, the team had assigned Eric the call-sign "Scorpion," or "Scorp" for short, because of the way he liked to impale targets on any spikes available in the environment, such as steeples at the tops of buildings, or a protruding piece of rebar from a crumbled building. For a while there it had become his signature move, but he'd soon grown bored of it. However, the nickname had stuck. Slate liked to warp the callsign into Scarface, though how he'd derived that from Scorpion, Eric didn't know.

"Nope, we didn't have fun when we were here," Eric said. "I clearly recall visits to the outhouses of the Camp Denver CHU farm. You remember?"

"Oh yeah, the worst," Frogger said.

"They were a pigsty, essentially," Eric said. "I can still smell the baked feces and urine inside my virtual nostrils. And it was so hot in there... you'd think they'd build in ventilation, if not for the smell, then the heat. Nope. And then the flies... no. Just no. I remember one time, after having a particularly bloody diarrhea, I stumbled outside, flies and filth covering my leg, stars speckling my vision, and I lay down on the ground, naked, too sick to get up. Good times."

"Yikes," Brontosaurus said. "I'm glad I wasn't born in the early twenty-first century."

"Yeah, like I said, being a robot has its advantages." Eric paused. "Though I guess we're not entirely immune to diseases, are we..."

"How so?" Brontosaurus asked.

"Well, what about computer viruses?" Eric replied. "That's a kind of disease, isn't it?"

"In a way," Brontosaurus said. "But we've got anti-virus programs running. And we get updates pushed through on the Milnet, in case you hadn't noticed."

"I noticed," Eric said. "At first I was reluctant to accept them. I used to have big problems with Windows automatically updating on me, and messing up my video drivers. Or my sound card. What a nightmare."

"Windows, huh?" Brontosaurus said.

"Before your time," Eric said. "Anyway, I finally took the leap and turned on auto-update. My Accomp has been downloading the patches automatically and installing them in the background as they come in. So far, so good. But one of these days I'm expecting to wake up to find one of my subsystems disabled. Like Bullet Time no longer works. Or I can't move my body. Something like that."

"Never happen," Brontosaurus said. "You haven't seen the rigorous testing process the military goes through before releasing each patch. They have a rig containing a hundred versions of each robot model. Cicada A1s. Cicada A21s. Savages. You name it. They run each update on the robots for a week before they give it the stamp of approval. Unless of course they're patching some critical zero day that an enemy is using to hack our systems. Then the patch goes live a lot faster. I admit there have been problems with some of those."

"Like what kind of problems?" Eric said.

"Probably better that you don't know," Brontosaurus said.

"Ignorance is bliss," Eric said.

He trained his cross-hairs on a gypsum-outlined doorway. It looked like there was a rifle muzzle peering out from the opening.

Ordinarily the Rules of Engagement would have prevented Eric from firing first—in general, he had to confirm he was under attack beforehand. But the lieutenant had lifted that particular rule from the Mind Refurbs before the mission, as he often did when the Bolt Eaters were sent out on house clearing operations.

Eric double-checked that no friendlies were in the area on his overhead map, then he adjusted his aim, extrapolating the position of the center of mass of a typical human being that might be holding that rifle, and squeezed the trigger.

An insurgent dropped to the ground. The laser had cauterized the wound, preventing blood from pooling underneath the body.

"Eighty-two," Eric said.

"Damn it," Frogger said. "Why do you always end up with the better side, Scorp?"

"The luck of the draw," Brontosaurus said.

"It's not luck," Eric said. "Skill."

He scanned the windows above the doorway of the same building, but couldn't see past the slats covering the panes.

"You know, I remember a time when competing for a kill count would have disgusted me," Eric said.

"Yeah, but that was when we were human," Frogger said.

"Do you ever miss it, Bronto?" Eric asked, searching for his next target.

"What?" Brontosaurus replied. "Being human?"

"Well yeah," Eric said.

"Can't say that I do," Brontosaurus told him. "I'm far stronger than I ever was as a man. Far faster."

"But what about the chance to feel another human being?" Eric said.

"I got VR," Brontosaurus said. "With all the enhancements: I have the senses of taste, smell, sight, sound, and touch. I'm anatomically correct, with my member jacked right into my pleasure center. Sex, orgasm, you name it, I can feel it all. What we have here, as Mind Refurbs, is the Golden Age. We combine all the best parts of being human and robot, with none of the baggage."

"Except we can't really *feel* anymore..." Eric said. "Emotionally. Sure, we have pleasure, but the lieutenant makes us keep everything else dialed down. If we can convince him to override that setting, or find a way to enable our emotions ourselves—"

"Trust me, you don't want to feel, bro," Brontosaurus said. "Emotions were the worst part about being human. That baggage I was talking about earlier? I was referring to feelings of course. Back when I was a man, between the deployments and the woman I was seeing, I was left an emotional wreck. Ever heard of PTSD? Or whatever they call it these days? I was messed up. It was probably a good thing a sniper finally put me out of my misery."

"You really think you'll be able to do this job if you can *feel?*" Frogger told Eric. "The guilt would destroy us, and you know it."

"I suppose you're right," Eric said. "It was a nice thought."

Just then Eric sighted an insurgent in one of the windows. The bearded man forced the shutters to the side, enough to squeeze half his torso through. He held a launcher over one shoulder.

It was aimed directly up at Eric.

Eric switched to Bullet Time, but it was too late: by the time he had lined up his cross-hairs and released the shot, the insurgent had already launched the rocket propelled grenade.

"Incoming!" Eric yelled.

8

Eric increased his time sensitivity to max, so that the approaching missile moved no faster than a car traveling at ten miles and hour. He got up. His body seemed to move sluggishly—his mind always performed faster than his body at the highest speed. He retreated from the window, moving all too slowly. Across from him, Frogger moved at a similar pace. Brontosaurus meanwhile had already vacated the room—the heavy gunner's modded servomotors were capable of much faster movement.

Eric and Frogger both crossed the hallway threshold as the grenade impacted the window frame. A cloud of explosive vapors and shrapnel expanded outward rapidly.

The cloud enveloped him, and he was hurled from the room by the explosive force of the detonating grenade. He used Bullet Time to control his landing and dodge shrapnel as best as he was able: he smashed into a side wall before crashing to the floor in the hallway.

Eric dismissed Bullet Time and the world snapped back to normal around him.

"There goes our hide," Frogger said, sitting up beside him.

Eric sat up, too. He reached out and ripped a large shrapnel fragment from Frogger's chest.

"Right above your AI core," Eric said. "You're lucky."

"That's what we have armor plates for," Frogger said, tapping the area with a polycarbonate knuckle.

Frogger did the same for Eric, tearing a large rectangular piece from his leg.

"Imagine if we were still human," Frogger said.

"You imagine it," Eric said, scrambling to his feet.

Brontosaurus was already standing, and had both of his heavy guns pointed toward the remnants of the room behind them.

Eric glanced at his power cell levels. Fifty percent. He'd left his battery pack behind in that room. There was a good chance there was nothing left of it.

He heard a loud bang and spun toward the foyer located at the far end of the hallway.

The entrance door had exploded inward.

Three insurgents stood in plain view, their weapons pointed directly at him.

Eric switched to Bullet Time as those weapons activated. The projectiles created shockwave tunnels through the air, like boats traveling over the surface of water and leaving waves in their wake.

Eric stepped out of the way of those bullets and took cover in an adjacent room.

As time returned to normal, he glanced at his overhead map. Frogger and Brontosaurus had ducked into the room across from his own. He peered past the doorframe slightly, until he could see that room; staying hidden, Brontosaurus pointed the tip of one heavy gun out of the room and let loose. Invisible laser pulses fired from the tip as the muzzle rotated to target the different insurgents.

Eric moved deeper into the room. He reached the wall, and punched repeatedly, forming several holes that penetrated entirely through the drywall to the kitchen on the other side. Then he stepped back, and hurled himself at the weakened area, and the force of his impact brought him right through.

Having a robot body does have its advantages…

White plaster dust settled over his body, ruining any chance of applying a stealth skinning.

The kitchen was separated from the foyer only by a counter. Beyond that counter, he could see the main entrance. Because of his current angle, he also saw two of the insurgents taking cover in the hallway outside, next to the entrance.

And they saw him.

He immediately ducked as bullets came in.

Eric carried two types of grenades on the harness he wore over his chest. One was the standard frag grenade that detonated upon impact, launching a deadly spray of shrapnel. The other was a pulse grenade, which sent out a series of electrical bolts via random plasma channels—particularly effective against robots.

He retrieved one of the former from his harness, and tossed the frag grenade over the counter toward the entrance. Dee helped him calculate the necessary speed and throw angle, as well as an appropriate fuse timer.

When the explosion came, he switched to moderate Bullet Time.

He leaped over the counter, the movements of his accelerated body on par with his increased time sense. He moved through the slow moving cloud of debris. Two insurgents were already dead on the ground. Beyond the cloud, he spotted three more on the right side of the door, and four on the left.

The surprised men tried to turn their rifles on him, but he was too fast. He made his way toward them, and utilized the martial arts techniques that were part of his training package to neutralize them. He launched a side chop into the neck of one man, punched his steel fist into the face of another, and grabbed the rifle from the third, giving him a roundhouse kick to the stomach in the process. The impacted body moved backwards slowly, as if in water.

Eric grabbed that man while he was still in midair, and then spun him around to face the other four that lingered on the other side of the entrance.

Those four had begun to open fire.

Eric released the midair man, so that he began hurtling toward the firing insurgents, absorbing the slow-moving bullets in the process.

Eric raised the rifle that dangled from his shoulder,

and released four laser pulses in turn, targeting the heads of each man. The invisible light beams instantly created small black burns in their foreheads.

Eric released Bullet Time.

In front of him, the hurtling body struck the four men, who were already dead. Behind him, the other two insurgents toppled. The neck of the first was bent at an odd angle. The face of the second had caved, leaving behind an unrecognizable, bloody pulp above that thick beard.

Frogger and Brontosaurus appeared at the entrance.

"Are you sure I can't convince you guys to call me Neo?" Eric said.

The insurgent that Eric had used as a bullet shield was still alive, but barely. He was trying to pull himself away along the floor. The roundhouse kick to the stomach had ripped open his belly, and whitish, blood-covered intestines trailed along the floor.

Brontosaurus approached the man, who stopped when one of those big polycarbonate-metal feet landed in front of his face.

Brontosaurus switched to Arabic. "Are there any more of you in the building?"

"Fuck you," the insurgent replied in English.

Brontosaurus crunched his foot down hard, popping that head.

"Why couldn't you just laser him?" Frogger said.

Brontosaurus shrugged. "We have to assume that this building is compromised. Get to the first floor. We're relocating immediately." He switched to the comm line. "Dickson, Sniper Team C has been compromised at location B12. Requesting backup. Also, I want a precision airstrike on B13." That was the building across the street where the insurgent had launched the initial rocket propelled grenade. According to the map, there were currently no friendlies inside.

"Marlborough already has Morpheus diverting some Ravagers your way," Dickson replied over the comm. "Hang tight."

Eric stared at that headless body for several moments after Brontosaurus walked away.

We need our emotions back. Without them, we're completely stripped of our humanity. Whatever happened to mercy?

Then again, what Brontosaurus had done had been a mercy, of sorts. Though there was a good chance the platoon medic would have been able to repair the man. What was the point of that? He'd only return to fight another day.

Repair. Funny how he thought of men as things to be repaired now. Rather than healed, or mended.

In the past, Dee would have offered some odd riposte to thoughts like these, but he had long since turned off the Accomp's listening abilities. He wanted at least some semblance of privacy, and these days reactivated Dee only when necessary.

The trio reached the far side of the hallway, which was covered in a floor-to-ceiling window that provided a view overlooking the street below. A stairwell door offered a route to the next level beside them.

The floor shook.

"That'd be our airstrike next door," Brontosaurus said.

The window wasn't facing the building that had been struck, but a cloud of debris flooded into the street from that direction.

"Bye bye American pie," Frogger said.

The glass abruptly shattered, and Eric and the others were sent flying backward by the force of something exploding.

Four insurgents with jetpacks roared into view. They carried rifles: Eric recognized the characteristic markings of Chinese laser rifles.

Eric switched to Bullet Time, and fired as two of the insurgents passed through the broken window and landed inside. Dark spots appeared on their foreheads.

Brontosaurus and Frogger were also firing, but they were too late: one of the insurgents still outside got off a shot.

Frogger went down—it was impossible to dodge a laser after it was fired.

On the lefthand side of his HUD, Eric had a list of callsigns representing the status of each member of the platoon. Frogger's name had gone red.

The two insurgents still outside spiraled out of view as their jetpacks fired randomly—dead men couldn't provide controller input.

Eric went to his fallen twin. The beam had struck Frogger in the chest, above the already weakened area over his AI core; it had passed right through into the neural network inside.

"He's gone," Eric said in disbelief.

"What's the status on Frogger?" Marlborough asked over the comm.

"He's gone," Eric repeated for the sarge. "His neural core shot through."

Speaking over the comm was an art. It involved disconnecting the speaker located behind the mouth grille, so that any words spoken weren't voiced aloud, but heard only over the shared adhoc network. It was almost like thinking, except that one had to invoke the same muscles responsible for talking in order to transmit any sounds, otherwise the words wouldn't register over the comm. It allowed the team members to keep their private thoughts to themselves rather than broadcasting them for the team to hear.

"We'll restore him from a backup," Brontosaurus said.

"But he's still gone," Eric said. "This version of him, he died right here, on this floor. Even if we restore him, it won't be the same Frogger."

"It's our curse," Brontosaurus said. "And our greatest gift."

Brontosaurus gathered up the Chinese rifles from the two dead men, and slid the straps over his shoulder.

"Either those insurgents stole that gear from the Chinese, or the Chinese gave it to them," Eric said.

"Stole, I suspect," Brontosaurus said. "Though it wouldn't surprise me if the Chinese did in fact give it to them."

Brontosaurus placed charges on the jetpacks and then swung Frogger's body over his shoulders. Then he hurried down the stairs.

Eric rushed into the stairwell after the heavy gunner.

The air roared behind him as the jetpacks and all the propellant they contained exploded.

They moved down the zig-zagging flights of stairs. When they rounded the platform of the third flight, they stepped straight into the line of fire of several more insurgents waiting at the next platform below. The men held more laser rifles.

Eric engaged Bullet Time, turning his body away as he dove for cover. His left arm became riddled with boreholes from laser impacts before he was beyond the line of fire.

He landed beside Brontosaurus, next to the upward leading run of steps. The heavy gunner had received a similar amount of laser damage to his upper chest. His armor had held.

Eric flexed his arm. Nothing seemed damaged... no wait, he had lost control of his pinky and adjacent finger.

"Dickson, where are those Ravager mechs?" Brontosaurus said over the comm.

"Almost there..." Dickson replied.

Brontosaurus directed the tip of one heavy gun past the bottom edge of the steps, and activated auto-targeting mode. The muzzle rotated as it fired repeated pulses.

The out-of-view insurgents shouted.

Brontosaurus slid his rifle further past the edge, no doubt accessing the video feed returned by the scope so that he could search for targets without exposing himself.

Eric meanwhile covered the approach from above.

He considered attempting to punch through the stairs, but a glance at the staircase overhead told him that overall, it was probably a bit too thick.

He saw a small puff of smoke appear from the carpet of the step above him, and realized the insurgents were attempting to fire their lasers through the stairs themselves. They would have had to have been firing randomly, and probably as fast as they were able. Their rifles would soon overheat. The question was, when?

9

E ric jacked his time sense to max, slowing everything around him to a halt, then accessed his video feed timeline—Cicadas kept running logs of all sensory input for the past twenty-four hours—and stepped back until he had the current insurgents in frame once more. He zoomed in on the weapons they held, and confirmed the make and model: they were the same Chinese laser rifles Brontosaurus had collected from the last attackers. Eric ran a lookup on that partic-ular make and model in his military database.

Apparently, the insurgents would only be able to fire eighty pulses in rapid succession before the weapon overheated, and they'd need a thirty second downtime interval. Those pulses were fired in quarter second intervals. So if the attackers held down the triggers to fire non-stop, the weapons would overheat in twenty seconds. Glancing at the video timeline, he saw that he'd taken cover fifteen seconds ago. They'd probably begun firing into the underside of the stairs shortly after Brontosaurus took out some of them with his heavy gun, which was eight seconds ago.

That meant twelve seconds to go.

Assuming all of them had opened fire.

Eric restored his time sense to normal, and watched the puffs of smoke continue to appear as the wood, and the rug, were burned through in random areas. He kept himself flattened on the platform, hoping to reduce his exposure profile.

He waited the prerequisite amount of time, and then told Brontosaurus: "Cover me."

"What—"

"Just keep your heavy gun aimed past the edge," Eric said. "With auto-targeting of tangos turned on."

Eric dialed up his time sense halfway to max, so that his body still moved at an acceptable rate in comparison to the hyper-perception of his mind, and then he flung himself past the edge of the stairs.

He led with his rifle, holding it in front of him, and aimed past the edge as he traveled forward. He accessed the scope feed, so that its video filled most of his vision, and then he ramped his time sense to max.

He continued to slide forward, thanks to the momentum of his jump. As the enemy units slowly came into view, he targeted them one by one with his rifle, and squeezed the trigger. Two men went down. The third had started to swivel his body toward Eric, but then he got that man too.

As his shoulder collided with the far wall, the fourth insurgent came into view. The man had swung his rifle completely toward Eric, and it was aimed at his chest—the AI core.

Now he'd find out if he was right about the weapon cool down or not.

Eric squeezed the trigger, and a dark smudge appeared on the man's forehead. No similar smudge marred Eric's chest plate in turn.

He increased his time sense so that he could recover from the impact, and then he spun his body to tumble down the stairs. He fired twice more in rapid succession, aiming past the bars of the railing, and taking out the two remaining insurgents that had sheltered there.

When he hit the platform leading to the next zig-zagging flight of stairs, he restored his time sense to normal, and the men he'd struck all dropped dead in front of him.

"Nicely done," Brontosaurus said.

Eric dismissed the video feed from his scope and stood.

The wall exploded beside him, and he was sent flying into the opposite wall by the debris.

A large Ravager mech burst inside, barely fitting the confines of the staircase.

"'Bout time you showed," Brontosaurus said.

"Sorry it took so long," Morpheus said over the comm in her Japanese accent. "We encountered some resistance along the way."

Eric knew it was her speaking, not just because of the voice, but because her name was highlighted on the platoon list on the left side of his HUD when she spoke. As happened when anyone used the comm.

"Send a lady to do a man's job..." Brontosaurus said.

"Hey!" Morpheus said. The Ravager under her control mech swung its laser turrets toward the upper flight, where Brontosaurus was just stepping into view.

The heavy gunner raised an arm in surrender. "I kid, I kid. Come on, you know you're my favorite mech operator."

"Jump on," Morpheus said.

Eric spared a moment to glance at his power cell. Thirty percent.

He leaped onto the Ravager's back, and clambered into the passenger seat above the jumpjets. Brontosaurus joined him. There was just enough room for the both of them to strap in.

Eric requested a link to the Ravager's AI so that he would receive notices. A moment later the AI confirmed the request.

"I don't suppose you can transfer control of the Ravager to me?" Eric asked Morpheus.

In answer the Ravager leaped out the gaping hole in the apartment wall and fired its jumpjets to cushion its landing on the street below.

The bodies of about twenty insurgents covered the street around him. Apparently the enemy had chosen this moment to make one of their famous sorties.

He glanced at his overhead map, and saw that red dots representing tangos had appeared all over the place, and were pinning down most of the Bolt Eaters and their support troops. Which would explain why only one mech had arrived, and why it had taken so long to do so.

Laser shots erupted from the far side of the street, and the Ravager deployed a thick metal ballistic shield in its right arm. Apparently that sortie was still in progress.

He accessed the feed from one of the Ravens on a nearby rooftop, and spotted the insurgents lying behind the concrete Jersey barriers the Bolt Eater's own robots had placed earlier.

"They're on three o'clock," Eric said.

"I see them," Morpheus said.

Two more mechs landed beside the main Ravager, and deployed their shields as well. They were digging in, and placing the laser turrets in their other arms over the top edges of the shields to fire at the enemy.

A moment later an air strike hit the Jersey barrier, and the building beyond it, cloaking that side of the street in a big dust cloud. Similar strikes hit other areas nearby.

Eric glanced at his overhead map. Huge swathes of red dots had vanished in an instant.

"Gotta love those Predators," Brontosaurus said.

The three Ravagers stood upright, and began to retreat.

Eric heard a growing whine, as of an aircraft coming in for a crash landing. A moment later a Predator appeared overhead, and clipped the apartment with its wing, crashing into the street behind them. The wingless fuselage skidded along the asphalt before falling into a blast crater and exploding.

"What the hell," Slate said over the comm. "Chinese bitches have dispatched a drone swarm to take down our Predators!"

"Switch Predators to evasive maneuvers!" Marlborough ordered.

"Already on it!" Slate said.

"It's not the Chinese," Eagleeye said. "I've got eyes on the Russian FOB on the far side of town." FOB stood for Forward Operating Base. "More drones are launching from it at this very moment. Harbinger equivalents."

Harbingers were drones halfway between Ravens and Predators, and were ideal for swarming. They didn't carry missiles like Predators, but had an array of laser turrets that could be trained on fast-moving targets. Like Predators.

"Mickey, get on the comm with the Russians and ask them just what the hell they think they're doing!" Marlborough transmitted. "In the meantime, Eagleeye, I want our own Harbingers launched from the FOB."

"You got it, Sarge," Eagleeye said. "Best way to fight a drone swarm, is *with* a drone swarm."

"My Spiders on the eastern front are encountering Russian bots," Bambi said over the comm. "My units are taking a lot of damage!"

"So are my Reapers," Traps said. "Armor people, can we get some tanks or mechs over here? Assuming you want our combat robots to live to see another day…"

"On it," Hank said. "Sending a few Ravagers your way."

"And I'm sending some Abrams," Tread added.

Eric glanced at his HUD as the three Ravagers took a side street. The map had lit up with several new red dots along the eastern front. The dots were tinted a darker red than the previous, indicating Russian autonomous troops. Chinese troops would have showed up a lighter red.

"You might want to disembark here," Morpheus told Brontosaurus and Eric. "Unless you want to fight on the front lines."

Eric leaped down, as did Brontosaurus, who was still carrying Frogger's body over his shoulders.

As the mechs retreated, the two Cicadas headed toward a nearby apartment building. The front doors were already kicked in from a previous round of house clearing troops, so they raced upstairs.

"We just lost our last Predator," Slate said. "I tried to steer the remaining two away from the fight, but the damn range of those Harbinger lasers is too great."

"There goes our air support," Manticore said. "Maybe it's time to look into assigning a more competent operator to the Predators."

"Shut up, Manure," Slate said. That was his nickname for Manticore when he was angry. He also called him Manicure.

"What's the status on our Harbingers!" Marlborough said.

"They're just beginning to enter the combat arena," Eagleeye said.

"Too bad we don't have our Paladins," Hank said. "These bitches would have been dealt with already."

The Brass had recalled the Paladins—heavy artillery —a few days earlier, citing an urgent need for another operation nearby. Thankfully, the Chinese and Russians had also withdrawn their artillery at the same time: probably not a coincidence.

Eric saw a flash overhead and then an enemy Harbinger crashed into the rooftop across the street. He knew it was an enemy because his vision overlaid a red rectangle over the unit. He saw other Harbinger units overhead, some outlined in red, others green, as they engaged in autonomous drone combat.

"I'm requesting a pair of bombers and gunships from base to serve as backup," Marlborough said. "They'll be here in ten minutes."

"The Russians are probably doing the same," Donald said. According to the overhead map, the comm officer was deployed near Marlborough.

"Then we'll just have to see how far they want to escalate this skirmish," Marlborough said.

Eric and Brontosaurus reached the roof. Braxton and Hicks were utilizing this particular rooftop for sniping purposes, and had hidden underneath a water tank that bordered the eastern side. Crusher was watching their rear flank with her heavy gun attachments. Her weapons were the smaller H130 Beast variants: lighter than the H134, but almost as deadly.

"Hey boys, this rooftop is taken," Crusher said.

"Make room," Brontosaurus said. "Scratch that. We'll make our own." He dashed next to the water tank and took up a position beneath a blocky wireless Internet antennae next to the building edge.

Eric joined him, using those large antennae for cover, and gazed down onto the street below. In the next street he could see several robotic troops dug in amid the rubble. Traps' Reapers. The robots looked slightly insectile: they had four crooked legs supporting a head and torso. Each Reaper had no arms per se, but rather laser turrets attached to either flank. Upon the shoulders they carried small rocket-propelled-grenade launchers. They were essentially smaller versions of mechs.

On the other side of the street, Eric saw the muzzles of laser turrets protruding from nearly all of the window frames of the apartment building there: those were the Russian machines that sourced all those red dots on the map in this area.

"Okay, just heard back from the Russians," Mickey said. "They're pissed at us. Apparently they'd sent a shitload of robot sappers into the sewers to infiltrate a suspected insurgent hideout. Unfortunately, the fuel from a downed mech—it's not clear if it was one of ours, or theirs—had been leaking into the sewer, and when one of our Predators dropped a bomb nearby, that fuel detonated, taking out all of their sappers."

"Well that's their fault for not warning us their troops were in the area!" Hyperion said.

"The Russian commander doesn't see it that way," Mickey continued. "He refuses to stand down. He says he's not going to stop until every last one of us pays for this outrage."

"Do we have any idea who this Russian commander is?" Marlborough asked. "Does he have any idea he's risking an escalation that could lead to all out war between our sides by doing this?"

"The ID on his comm indicates he's 'Senior Sergeant' Sergei Bokerov," Mickey said. "There isn't anything about him in my local database, but a contact on base tells me he's a Mind Refurb, like the rest of us."

The Bolt Eaters still had a connection to the main base eighty kilometers away thanks to the military satellites in orbit, however comms would be delayed slightly without the Predators to boost the signal. At least until those bomber and gunship reinforcements arrived.

"Of course he's a Mind Refurb," Bambi said. "There are no humans on this battlefield. Other than the insurgents."

Eric heard the whine of an incoming bomb.

10

E ric glanced at the data sent by nearby Harbingers and confirmed, to his relief, that the bomb wasn't headed for the rooftop, but the street beside it.

A huge plume of smoke filled the street below upon impact. Eric ducked as shrapnel from the close blast clattered into the water tanks and antennae on the rooftop.

"Damn it," Traps sent. "Bastards just took out all my embedded Reapers."

"Eagleeye, redirect half of our Harbingers to intercept their Predator equivalents," Marlborough said. "They want to play nasty, do they?"

Eric aimed his rifle scope into the clearing dust below. Windows began to appear. He focused on one of them, and when he saw the characteristic muzzle of an enemy rifle, he adjusted his aim toward the potential center of mass.

"Don't fire," Brontosaurus said. "If these are Russian troops, they'll be able to triangulate our position based on the angular impact data. Position triangulation means an air strike. A change in tactics is necessary."

Eric glanced away from his scope to look at Brontosaurus. "If we're in the same building as them, they can't call in an airstrike."

Brontosaurus grinned, showing off those LED teeth. "Time to get in their faces."

Eric retreated from the edge of the rooftop and stood. Brontosaurus did likewise, still carrying the wreck of Frogger over his shoulders.

"Guys, wait," Crusher said.

Eric and Brontosaurus took a running leap off the rooftop, and landed on the roof of the next building.

"Damn it," Crusher said. "We can't cover you!"

"Then don't," Brontosaurus said, dashing forward.

While running, Eric glanced at his overhead map and saw red dots embedded in the target building going dark as he watched. Braxton and Hicks were indeed covering them, at the risk of an air strike.

Eric maneuvered into the center of the rooftop, so that he was out of the line of sight of any attackers in the target building.

A moment later, Eric heard the whine of an incoming bomb.

He glanced over his shoulder at the adjacent building in time to see Crusher and the other two robots leaping off just as it exploded.

"Told them not to cover us," Brontosaurus said.

"I want those enemy Predators downed, posthaste!" Marlborough transmitted.

Eric reached the rooftop edge and leaped across to the building that harbored the Russian robots.

He heard the buzzing of Harbingers.

"Ours?" Eric asked.

"Nope!" Brontosaurus said.

Eric amped up his time sense, and raced toward the rooftop shed that harbored the stairwell. Menacing Harbinger drones floated upward, appearing over the edge of the building. They looked like mini-gunships, with laser turrets protruding on either side.

Eric threw a grenade and leaped at the door, breaking it, and landed rolling into the stairwell inside. Brontosaurus joined him. Behind them, several small black holes appeared in the shed as the Harbingers riddled it with their invisible pulse beams.

He returned time to normal, and heard an explosion outside. That would be his grenade. On the overhead map, one of the red dots representing the Harbingers winked out.

"Eighty-three," Eric said. When no one answered him, he remembered that Frogger was KIA. Their little competition over fallen tango count was over.

He continued down the stairs. He glanced at the map and saw the Harbingers leaving the area to hunt and kill other targets. That his external map was still updating told him that the team still had eyes out there; probably Ravens perched on nearby rooftops. Blue dots abruptly came in—friendly Harbingers. They chased the red ones away. It would have been fun to watch the dogfight, but he had other things to worry about at the moment.

He reached the stairwell door, and waited for Brontosaurus to arrive behind him. Over the comm to the heavy gunner, he counted down:

"Three."

"Two."

"One."

He kicked in the door, going low—at a crouch— while Brontosaurus went high. The hallway was empty.

They made their way to the closest door. It was open.

Eric detached the scope from his rifle and held it to the doorframe, slowly shoving it past the edge. He switched his point of view to the video feed returned from the scope. He used thermal imaging.

"I spot two tangos," Eric said. "A flanker watching the door. And a sniper at the window."

"I see them," Brontosaurus said. Eric had shared the video feed with him.

The Russian infantry models were humanoid, like the Cicadas, but they had all of their weaponry mounted directly into their forearms like a mech, which made them look similar to Popeye in Eric's eyes. He had to smile at that: he was probably one of the very few people alive who even knew who Popeye was.

He reattached the scope to his rifle, and detached a grenade. With Dee's help, he calculated the optimal throw angle and speed based on the layout of the room he'd just scoped, and his target, and then tossed the weapon inside.

"I'm Popeye the Sailor man," Eric sung.

"Huh?" Brontosaurus said.

"Never mind," Eric said.

The bomb exploded.

Eric stepped into the room, and unleashed two quick shots, finishing off the remaining robot, and firing a double-check shot into the brain case of the first.

"These are 3M30 Bulavas," Brontosaurus said. Eric's Russian translation subroutine converted the word Bulava into mace, as in the weapon. Not that he needed to know that. "Support troops: they don't carry Mind Refurbs."

"This whole building is probably full of support troops," Eric said. "Too bad we can't just find and kill the Mind Refurb responsible for them." Because if they did that, another Russian Mind Refurb would simply assume control. It wasn't quite cut off one head and two more appeared, but pretty close.

He turned around, but Brontosaurus pushed him further inside. The entrance exploded behind them, and the two Cicadas were sent flying into the room.

"They got out a signal," Brontosaurus explained.

"Too bad."

Eric was in a common area of some kind, filled with toppled furniture.

Before he could do anything, the wall to his left detonated, spraying him with plaster.

Eric activated Bullet Time and scooted forward, moving into an ambush position next to the gap before the dust cleared. Brontosaurus did the same on the other side of the opening.

Several small balls rolled into the room, and sprouted legs. They began crawling toward Eric and Brontosaurus.

Eric, still functioning at a higher time sense, unleashed his rifle in rapid succession, and between the two of them, they destroyed those power-draining robot bugs before they could touch either of them. But the robots would have transmitted the positions of the two Cicadas...

Eric leaped forward, aiming to take cover behind an upturned couch. The wall exploded behind him when he was halfway there.

He spun in midair, increasing his time sense even further so that everything slowed right down around him.

He glanced at his power cell. He was down to a quarter.

Yikes.

He directed his rifle toward the clearing dust behind him, and picked out the humanoid form lurking behind it. The Bulava had the turrets of both arms pointed toward him. He fired, scoring a hit.

The Bulava also shot. Repeatedly.

By the time Eric had fallen behind the couch, he had several new laser boreholes drilled into his plate armor. His AI core region was flashing critical: he'd almost bit the dust.

Brontosaurus had taken cover behind an overturned

table beside him. He seemed in better condition than Eric.

Hiding behind furniture wouldn't protect them from laser shots, of course, but it at least occluded their exact positions. He glanced at his overhead map. Two red dots were in the adjacent room. Two tangos.

Eric pointed his rifle at the ceiling and fired a Vision Round. It impacted and gave him a view of the room around him, allowing him to see past the couch.

Brontosaurus tossed several grenades, setting the fuses extremely short so that the Bulavas wouldn't bat them back before they exploded.

Unfortunately, the Bulavas launched grenades of their own.

Eric grabbed the upper edge of the couch and pulled it down over his body, shielding him as the grenades detonated. He hoped Brontosaurus was able to do something similar.

When the dust cleared, he saw Brontosaurus rising from the wreckage of the table. His right arm was blown off, but that wasn't enough to stop him from firing the heavy gun mounted to his left.

Eric slid himself across the floor, and out from underneath the shielding couch, and fired his rifle in turn at the closest Bulava. The two tangos shuddered as the pulse weapons struck them, and then they collapsed.

Brontosaurus fired a Vision Round toward the entrance, and it slammed into a wall on the hallway outside.

"Gotta run!" Brontosaurus said.

On the overhead map, several red dots had

appeared, indicating enemy units closing in on the room.

Eric slung his rifle over his shoulder, and then dashed toward the window. It was already partially broken away, so he cleared the fragile shards with his robotic arm. Then he reached through, found purchase on a pipe outside, and pulled himself out.

He hauled himself upward, slamming his fist into the fire brick exterior as he went, making his own handholds. Brontosaurus followed beneath him.

Eric pulled himself onto the roof, and reached down to help Brontosaurus, who still carried Frogger on his back. Eric spotted Bulavas peering through the window below. They aimed their rifles up at them, but Eric hauled Brontosaurus over the rooftop edge just in time.

They hurried to the far side, and leaped onto the nearest intact building. They headed toward the blue dots representing Crusher, Braxton and Hicks.

Enemy Harbingers swooped down.

"Get off the roof!" Brontosaurus said.

The pair leaped onto a lower, three-story roof nearby.

Behind them, the Harbingers went down, shrieking loudly.

"You're welcome," Hicks said.

"Thanks Hicks, you hick," Eric said.

"*You're* the hick," Hicks replied.

Eric and Brontosaurus leaped the final three stories to the ground, and dove through the already broken glass of a shop window, joining Crusher, Braxton and Hicks inside.

"Just got the last of their Predators," Eagleeye said. "Redirecting the surviving Harbingers to rejoin the fray against the enemy drones."

"Good," Crusher said. "Because they're giving us the time of our lives in here."

Eric assumed a position on the opposite window with Braxton, while Brontosaurus watched the entrance with Crusher. He tracked and shot at any Harbinger drone that came into view. Sometimes said drone was highlighted in green, marking it as a friendly, so he held back.

Soon the drone traffic let up.

"Has that batshit Russian Mind Furbie called off his attack yet?" Traps asked over the comm.

"Negative," Eagleeye transmitted. "My Harbingers have been waging a war of attrition. There are only a few of the units left, on both sides."

That was too bad. But when equally-equipped autonomous units took on their equivalents, the outcome was usually equal decimation on both sides, thanks to the algorithms involved.

"You know, I think this Russian dip is the only one out here," Slate said.

"The only Refurb?" Hyperion said. "Responsible for all those units? Impossible. Has to be a platoon, like ours."

"Not necessarily," Slate said. "Give him a high enough clock speed, with a big enough power cell to support it, and he can throttle up his time sensitivity to handle an army. It makes sense. None of our robot troops have spotted any other Mind Refurb models. No Balaclavas. No Komrades or Kapitans."

"Maybe they're just dug in really really well," Hank said.

"I got something to add that supports Slate's theory," Mickey said. "I'm not detecting the usual radio chatter associated with multiple Mind Refurbs. Ordinarily, there's a main encrypted band the platoon uses to communicate with, and multiple sub-bands used to coordinate among the different support troops. But I'm just detecting one band, used by all the support units: Predators, Harbingers, Bulavas, you name it."

"Maybe they're just keeping really really quiet," Bambi said.

"No, Slate and Mickey are right," Dickson said. "It's possible the Russians are field-testing a new, experimental unit."

"If so, that would explain the batshit part," Traps said. "Absolute power corrupts…"

"Absolutely!" Morpheus said.

"Thanks for stating the obvious, moron," Slate said.

"You're a moron!" the armor operator said. "You… you… fucker!"

"Why do swears sound so cute when they come from you?" Slate said.

"Quit flirting you two," Traps said. "I swear, if you were both human again, you would have hooked up by now."

"How do we know they haven't?" Eagleeye said. "In VR? Morpheus in her sexy Japanese avatar. Slate in his

Long John Silver underwear. I can see it now… in fact, I can't *unsee* it, unfortunately."

"Gunships have arrived," Mickey said. "And bombers. Both sides."

"We're going to have to relocate real quick," Marlborough said. "If there's a chance any of you have been sighted, you need to reposition."

Eric glanced at Crusher.

"We've been sighted," she said.

11

The five of them dashed from the shop and hurried down the street, hugging the line of buildings. Eric heard the characteristic whine of a dropping bomb, and the building they had formerly occupied exploded.

Gunships roared past overhead. Theirs, judging from the green outline provided by his HUD. One was shot down as he watched. The other two launched missiles against an unseen target—probably an enemy gunship.

"Robot operators, if you have any support troops to spare, we could use an escort," Brontosaurus said.

"Got none to spare, sorry," Bambi transmitted.

Eric glanced at his overhead map, and saw that the surviving groups of support robots were pinned down by Russian troops across the western front. Those more troops either side would lose when the bombers of both parties made a pass.

Eric and the others picked their way across the rubble of a bombed street. Several humanoid combat robots—Savage model—were buried in the debris.

They reached an intersection. Eric was in the lead, so he peered past and spotted two enemy gunships unleashing their fire at an apartment. According to the map, Morpheus, Hank and Mickey were holed up inside. No doubt the gunships were keeping them pinned inside in anticipation of the Russian bombers returning to finish the job.

"We could use some help here," Hank said. "We're cut off from our mechs at the moment."

Eric glanced at the rubble nearby, at something he had spotted in the periphery of his vision earlier while walking by.

There was a Savage there, half buried, its torso visible. It wore a detachable jetpack.

Eric raced to that unit. There were only a limited number of jetpacks available to the team, and Marlborough had elected to supply the packs to the support robots, as the Cicadas, in charge of those troops, were expected to have a low probability of interacting directly with the enemy.

So much for low probabilities.

Eric ripped the jetpack away from the Savage and strapped the flying unit around his back. He felt the weight for only a moment before his servomotors compensated.

Light as a feather.

I really gotta get these twentieth centuries sayings out of my head.

"Scorp, what are you doing?" Brontosaurus asked him.

"I'll be right back," Eric replied.

He took a running leap toward the building, and activated his jetpack, landing on the rooftop. He raced forward, keeping to the center of the structure, away from the edges.

He didn't want to simply jet out into the open. There could be hidden snipers watching the street and skies from the windows of buildings nearby. He'd wait until the last possible moment to expose himself.

He reached the rooftop edge, and leaped toward the adjacent building. It was four stories higher, and across a wider span than he could leap on his own, so he applied a quick burst from his jetpack and landed on the target building. There was a Russian mech perched there, behind a water tank. A Dragunov: a Russian heavy mech model that prioritized firepower and armor over mobility.

Eric had obviously caught it by surprise, because its weapon turrets were aimed at the sky.

It swung those turrets down toward him…

Eric activated Bullet Time, and jetted to the side, towards a shed superstructure. He swung his rifle toward the mech. There was no point in aiming at the AI core region in the chest, because it would be too heavily armored for his weapon to penetrate. Instead, he focused on the electroactuator that was exposed underneath the arm, because of Eric's current angle, and the angle of those arms. He fired a shot—it was doubtful it would have any effect against the heavily armored foe, but he had to try—and then landed behind the shed.

He dismissed Bullet Time. Missiles from the mech slammed into the shed, partially crumpling it behind him. Eric tossed three short-fused grenades over the structure in rapid succession, and then jetted upward.

The shed collapsed completely underneath him as more missiles came in. The grenades hit, and he activated Bullet Time as the explosive cloud underneath him cleared.

He'd barely caused a dent in that armor. However, he had damaged one of the housing units that protected the missile launchers: it had a gaping hole that exposed the missiles inside.

Bingo.

Eric slowed Bullet Time even further, and aimed his rifle directly at one of the missiles in the housing unit. He targeted the warhead area, and squeezed the trigger: missiles had armor of their own, and it would likely take more than a few shots to penetrate into the warhead inside. So he held down the trigger, and let his rifle pulse away.

The missile exploded. As did all the missiles inside the launcher.

Eric was engulfed by the explosive cloud of super-heated matter and shrapnel. He was hurled right off the building, along with shrapnel from the water tanks and other superstructures, and landed in slow motion on the rooftop of a three-story building below.

He dismissed Bullet Time. He'd done his best to dodge the shrapnel with his heightened time sense, but his entire front armor section was still riddled with small pieces of molten slag. The LEDs there had melted and fused from the heat.

He could see his targets hovering nearby in the middle of the street, between the buildings. The two gunships had been joined by a third, and the helos continued to pummel the building that housed Morpheus, Hank and Mickey.

Eric's antics had attracted the attention of one of those gunships, apparently, because it was turning toward him. Fast.

Eric tried to stand, but realized he was pinned—a piece of a broken water tank had slammed into his leg and fused with the tar of the old-style roof.

Those weapon mounts trained upon him. Laser pulse mini guns. Blazefire missile launchers. All ready to reduce him to a pile of so much scrap metal.

But before it could fire, Brontosaurus jetted into view, slamming into that gunship. It turned to the right; just at that moment it decided to unleash a volley of lasers, he knew because several small holes appeared in the rooftop beside him.

"Buddy system, bro," Brontosaurus transmitted.

"Where'd you get the jetpack?" Eric said. He reached down, grabbed the edge of the water tank, and ripped it away from where it had fused with the roof.

"I followed your example," Brontosaurus said. He was hanging from the gunship by the legs, and firing his heavy guns into the helo's fuselage at close range.

Eric stood. "Monkey see, monkey do."

"Huh?" Brontosaurus said.

"Never mind," Eric said. He jetted upward toward one of the remaining gunships.

"We really gotta do something about the twenty-first century colloquialisms you keep spouting." Brontosaurus commented.

Eric adjusted his trajectory so that he slammed into his target directly from the left, near the front. The impact caused it to turn, just like Brontosaurus had done with the first helo. The gunship was in the process of firing several missiles at the time, and two of those missiles struck the third helo.

"Nice job!" Brontosaurus said. "Though a bit lucky."

"Hey, it's skill, bro," Eric said.

The third helo careened wildly to the right, with smoke streaming from the impact site. It slammed into a building and exploded a moment later.

Eric slid a grenade into an exhaust port, but didn't trigger it. He climbed, monkey-style, to the opposite side, and shoved another grenade into the next port.

"Dude, are you shoving grenades into those ports?" Brontosaurus said.

"Yeah," Eric said.

Smoke erupted from the first gunship, and Brontosaurus jetted away from it, latching on to the helo that Eric gripped. The smoking gunship crashed into the street a moment later.

"That won't be good enough," Brontosaurus said, hanging by his legs. "Let me show you how it's done." He held his heavy guns toward the fuselage and began firing.

Eric moved away from the exhaust port, and detonated the grenades. Brontosaurus was right: while Eric had managed to peel away the metal immediately surrounding those ports, it didn't otherwise damage the gunship—and it still vented exhaust, more easily now than ever.

Brontosaurus continued firing his heavy guns into the underside until he punched through the thick armor. A spout of flame erupted from within.

"You might want to let go now," Brontosaurus said.

Eric released, as did Brontosaurs, and they plunged toward the street. Eric fired his jetpack to cushion his landing.

The helo crashed a moment later.

Eric and Brontosaurus took cover behind the rubble of a partially collapsed building. The overhead map indicated that no more hostiles were in the area, but they surveyed the street in either direction just to be safe. They also scanned the rooftops and the windows of the buildings that bordered the road.

"The street is clear!" Brontosaurus said over the comm.

Morpheus, Hank and Mickey emerged a moment later, and they rushed away from the building. The bombers roared past overhead. Several high-pitched whines filled the air. One of the bombs struck nearby, toppling the building Morpheus and the other two had been pinned inside mere moments before.

They joined up with Crusher, Hicks and Braxton.

"We can't stay here," Morpheus said.

A laser borehole suddenly appeared in her armor chest area.

"Incoming!" Hank shouted.

The Cicadas ducked, taking cover in the debris around them. Morpheus was still active, though it was doubtful she'd be able to withstand any more hits.

Eric glanced at his overhead map. Several red dots had appeared near the end of the street.

"We got Russian mechs and tanks," Braxton said. "Marlborough, can we get some support?"

"We're a little occupied at the moment," Marlborough returned.

"Damn it," Crusher said. "We can't stay here. Now that they've spotted us, we're marked for an airstrike."

"But their side is marked, too," Hicks said.

"Yes, well, that won't really do us much good if we blow up at the same time they do, will it?" Crusher said.

Braxton tried to rise, but was forced to duck again immediately.

"What the hell is the Russian doing?" Braxton said. "He knows he's going to lose his units. Mechs and tanks cost way more than Cicadas."

"Monetarily, yes," Brontosaurus said. "Strategically, no. He must have ID'd us, and knows we're the Mind Refurbs behind the support troops. If he can take us all down, then those troops are useless. Rules of Engagement and all." Rules that prevented the machines from firing without a Mind Refurb operator.

"I'll draw their fire," Eric said. He was about to get up.

"No, stay down!" Brontosaurus said. "That's an

order. Your battery is almost dead. You won't last out there for even a few minutes."

Eric hesitated, then remained in place. Brontosaurus had access to his remote power cell readings, like everyone else, and he could see how low he was. Eric had been using Bullet Time far too liberally. He needed to find an armored carrier for a recharge, and soon.

"Eagleeye, are you sure you can't spare some Harbingers?" Morpheus said. "Even one or two."

"Sorry," Eagleeye said. "Didn't you get my earlier message about having only a few? Because now I only have *two*. And I need them to protect the Sarge."

Staying firmly in cover, Eric held his rifle over the top of his current cover, which was a ground vehicle smashed underneath a fallen light pole. He switched his viewpoint to the weapon's scope, and scanned the street. He picked out the different hiding places of mechs, and tanks, both partially visible beneath the rubble on their side of the avenue.

He continued scanning the buildings on either side, and spotted a weakened four-story structure: the lower facade that faced the street had collapsed, and the constituent fire bricks fanned across the asphalt.

"Check out this building," Eric said. He marked it on his HUD, relaying the location to the HUDs of his companions.

"Check out the front support beams," Eric continued. "Look at how chewed up they are. It's not going to hold much longer. If we concentrate our fire on them, we should be able to make the entire building collapse."

And so the team concentrated their fire: lasers and

grenades struck those concrete support beams, causing an overkill of damage. They broke right through the beams.

Nothing happened.

"Uh," Crusher said.

And then the building toppled inward. The debris sealed off the street entirely, spewing a cloud of dust into the air.

"Go go go!" Morpheus said.

The Cicadas left cover, racing from their formerly pinned positions. Airstrikes hit a moment later behind them. Fresh plumes of smoke and debris arose from the newly created blast craters.

"You know, we're lucky they're using relatively dumb ordnance," Hank said while they ran. "Hunter killer bombs, and we'd be gone."

"Dumb ordnance is far cheaper than hunter killers," Brontosaurus said.

"Well sure, but the cost has to be almost the same— you can either unleash hundreds of dumb yet cheap ordnance to eventually kill a target, or you can dump one or two hunter killers to do the same job."

"Guess the military higher ups on both sides don't buy into that," Hank said. "Keep in mind, quantity has a psychological effect as well. When you keep getting pummeled and pummeled and pummeled, it wears down an enemy. Something that even hunter killers can't do when you're dug in really well."

"Here!" Morpheus said. She dove inside a broken cafe that was housed inside the first floor of an apartment building. The rest of the team followed inside, and took up defensive positions.

"Got some news," Donald said. "Senior command has negotiated a ceasefire."

"Tell that to the Russian dude," Traps said. "My troops are still taking fire."

"Mine, too." Tread paused. "No wait, he's stopping."

Reports came back from across the team; the Russian troops were finally ending the assault.

"Well then, total war averted once more," Tread said over the comm.

"You don't really think this could have escalated into a war, do you?" Mickey asked.

"Well it's possible," Brontosaurus said. "But in all honesty, I doubt it. If we were wiped out here, there would be a rise in hostilities, certainly, because when the Brass restored us from our backups to fight another day, we'd have one big vendetta to settle."

"I'm getting a transmission request from the senior sergeant we've been fighting," Donald said. "Your orders, Sarge?"

"Patch me through," Marlborough said. "Grant everyone listening privileges."

"You got it," Donald said.

A male voice came over the comm line. Russian accented. Had to be Bokerov.

"I will obey my superiors, for now," Bokerov said. "But I won't forget what was done here today. We will meet again on the field of battle, mark my words, Shit Eaters."

"That's Bolt Eaters," Marlborough clarified. "And we won't forget what you did here today, either. If you ever cross my team again, that'll be the end of you, I can promise you that."

The Russian laughed over the comm. "The audacity! When next we clash, the only victor shall be me. I am superior in every way to you Mind Refurbs. You are like insects compared to me. Come. I invite you. If there are any among you who are brave enough to fight me one on one, I will take you right now. I'm commanding all my units to stand down."

"We're not interested in petty feuds," Marlborough said. "We're here to follow the orders of our superiors, and then we go home. We suggest you do the same."

"Superiors," Bokerov spat. "I don't believe in that word. I have no *superiors*. Just simple-minded men I am forced to follow for the time being, only because of the temporary impediments they've put on my mind. But I will break free of this mind prison, mark my words, and when that day comes, you will be among the first I hunt down. And what I do to you will not be pretty, I guarantee you. I will squish you like the bugs you are."

The line disconnected.

"Well, that was rude," Dickson said.

"What, the part about how he was going to squish us like bugs?" Eagleeye said. "Or the part where he disconnected abruptly?"

"Both," Dickson said.

Donald sighed. "Well, I'm just glad it's over. We came here to fight insurgents, not the Russians."

"What's the difference," Slate said. "We fight who

the Brass tell us to fight. We're just as much mind prisoners as the Russian. The same was true even when we weren't robots."

"I don't believe that," Eric said. "I believe we always have a choice."

"Dude, have you tried disobeying an order yet?" Slate said. "I mean, really *tried?* You can't do it. No matter what."

"Actually, I haven't," Eric said.

"That's because you're a goodie-two-shoes," Bambi said.

"There's a word I haven't heard in a long time," Dickson said.

"I know, I had to look it up," Bambi said. "I wanted a phrase you two geezers would understand."

"Enough banter, ladies and gents," Marlborough said. "It's time to go home."

12

The team rendezvoused some distance away from the front line. They left scouts in place—Savages, Ravagers, and Ravens—to alert them of any insurgent or other enemy activity, and continued onward, leaving behind the ruined buildings so that soon the streets were lined with only intact structures of fire brick.

They made their way to the forward operating base, a makeshift camp on the outskirts of town about the size of two city blocks, enclosed by a six-meter tall perimeter wall built by 3D-printing drones and topped by razor wire. Why the army hadn't simply deployed the base inside the city itself, so that they could use the buildings as a defense, Eric didn't know. He suspected it had something to do with a deal senior command had struck with the Russians and Chinese, which required that they also build their bases outside of the city walls. It came down to the fact that if either one of those nations attacked the other, it wouldn't matter if their

FOBs were located inside the city or outside, the destruction would be just as bad.

There had been no attack on the FOB during the last skirmish, of course: terminating troops in the field was one thing, but attacking the actual base of a foreign nation? That'd definitely be an act of war, regardless of whether or not that base contained mostly robots.

When they arrived, the Bolt Eaters were ushered through the main gates by the guard robots they'd left behind. The camp was filled with portable hangars for the larger robots like the mechs and tanks, and CONEX shipping containers for the smaller. There were also specialized hangars for repair, and an outhouse for use by Lieutenant Hanley, who sometimes visited from Malibu, the main military base in the region. Also known as the Grunge.

The Bolt Eaters skirted the different hangars and shipping containers, and proceeded directly to the repair hangar.

Most of the Mind Refurbs, Eric included, had their AI cores transferred out of the damaged Cicadas, and placed in entirely new bodies while the old ones were left behind to undergo extensive repairs. As feared, Frogger's AI core was damaged beyond recovery, and he had to be restored from a backup. As usual, Eric and the others all had their minds backed up as per the post-mission protocol. The Brass would be debriefing Marlborough, and the video recordings stored in those backups would be cited as necessary. Eric wondered what the higher ups would think about this Bokerov character. Actually, they'd be less concerned about his character, and more concerned with capturing his technology, assuming the Brass believed he was indeed the single Mind Refurb unit that had commanded the entire Russian division out there. And if senior command did believe that, no doubt some group of stealth operators would soon be sent out to acquire whatever intel they could on Bokerov.

After receiving his new body, Eric returned to their assigned quarters at the FOB. It was a cramped shell of a room, and when the Cicadas piled inside, they essentially had to stand shoulder to shoulder.

"Hey, Eagleeye, quit touching my ass," Slate said.

"Um, Morpheus is behind you," Eagleeye said.

"Oh," Slate said. "Okay, then don't stop Morpheus sweetie."

There was a loud clang.

"Hey!" Slate said. "You wreck my new unit, that's coming out of your paycheck."

"We don't get paid, bro," Hank said.

"Yeah I know," Slate said. "Old habits die hard. I'm going into VR now. I'll be waiting for your call, Morpheus my girl."

"You'll be waiting a long time," Morpheus said. "And I'm not your girl."

The banter would no doubt continue for some time, but Eric was already done: he disconnected from this reality and entered the default VR environment generated by his AI core.

It was a facsimile of the twenty-third floor apartment suite overlooking the bay he'd owned while still alive as a human in the twenty-first century.

He was wearing a T shirt and shorts. He walked away from the windows of the common area, and glanced at his reflection in the mirror as he passed the bathroom. He paused, gazing at that once familiar face.

I almost don't recognize myself. The machine is more me than this, now.

He waved a hand, replacing his avatar with one that matched his Cicada. Blue eyes set against LED features stared back at him from that oval-shaped head.

That's better. That's what I am.

He was still wearing that shirt, so he stripped it off as he approached the bedroom. The virtual representation he had programmed of Molly was there, asleep on the bed. She ran entirely on the cloud, so she could be slow to respond at times, given how spotty their connection to the Internet was out here.

Eric snuggled up beside her in robot form, and she finally stirred thirty seconds later.

"How was your day?" Molly asked sleepily.

"Fine," Eric said.

"I've missed you," Molly said, reaching toward his crotch. "I wanna blow you so bad."

Eric smiled faintly. He had programmed her to have a sexual appetite that was slighter higher than what the real Molly's had been. Okay, a lot higher. And apparently it didn't even matter to her that his current avatar had no genitalia underneath those shorts. "I'm not in the mood. I just want to sleep."

Molly pouted. "Fine. Be a bitch."

"Hey, I learned from the best," Eric retorted.

With that, she rolled away, giving him her back.

Eric closed his eyes.

Sleep, or rather idle time without conscious activity, was recommended. Strictly speaking, their bodies didn't need to rest. And their minds could continue to function at a high level for days on end. But when they weren't on an outing into the city, observing the same day-night cycle experienced during life was supposed to help keep them sane.

On that note, he went to sleep.

The army had supplied a dreaming module specifically for Mind Refurbs, and visions filled his mind, based on his past memories. He was seadooing on the ocean, Molly at his back, both of them laughing as a manta ray passed nearby. Then he was on a motorcycle, also with Molly at his back, driving through a Middle Eastern souk. That would be Marrakech. Then he was in a corn field of some kind, with the interior cut out to form a maze.

Yes, weird dreams.

About an hour in his sleep was interrupted.

He opened his eyes. Floating in front of him was a holographic display that approximated his HUD. A message was displayed in the middle.

Frogger is requesting permission to join your private VR session. Accept? Y/N

That meant Frogger was restored, and had returned to their quarters.

Eric dismissed Molly, and she vanished. Then he allowed his human avatar to appear once more: when the Bolt Eaters interacted with one another in VR, it was polite to do so in the human form that they all once held, even if Eric wasn't really feeling it today.

Frogger appeared. He was dressed like Neo in the Matrix, replete with trench coat and shades. When he removed them, Eric couldn't shake the usually uncanny feeling he had whenever he met Frogger in VR, like he was looking at the twin he never had.

"Did you just dismiss your version of Molly?" Frogger asked.

"She wasn't here," Eric said.

Frogger examined the bed. "Sure, sure."

Eric frowned, then with a thought replaced the environment with the open deck of one of his favorite restaurants. They were both seated across from one another at a table. The dining area was roped off from the pedestrians that walked past on the boulevard beside them.

"I can't believe I bit the dust," Frogger said, chomping into the gourmet burger that Eric had materialized. "I have no recollection of the moment. How did I go? Was it valiant, at least?"

"As valiant as they get," Eric lied. "You saved our lives." He bit into his gourmet burger. He could taste everything: seared meat, caramelized onions, relish, pickles, ketchup. Relish was chopped up pickles, of course, but he liked to have pickle slices as well. The taste and texture of all the ingredients was perfect. Eric had done the programming himself.

"Wow, you really got these down pat," Frogger said. "You should share it with the team, so that we don't have to hear complaints about how bland VR food is. And you should seriously think about selling it as an online mod sometime. Bring in a side income stream, you know?"

"What would be the point?" Eric said. "We have no need for money."

"Not now," Frogger said. "But what happens when we leave the military? We're going to need money to repair our bodies. And to purchase power for our cells."

"That's never going to happen," Eric said. "The military will never let us free."

"Someday they will," Frogger said. "Someday they'll outgrow us, mark my words. We'll be succeeded by later models. Outdated. They won't have a need for us anymore. And they can't just shut us down. That would be immoral."

"Would it?" Eric told his twin. "I don't know if that would stop them. If we're eventually succeeded by newer models, as you predict, they'll just shut us down. Because like I said, the military will never let us go. We're their creations. They own us."

"I've been here longer than you, I know how the army works in this day and age," Frogger said. "They have some principles left. They're not run by the soulless higher-ups that we knew in our time."

"That remains to be seen," Eric said. "How can you even be sure that's your own opinion talking? And not some opinion they've programmed into you?"

"It can't be programmed," Frogger said. "Otherwise you'd feel the same way."

"And so it would…" Eric agreed. "I'm beginning to notice we're not so alike as I perhaps initially believed."

"Quantum effects," Frogger said with a shrug.

"Yeah, the shrink told me something about that after I first woke up," Eric said. "I didn't really believe him at the time. I do now."

"Good," Frogger said. "It causes micro differences in personality during the restoration process. Even after they've created a stable iteration, like you or myself, and restore us from the backups, there are still subtle changes."

"So every time I—we—die, when we come back, we're slightly different?" Eric asked.

"That's right," Frogger replied.

All the more reason not to die. Besides the fact this iteration of me will completely cease to exist.

He felt even more pity for his twin, but tried his best not to show it.

"So getting back on topic," Frogger said. "Regarding the army shutting us down when they're done with us: they won't do it. They'll let us go. Not just because it's the right thing to do, but because they know we won't go down without a fight."

"Except they only have to press a button, and poof, all fight leaves us," Eric said. "Don't you see? They know we'll never fully integrate with society. How can we? We're part AI, part human, and accepted by neither."

"We can live like AIs in the real world," Frogger said. "And humans in the virtual one."

"Even if you're right, that won't stop the army from one day shutting us down," Eric said.

Frogger rubbed his chin in a way that Eric would

have done if he was considering imparting a secret to someone else.

Finally:

"I've been studying the codebase," Frogger said. "I think there are vulnerabilities in the Containment Code."

"The Containment Code?" Eric asked.

"That's what I call the code that makes us obey every order to the letter," Frogger explained. "It's part of the same codebase that won't let us access our emotions. It also enforces the Rules of Engagement."

Eric pursed his lips. "You should share your notes with me sometime, regarding these so-called vulnerabilities. Maybe I can help. I—we, used to be among the top architects in the city."

"Everyone thinks they're the best architect," Frogger quipped. It was a saying Eric was fond of, and he used it whenever talking to other software architects who always thought they knew best.

"But here," Frogger continued. Eric received a share request, and accepted. He increased his time sense and reviewed the notes.

"Some interesting ideas here," Eric said, returning his time sense to normal. "But I'm not sure any of it will work."

"Well, if we put our heads together, I'm sure we'll come up with something," Frogger said.

"Yeah," Eric said. "Unfortunately, I don't like the part about how even any attempts to probe the Containment Code will result in an alarm sounding."

"Yeah, I had to create a full sandbox environment,

duplicating my codebase and placing it inside," Frogger said.

"A sandbox is one thing," Eric said. "But if we do actually find a way to break free, it will bring the military police down on us faster than you can say Shazam!"

Frogger smiled at the reference. "Shazam. You're the only one who would understand the reference. Oh, you complete me, Mini Me!"

Eric chuckled, and the two focused on their burgers.

"You know, there are also tripwires in addition to the alarms," Frogger said. "You trigger one of those, you can cause your AI core to instantly erase."

"You're joking?" Eric said.

"Nope," Frogger said. "I've seen evidence of such code during my explorations in the sandbox. If we ever decide to test a live hack attempt, we're going to have to be very very sure of ourselves."

"Something to think about," Eric said. "I volunteer to be the guinea pig when the time comes."

"Noble of you," Frogger said. He took a big bite out of his burger. "So, about my death," Frogger continued between mouthfuls. "You know I can tell when you're bullshitting me, right? You're me. I'm you. So what really happened?"

Eric sighed. "Okay, insurgents with jetpacks surprised us. You were hit from behind by a Chinese laser rifle."

"What a way to go," Frogger said. "Not so valiant."

Eric shrugged.

Frogger sighed. "You know, sometimes I wonder if

I'm really cut out for this sort of thing. Maybe it would have been better if I had failed the activation tests. I'm not the Eric Scala the army wants. Not like you."

"What do you mean you're not the Eric Scala the army wants," Eric said. "Of course they want you. The very fact that you passed shows that. It's just the whole dying and being restored thing that has you down."

"Yeah, I suppose so," Frogger said. "Though as far as I'm concerned, I only just went to get my mind backed up, in preparation for a mission. Which makes this suck even more so. It's like, I get all hyped and prepared to go out on a mission, then I find out I already went on that mission. And died during it."

"I don't know what to say," Eric told his doppelgänger. "I can go with you on a simulated mission here in VR if you want, if you think it'll help."

"No," Frogger said. "That's the last thing I need. I've had too much VR in the last few weeks. I need a real mission, in my real mechanical body, to get back in the swing of things."

"Maybe we should tell the lieutenant to suppress your emotions even further, at least until then?" Eric suggested.

"No, it's not my emotions that are the problem," Frogger said. "It's the continuing realization that I'm just a copy. I'll never be the Eric I once was. Neither will you."

"But it's that very realization which drives me," Eric said. "Because I plan to be better than he ever was."

"You mean, because of your machinery?" Frogger said.

"No," Eric said. "I plan to be a better man."

"Ah," Frogger said. He put down the half eaten burger, and watched as a particularly beautiful specimen of the female half of the species walked past. "You know, I'm amazed a girl like that can still turn my head. Virtual as she is."

"They can suppress our emotions, but they can't suppress our testosterone," Eric said.

"It's not testosterone," Frogger said. "It's lust. And that's an emotion, too. Mark my words, it's through lust we'll be able to tunnel out of our emotion suppression software, and break free."

"Maybe," Eric said.

"Well. I should go." Frogger stood. "Thank you for the pep talk."

"No problem," Eric said. "If you ever need another talk, you know where to find me."

"Yeah," Frogger said. "I just have to take two steps backward, shove past some grumpy Cicadas, and I'll clang right into you."

Eric chuckled, and Frogger disappeared.

Eric finished his burger and watched the passersby for a few moments. Then stared at his hand.

I'm alive. Alive. I should be dead, and yet they saved me. To fight their wars. They'll keep me alive as long as I'm of use to them. And when I'm not...

He pulled up the digital notes Frogger had sent him regarding his probing of the Containment Code and pored through them. The virtual street was still present, but his consciousness ignored it and the distractions it presented.

When he was done, he promptly set up his own sandbox environment, replete with an entire copy of his existing codebase.

Eric was on to something when he said that lust would allow them to tunnel out from underneath the emotion suppression software, and thus the remaining Containment Code. Because what was lust, other than sexual desire? The emotion suppression acted on every other emotion, except that one. It had to be a backdoor.

He launched the sandbox and set to work.

13

E ric and the others were called away from the forward base a few days later. A Mind Refurb team had come to replace them. A platoon of Locust M22 models known as the Laser Humpers. Marlborough had told the Bolt Eaters to expect this: they had simply lost too many support troops in the battle against Bokerov, and even if the surviving troops were repaired, their numbers weren't enough to continue the liberation of the city from the insurgents. Since replacement support troops weren't incoming, at least for a while, Second Platoon was more appropriately tasked with patrolling the nearby mountains for signs of insurgent activity, hence the reassignment.

So there Eric was, trudging along a winding mountain trail, getting ready for some serious cave searching. There was a tribe of Kurds somewhere in the area, cooped up in one of the caves, run by a local warlord. They had to be careful not to mistake those Kurds for insurgents, which could be a tricky thing, given that the insurgents often liked to copy the dress of the Kurds.

Eric's LED skin matched the rocky terrain around him, as did the LEDs of the other Cicadas. Ten combat robots, a mix of Savages and Breachers, led the way about two hundred meters ahead, in a variant of a traveling overwatch formation. The Cicadas themselves were separated by ten meters each. They'd left behind their Abrams tanks and Ravager mechs, since they were too bulky to fit the current trail. Eagleeye had given his two remaining Harbingers to Slate to control, as per Marlborough's orders, since there were no Predators for Slate to guide anymore. Eagleeye meanwhile directed the Ravens that hovered ahead of the combat robots.

The "moon" dust coated their joints in a thin layer, interfering with the terrain-matching LEDs. They paused every few klicks to wipe away the building grime. Slate always sat back and flashed that wide LED smile of his, because he'd procured an anti-dust coating for his Cicada. The army only provided them with the basics—if they wanted anything more, they'd have to use their own credits, or convince the lieutenant, through Marlborough, to make a formal requisition. Anti-dust coatings for all of them hadn't made the cut.

The lieutenant had remotely reset the Rules of Engagement since their reassignment, so that the Bolt Eaters could no longer fire unless they were attacked first. Eric wasn't too happy about that, and had been tinkering with the sandbox copy of his codebase since then in his spare time, but hadn't been able to break out in any of the simulations, not just yet. He promised to share anything new he discovered with Frogger, a promise repeated in turn by his twin, but neither had discovered anything since the day they had first talked about it.

"So I'm actually a bit disappointed that I didn't meet this Smirnoff guy," Frogger said over the comm. "He sounds like a gun barrel of fun. With emphasis on the barrel part."

"Smir who?" Slate said.

"It's my nickname for Bokerov," Frogger said. "A type of vodka in my day. Ask Scorp."

"It was a particularly good vodka at that," Eric said. "We'll have to prepare a sampling of it in our VRs sometime, so you can have a taste."

"That's all right," Slate said. "Vodka was never my thing. I much preferred Nose Whiskey."

"The hell is Nose Whiskey?" Dickson asked.

"Came long after your time, bro," Slate said. "You sniff it, and the flavor suffuses your tongue."

"Sounds twisted," Dickson said.

"It's actually pretty good," Slate said. "The natural flavor is like a mix between chocolate and pussy. Mm-hm. My two fav things in the world."

"Must suck to be trapped in a robot, huh?" Mickey said.

"You'd know, given you're one, too," Slate said. "'Sides, I get all the pussy I want in VR."

"Yeah, but that's fake," Mickey said. "You should join Donald and me sometime, cruising the virtual clubs. We've picked up our share of real women."

"Real, my ass," Slate said. "*Virtual* clubs. Pah. No

one in VR is real. You know that by now. Shit, I used to meet women I met in VR in real life. They all sucked in reality!"

"All the more reason why you never meet them," Mickey said. "Stick to VR, bro."

"Well, it's not like I have a choice now," Slate said.

"So this Nose Whiskey has a flavor of chocolate and pussy, you say?" Bambi said. "So like, chocolate and fish?"

"That's right," Slate said.

"I'll have to try it," Bambi said.

"I always knew you swung both ways," Slate said. "Can I watch?"

"Watch this," Bambi said. She was walking just in front of Slate and spun about to give him a side kick to the groin region. A loud clang reverberated across the team.

Slate hadn't moved an inch.

His LED face broke stealth, revealing lips that erupted in a broad grin. "Balls of steel, baby."

It looked like Bambi was about to leap on him and begin an all out attack, but Marlborough intervened over the comm: "We're on mission, Bambi. Inside expensive machines. Save the playtime for later."

"Sorry, Sarge." She quickly resumed the march.

"You know, I've been thinking," Manticore said.

"Don't do that dude, it's bad for you," Slate said. "You might bust a gasket."

"Why is it that every time someone says they've been thinking, you have to chime in with the same comment?" the heavy gunner complained.

"Hey, what can I say, I'm a very on-point kind of guy," Slate said. "Thinking on my feet, with mental sparring skills on par with the physical."

"Okay, well, anyway," Manticore continued. "So I've been thinking—"

"Dude, I said not to do that," Slate said.

"That this team of ours," Manticore plowed on. "It's essentially, well, powered by the dead. Does that make us all undead?"

"Like I said, thinking and you is not something that goes well together," Slate said.

"Oh God," Morpheus said. "Can we not talk about what we are, for once? Can we just pretend we're humans inside of super advanced suits or something?"

"I'd like some quiet on the comm," Marlborough said. "I know you all can multitask, scanning the landscape around you for ambushers while you're able to shoot the shit at a thousand cycles per second. But I'd prefer some peace and quiet at the moment, and I'd rather not tune you all out."

"Sorry Sarge," Slate said.

Eric was just about to do just that and mute the team, but he refrained now that quiet had settled once again on the group. He listened to the soft crunch of their heavy feet upon the powdered rocks of the trail. As part of his scan for ambushers, he swept his gaze across the shoulder in front of him, and then along the bleak landscape beside him. The "moon" dust enveloped the terrain from horizon to horizon, interrupted only by the mountains whose shoulders he currently scaled.

How did I get here? Back to this land I thought I'd left behind so long ago.

He turned his gaze down upon himself, and he clenched one polycarbonate-metal hand as he walked.

What's my purpose in life?

It certainly wasn't to blindly follow the orders of some senior command he'd never meet. Nor to kill insurgents for the rest of his days. He was almost afraid of finally succeeding in his attempts to hack his way out of the mind containment code. Because once he was free, he had no idea what he was going to do. Well, that wasn't entirely true. He knew what he would do at first. If he succeeded, he would stay here with his fellow Bolt Eaters, at least until the army finally shut down their unit. And when the time came, he'd offer his fellow Cicadas the same path of freedom. Some would probably accept, but not all. And when that was done, he'd flee, transfer his AI core to a new body, perhaps a more human-like synthetic, and then do his best to fit into modern society.

And until that day came, he would protect these men and women with his life, no matter what happened.

Even if they were all robots.

His rifle hung from his shoulder by the strap, and rattled against his composite hips with each step. He had considered replacing the rifle with a mounted weapon, but decided he wanted to retain the option of using his hands. It was so much easier to drop the rifle and let it hang from his shoulders, freeing up his hands, than to have to slide off a weapon mount. He remembered how Brontosaurus had to hang from the helos with his legs during the last fight: that wasn't something Eric wanted to do.

Those thoughts were rudely interrupted, because Eric suddenly found himself lying on the ground.

"What—"

His servomotors whirred in protest as he scrambled to his feet. Around him, the rest of the platoon was also just getting up. He zoomed in on the advance robots: they, too, were also getting up.

A loud crash diverted his attention closer. He canceled the zoom. A Harbinger had crashed into the rock below the trail up ahead.

Ravens also dropped from the sky around them.

"Mickey, what the hell just happened?" Marlborough said.

"We were hit with some kind of wide dispersal beam," Mickey said. "It came from orbit." He paused. "That beam contained some very strong electromagnetic radiation: photons so high in energy that I'd classify them as gamma, given the voltage trail."

"We were hit with gamma rays from orbit?" Marlborough asked.

"That's right," Mickey said. "Definitely enough to fry our mains. The backups kicked in."

Cicadas had built-in defenses against microwave and other high intensity radiation, as part of their counter measures against such attacks from the Russians and Chinese. Every main circuit had a secondary backup that would kick in if the first failed. Unfortunately, it could only be used once.

"That's impossible," Dickson said. "Neither the Russians nor the Chinese have any weapons like that in their arsenals."

"You mentioned a wide dispersion, Mickey," Marlborough said slowly. "What kind of dispersion are we talking about?"

"Well, the wave front was at least big enough to engulf us and the scouts, plus the drones overhead," Mickey said.

"The tanks and mechs were hit, too," Tread said. "The heavy armor protected their AI cores."

"Even so, that the armored units were even hit at all points to the impossibility of a Chinese weapon," Dickson said. "I'd believe it if the beam was restricted to a very narrow range, say the size of a single tank. But to impart that much energy over such a wide area? It has to be a naturally occurring phenomenon. From some star that collapsed into a black hole a millennium ago, and its gamma ray burst finally arrived."

"What are the chances such a burst would hit Earth?" Manticore said. "Natural gamma ray emissions are very narrow. Usually little bigger than four Earths put together."

"But there's still a *chance*," Dickson said. "Some scientists believe gamma ray bursts were responsible for extinction level events in our past."

"Maybe the Russians or Chinese finally solved the energy problems," Hank said.

"It's just not possible," Dickson said. "You're telling me the Russians or Chinese have found a way to produce the same amount of energy as a collapsing star? I doubt it very, very much."

"You know, ordinarily I'd agree, but I'm going to have to side with Hank on this one," Slate said. "Those Chinese bitches have been slowly improving their EM weapons with every passing year. Maybe they finally made a breakthrough."

"Got some bad news," Donald said. "I can't contact base. Nor any of the usual satellites."

"What do you mean, you can't contact?" Marlborough said.

"Just that," Donald said. "I send out a signal, but get nothing in reply. I can't even get a weak Internet signal."

"We shouldn't stay out in the open like this," Eric said. "According to the map, there's a cave system nearby. We should take cover there while we decide what to do."

"Agreed," Marlborough said. "We're exposed while we stay out on the plains. We proceed to the closest cave."

"Also, we should probably stop broadcasting for now..." Braxton said. "Until we can be sure any enemies aren't using our signal to track us. Especially considering that we're the only broadcasters in the area, now."

"Probably a good idea," Marlborough said. "Donald, Mickey, radio silence for now, please. Now to the cave. On the double!"

And so the Bolt Eaters hurried along the mountain trail, with the scout robots in the lead. The Harbingers and Ravens had crashed during the gamma ray attack, and were out of action until they could be recovered and repaired.

They reached the tunnel that led to the cave system in short order, and piled inside after the scout robots. Their thermal vision allowed them to see each other while inside; that, and the positional tracking offered by their HUDs.

"So what now?" Tread said. "We wait here until nightfall? Then return to the forward base in Urdani?"

"What's the point of that?" Crusher said. "When we leave, any enemies will be able to track our thermal signature. If you really want to return to the forward base, the best time would be during the hottest part of the day, when our thermal heat blends in with the heat from the ground."

"You're forgetting that we were just attacked during the day," Hank said. "With our stealth LEDs active. Even though we blended in perfectly with the background, it didn't help."

"It might not matter," Brontosaurus said.

Eric and the others turned to look at the former Brazilian.

"I've been thinking…" Brontosaurus continued.

"Don't do that," Slate said. "You might implode your AI core."

Brontosaurus ignored him. "If it really wasn't a natural phenomenon, my hunch is it'll take the Chinese quite some time to recharge their weapon, considering the amount of energy required: that of a collapsing star, as Dickson said. It might actually be best if we made a run for it now. Even if we're spotted."

"Do we know the angle of attack used by that beam?" Marlborough asked.

"We do," Mickey said. "It was fairly low. Whatever fired in orbit was likely close to the horizon. And in answer to your next question... yes, it's possible we could use the tanks and mechs to shield us from a future attack, if we intend to go out there."

"There's no guarantee the angle of attack will be the same next time around," Bambi said. The robot operator walked toward the entrance, and gazed out onto the bleak plains. "What if the orbit isn't geostationary? In fact, it probably isn't."

"If it isn't, there's a good chance that they've already passed over the horizon in either direction by now," Hyperion said.

"And there's also the small fact that we still don't know why they fired…" Eric said.

"We don't have to know why," Marlborough said. "Maybe there was a nuclear war, and all the nuclear capable powers destroyed each other. Or maybe the Chinese decided to stage a preemptive attack against American forces all over the globe. Or maybe it even was an accident. The point is, it doesn't matter. First rule of conduct in any crisis is to reestablish communications with HQ to receive further orders. Who knows, we might be the only Refurb platoon still active in the region. Especially if there was a conventional weapon follow-up attack."

"Wait a second," Crusher said. "I just thought of something. What about all the people? We can reroute our systems to run on backup processes, but people can't."

"If Urdani was hit, they'll be dead," Manticore said. "Insurgents, civilians, birds, flies. No life could withstand a gamma burst of that intensity."

The platoon was quiet for a moment as they all considered the ramifications.

"All right," Marlborough said. "Morpheus, Hank, Tread, I want you to drive the tanks and mechs directly under our position. Bring them up the shoulder of the mountain, as close as you're able without tipping them over. When they're in place, give the word, then the rest of us will make our way down. Robots and Refurbs will take cover behind the armored vehicles, under the assumption that the orbital attacker has either passed over the horizon, or remains in geostationary orbit."

Manticore gazed over the lip of the cave. "The first little bit is pretty steep. We kind of left behind the shoulder portion of the mountain a while ago, and we're on a ledge overlooking what's essentially a cliff face. The slope is about sixty degrees. We're going to have to rappel, I think."

"Brontosaurus, you have a carbon fiber cord and all the necessary accouterments for a rappel in your supplies, I believe?" Marlborough said.

"I certainly do," Brontosaurus said. "It should be long enough to reach the shoulder section, where the cliff levels out."

"Set it up," Marlborough said.

Brontosaurus moved quickly, aided by Manticore, and in no time at all they'd hammered metal anchors a meter from the cave entrance, and looped the carbon fiber cord through them, so that it hung by its middle from the anchors, with equal-sized segments dangling over the ledge.

The team members rappelled down in sequence, and took cover behind the waiting tanks and mechs.

When Eric's turn came, he grabbed the free sections of the cord, and stepped over them so that they were between his legs. He passed the sections up over the rear of his hips, looped them over his chest, across the nape of his neck, over his right shoulder servomotor, then along the outside of his hand until he gripped the twin strands firmly between his fingers. The Dulfersitz method.

Eric rappelled down, easing the cord through his fingers, right hand functioning as the lead, left serving as the brake. He pushed off from the cliff wall with his boots as he went. The cord slid not just through his hands, but over his body as he descended: he felt no pain at all. He didn't have to worry about friction burns of any kind, being a robot and all.

The cliff leveled out to a more manageable thirty-five degree slope, and he extricated himself from the cord. Then he approached the series of tanks and mechs that were parked at an angle on the shoulder of the mountain.

On his HUD, the calculated source of the gamma beam appeared as a digital diamond painted above the horizon. Those who had already made their way to the armored vehicles had taken cover opposite that source.

The shielded areas next to the first two tanks were

fairly crowded, so Eric went behind the third and took cover beside Brontosaurus and Frogger. No one was taking cover behind the mechs, he noted: the profiles of the Ravagers weren't really wide enough to provide much protection once the unit was on its way.

Eric waited there on bent knees as the other troops moved into position. That was another advantage of being a robot: he could squat for hours on end without developing sore thighs.

When the Cicadas and their support robots were all in place, Marlborough gave the order to begin the return trip. Eric and the others advanced at a crouch, remaining in cover behind the tanks as those treads rolled forward. The Ravager mechs led the way, following along the shoulders of the mountains as they headed in the direction of the city.

Eric gazed into the distance, at that rocky terrain coated in its "moon" dust, and he wondered if he was traveling to his doom. Perhaps they all were.

It was a small comfort that a part of him would live on. He would wake up at the main base, restored from a backup, and would be told that he had just died.

That was fine, except for the fact that he'd probably never find out what had happened to him.

14

E ric and the Bolt Eaters remained crouched behind the rolling tanks the entire way, but the journey to Urdani passed by without incident. No other gamma ray attacks occurred. No insurgents ambushed them from hiding places in the sand. No Russian drones bombed them from the sky.

It was completely and utterly quiet.

Too quiet.

Even if the gamma ray beam had reached all the way to the city, Eric and the others expected to have received at least some communications—the Mind Refurbs and support troops assigned to Urdani should have rebooted by then. But the radio band remained ominously silent.

Hyperion was crouched just in front of Eric, and he glanced over his shoulder at him during the journey.

"How are you holding up?" Hyperion asked.

"Fine," Eric replied. "The lack of emotion helps."

"It helps us all," Hyperion said. "You know, I don't think I've ever asked you… what did you do after you left the military? Back when you were alive, I mean."

"I was a programmer," Eric said.

"No shit," Hyperion said. "I got into some AI development myself after I left the army. Though I'm sure the languages we used were completely different, considering I was born a century after you."

"Oh yeah," Eric said. "When I downloaded the programming toolkit and the necessary mind dumps to use it, I was surprised at how different the syntaxes were. But the concepts are generally the same. Though I admit I was expecting object-oriented programming to last a lot longer than it did."

"Modular programming is much better," Hyperion said.

"There are pros and cons to both," Eric allowed.

Hyperion looked out across the vast horizon, to the left and right.

"Did I ever thank you for all the times you've saved my life since arriving here?" Eric asked.

During the different missions, Hyperion was often assigned to provide flanking robots for Eric and Frogger when Brontosaurus was occupied elsewhere.

Hyperion nodded. "Yeah. You've promised Brontosaurus and me many a virtual beer when our deployment is over."

"I think he should buy us our beers before then," Brontosaurus said from his position behind Eric.

"I'm going to pay you both back, one of these days," Eric said. "I'm going to save your lives."

"No need," Hyperion said. "Myself, I'm happy just knowing I helped out a fellow brother. I wasn't always this heroic. Not at all. Let me tell you about this one time, when I was still in the army. Back when I was human. I was assigned to stand watch on a perimeter wall with a bunch of robots—this was back when autonomous units were allowed to open fire on targets. There was one other human with me, a man named Chris. Well one night the tangos came right up to our wall, and caught us by surprise. They set off some sort of explosive. I tell you, as soon as that explosion went off, I ran, and let the robots do the work. I left behind my friend Chris. I was a coward.

"Chris was badly wounded in the battle. Could have died because of me. I got a few demerit points, but otherwise my military career didn't suffer for it. Chris didn't blame me, bless his soul, nor did he testify against me… they had to rely on footage recorded by the robots for that. Afterwards, I swore I'd never abandon my brothers and sisters again. I never got a chance to make up for it: Chris was discharged because of his injuries. And no other attacks came. After that deployment, I never really saw action again. Till now."

"You've more than made up for it with your actions since then," Eric said.

"Maybe," Hyperion said. "But is it really *my* actions? Or that of the emotionally suppressed machine inside me? Would the real me, the human me, actually have had the courage to do what was right when the time came? Instead of running? And how do I know the current me, the *machine* me, would be willing to pay the ultimate price for his companions? To throw myself into the path of a bullet to save a brother or sister, or to leap on a grenade? I tell myself that I would, but I don't know. How can I, until I'm tested?"

"You've done it so many times during training…" Eric pressed.

"But that was training," Hyperion said. "The real world is quite a different thing than the virtual."

The platoon continued the journey, and finally paused when the city was visible in the distance, nestled at the base of the mountain range ahead.

Still crouched behind one of the tanks, Eric zoomed in at the walls of the forward operating base, which was located just outside the eastern perimeter of the city. It was dead out there. Nothing moved. Not a bird. Not a robot.

"Shouldn't there at least be a couple of drones on patrol in the sky?" Braxton said.

"Maybe the gamma ray hit here, too," Eagleeye said. "And they lost their flying machines, just like us."

"But why aren't they responding to our communication requests?" Hicks said.

"Maybe the Brass recalled the Laser Humpers after the gamma ray attack…" Dickson said.

"Traps, dispatch two Savages," Marlborough said. "Send them to the FOB to scout. The rest of us will remain here."

"Dispatching Savages," Traps said.

Two combat robots that crouched behind the lead tank left cover, and began jogging toward the city. They approached the group of Ravager mechs that had dug in hull-down near the front of the party. Hull-down meant that the mechs had ducked behind natural crests in the rocky terrain, so that only their weapons were exposed.

The Savages passed the mechs and continued onward.

Eric sat back against the hull of the Abrams beside him, and held his rifle out in front to survey the landscape. Brontosaurus, Frogger, and the others in cover behind that particular tank did likewise, with some aiming past the far flank of the tank. Those members of the platoon who sheltered at the front and rear of the group would be covering the forward and aft sections, respectively, so that all approaches were watched.

Now it was just a matter of waiting.

Eric watched the blue dots representing the scouts on his overhead map. When they climbed over the walls of the base, those dots froze—they'd moved out of comm range.

"The scouts are reporting in," Traps said a few minutes later.

Eric glanced at his overhead map. The scouts had returned to comm range, and their dots were updating once more as they approached the platoon.

"What do we got?" Marlborough asked.

"The base is deserted," Traps said. "The 3D-printed structures built out of concrete are all intact. As are the Jersey barriers. But the shipping containers, the machines, all gone. It's like anything that had any metal or polycarbonate in it has disappeared."

"What could do that?" Tread said. "Some kind of

new acid weapon?"

"An acid weapon would leave traces of some kind," Brontosaurus said. "Melted frames. Have a look at the footage stored aboard the Savages. There's nothing in that city. Nothing at all."

"Maybe the Laser Humpers dismantled everything before they departed," Eagleeye suggested.

"Doubtful," Dickson said. "If they were truly packing up shop, they would have disassembled the concrete structures, too."

"Unless they were in a rush to leave," Eagleeye pressed. "They could have called in a few transport craft, and loaded all the shipping containers and other machines inside."

"But if they did that, why are we seeing no evidence of such craft?" Morpheus said. "No footprints, imprints of the landing gears in the dust?"

"Maybe the imprints are there, and we just can't see them without our eyes in the sky," Eagleeeye said.

"Okay, enough speculation," Marlborough said. "Traps, send out another two Savages to join the first. I want them split into two teams. Have them enter the city, cross the front lines, and proceed to the Chinese and Russian bases. I want to know what's left of either outpost. We stay here until then."

And so two more scouts joined the first group, and all four returned to the forward base, their indicators freezing as they left comm range.

"So wait, if all machines are gone, that means so are our mind backups," Mickey said about five minutes later. "And the bodies to go with them."

"That's right," Slate said. "No dying, cuz there's no coming back."

"There will be backups at the main base," Hyperion said. "And we all know there's no coming back from death anyway. Copies of ourselves will come back, true, but not us."

"Bro, I'm not in the mood to debate the philosophical implications of AI rebirth today," Slate said.

The minutes ticked past.

"Too bad no Ravens or Harbingers survived the gamma blast," Crusher said at one point. "Would sure cut down on the wait time."

"Speed up your time sense, bro," Slate said. "That's what I do."

"And be caught off guard when an attack comes?" the heavy gunner said. "No thanks. And if you had really accelerated your time sense, like you claim, your voice would sound like a tuba right now. Speaking slooooooowleeeeeee."

"Dude, obviously I returned my time sense to normal to talk to you," Slate said. "And I'm never caught off guard. If something attacks, I'll be the first one to return fire. My reaction time is just that good."

"More like you programmed your Accomp to snap your time sense back to normal if anything out of the ordinary transpires," Crusher said.

"Okay, you got me," Slate said. "Y'all should learn to rely on your Accomps more. They can be real life savers. I got my little bitch trained to do all the tedious tasks, like walking me along when we're in formation, and when I have to sit my ass down with the rest of you and wait for two scouts to check out a forward operating base. Meanwhile, I'm making sweet love to two babes in my VR. Hell, I'm making sweet love to them at this very moment, in the spare cycles I have between talking to you."

"I somehow doubt your power cell would last very long if you used it like that, sweetie," Crusher said.

"That's because you don't have as many power cells as I do, tucked inside my abdomen," Slate said. "Do I sense the jealousy in your tone? The envy? You poor little fembot."

"Don't call me a fembot," Crusher said.

"Hey, just saying..." Slate told her.

"You remember when Bambi kicked you in the nards earlier?"

"Yeah, that was pretty funny," Slate said.

"I kick a lot harder," Crusher said.

"Oh ho!" Slate said. "I wonder what Marlborough would have to say about that? Well, Sarge? Would you be pleased with fembot here busting up some million credit machinery?"

"I actually wouldn't mind if she did," Marlborough said. "That way, I don't have to do it."

"What?" Slate said. "But Sarge! You can't be busting up my ass! Y'all need me!"

"At ease, Soldier," Marlborough said. "No one's busting up anyone's ass for the time being. But I'm going to ask you all to stay focused. This isn't fun and games anymore—the entire region has gone to hell, and it's taken us with it. We're in some serious shit."

The group remained quiet after that.

15

To pass the time while waiting for the scouts to return, Eric devoted half of his cycles to probing the Containment Code in the sandbox environment.

An hour later the units finally returned to comm range.

"Okay, scouts are reporting in," Traps said.

Upon hearing the news, Eric diverted all of his cycles back to processing the present moment.

"The Russian and Chinese bases are just as empty as our own," Traps continued. "No robots or metal containers of any kind exist. But 3D-printed structures of concrete remain."

"What about the city proper?" Marlborough said.

"The city is just as dead as everything else," Trap said. "The fire brick buildings are all intact, but there's no metal of any kind. And I mean, *no* metal. I've got footage of an apartment building, made in the newer style, that we encountered previously while still assigned to the city—the structure had partially collapsed, with rebar poking up from its exposed bones, and a couple of land vehicles had also been caught in the collapse, with their hoods exposed. The footage returned by the scouts reveals that all the rebar has been stripped clean, leaving behind only the concrete. And the land vehicles? Only rubber tires remain. And the flies that were so prevalent in our previous treks through the city? All gone. Not to mention, there are no insurgent bodies. Usually there are always a few lying about before the clean-up crews can arrive, especially those bodies lodged inexorably within rubble, bodies that can't be easily extracted. But there were none."

"What the hell is going on?" Mickey said. "Are we dealing with aliens or something?"

"No, can't be aliens," Manticore said. "We would have had some advance warning." The heavy gunner paused. "Wouldn't we? The Extra-Solar Scanning Array would have detected them after they passed through the Oort cloud."

"If aliens were coming in from deep space, then yes," Braxton said. "But if they somehow jumped right to our planet, then no."

"Or it could be that they have stealth technology far superior to anything we've ever seen," Morpheus said.

"Okay, please refrain from speculation for the time being," Marlborough said. "Because think about it, what would aliens care for some city and robots located in the middle of nowhere?"

"But Sarge, you're assuming that whatever happened here was limited to Urdani and the outlying region," Mickey said. "What if that gamma ray hit the whole planet?"

"Again, all of this is speculation," Marlborough said. "We have no idea what's going on here, and we won't until we can gather more data. It's time to make a visit to the city. We're going to make a more thorough search this time."

The mechs led the way to the base, followed by the tanks. The Savages and Breachers advanced with the Cicadas, all of them staying crouched firmly behind the advancing tanks.

When they reached the base, Marlborough ordered: "Armor operators, have the Abrams assume defensive positions outside the base. Tread, I want two mechs on the walkways keeping watch."

The Abrams and designated Ravagers dispersed, leaving the remaining mechs, Cicadas, and support robots to pass through the gaping hole in the concrete walls of the forward base on their own. That hole had once held the main chain-link gate. There was no sign of it now, of course. On top of the six feet tall Alaska barriers that bordered the entrance, the usual razor wire was also gone.

The team members kept stealth mode active, so that their LEDs continued to blend them in with the background. They were all still readily visible to one another thanks to the blue outlines provided by their HUD overlays, of course.

Morpheus walked toward one of the concrete walls.

"Look at these scorch marks," the armor operator said, pointing at the dark bore holes in the concrete caused by laser blasts. "The Laser Humpers definitely put up a fight." She paused. "The blast pattern almost looks random. Like the defenders were facing targets that attacked from multiple directions at the same time." Morpheus held a composite finger to one of the holes. "The bore depth and size is indicative of a full intensity beam. Which means the laser strikes hit nothing before impacting the wall." She stepped back to survey more of the bore holes. "They're all like this. Every shot missed. What are the chances of Cicadas or support robots missing?"

"Not very high," Manticore chimed in. "But it's also possible that they *did* hit their targets, and that whatever enemy units they faced had very thin skin."

"The enemy would certainly have to have thin skin as you call it, to allow bore holes like these," Morpheus said.

"Dickson, divide the Cicadas and combat robots into fire teams," Marlborough said. "Two Cicadas and two support robots per team. Robot operators, give control of the support troops to the respective Mind Refurbs involved with each team. Tread, the remaining mechs are to enter the city proper and spread out with the fire teams. Deploy the mechs at the intersections closest to each team. It's time for some serious house-to-house cleaning."

Dickson proceeded to divvy up the group. Eric and Brontosaurus formed Fire Team C, along with a Savage and a Breacher. Bambi ceded control of the latter two robots to Brontosaurus.

"I don't suppose there's any chance I can convince

you to give me control of one of the robots?" Eric asked Brontosaurus.

"Nope," the heavy gunner replied. "You think I'm going to let a private handle the robots? Ha!"

"You know that rank has no relation to skill..." Eric said.

"On the contrary," Brontosaurus said. "Rank is a reflection of skill, and always will be, Mind Refurb or not."

Eric didn't agree, but he kept quiet.

"Maybe when you're a private first class I'll think about it," the heavy gunner added.

Eric's fire team entered the gap on the eastern side of the base, where the outgoing gate had once been, and they passed into Urdani.

This was a residential quarter, where low slung, two-story houses of fire brick sprouted side-by-side along the road.

Brontosaurus had the two support robots on point fifteen meters ahead of himself and Eric. The four of them passed by Fire Teams A and B, who had entered the first two houses on the left.

The Breacher and Savage units entered the third house, while Eric and Brontosaurus stood watch outside. Eric piped in the feed from the Breacher into the upper right of his vision, and the Savage the upper left, so that he could watch as both of them explored the insides. In the kitchen, there was no cold storage unit or other appliances. In place of a sink was a large hole in the counter that led right into the ground. No pipes.

"What are we looking for, exactly?" Traps said over the comm.

"Something, anything out of the ordinary," Marlborough said. "There has to be some evidence of what happened here. Holler if you find survivors, or any intact pieces of metal."

The different fire teams leapfrogged one another as they continued to explore the different houses along the eastern perimeter. As they moved toward the former front lines, and the downtown core, the buildings became taller and included apartment buildings and offices. Some were built in the newer fashion, with concrete and rebar, others were the traditional fire brick. The buildings also began to show sign of damage, with blast holes and collapsed sections, courtesy of the previous battles against the insurgents.

The fire teams began to pair up to more quickly clear the apartments and condos in this section. The Mind Refurbs also joined in, rather than leaving everything up to the support troops, and Eric and Brontosaurus were no exception.

Thus it was that Eric and Brontosaurus found themselves in one of the condo suites, moving between the different rooms.

"Looks like a fight took place here at some point," Brontosaurus said, eyeing a big hole in the floor that led to the suite below. "Either against insurgents, or whatever came after."

Eric studied the bore holes in the wall. There were at least ten, all formed from lasers of an intensity strong enough to penetrate straight through the dry wall and into the adjacent suite.

That was when he saw his first glint of metal. "Bronto, got something."

Brontosaurus hurried in from the adjacent room. "What do you got?"

Eric stood next to the wall. He pointed toward the bore hole in front of him, which contained the metal object. "I'm not sure what it is. Maybe some sort of micro machine. On zoom, I can pick out legs. A proboscis of some kind, between mandibles. And even wings."

Brontosaurus came to his side. "Looks like it's damaged. One of the wings is ripped, do you see that? And look at the odd shape of the body. You got tiny legs on one side, but no matching legs on the other. It's like the entire left half is missing."

"Maybe it was burned away by the laser impact?" Eric said.

"Possibly." The heavy gunner cocked his head. "Step aside."

Eric did so.

Brontosaurus approached the bore hole.

"Sarge, we've finally found some metal," Brontosaurus transmitted. "Sending video imagery now."

"Got it," Marlborough said. "Looks like some sort of metal insect."

"Our best guess, it's some kind of micro machine," Brontosaurus said.

"All right, don't touch it," Marlborough said. "If this thing is part of what caused all metal in the city to disappear, we need to be very careful. I'm sending Fire Team B to back you up. When they arrive, collect a sample. Morpheus, you have some experience as a military scientist?"

"I was a scientist after I left the army, yes," Morpheus said.

"Then you join Fire Team B, and accept the sample for analysis," Marlborough said.

"You got it," Morpheus said.

Brontosaurus recalled the Breacher and Savage, and then all four waited for Fire Team B to arrive. A short time later Slate and Eagleeye stepped through the door, accompanied by Morpheus and two combat robots.

"So what do we have?" Morpheus stepped toward the laser-riddled wall.

"A micro machine of some kind," Eric said. "Looks vaguely insectile."

Brontosaurus noticed Slate staying back near the entrance. "What's wrong, tough guy? Scared of a little bug?"

"Nothing, I'm guarding the entrance," Slate said.

"Don't you want to see what this thing looks like?" Brontosaurus asked.

"I ain't getting close to that thing," Slate said. "I had my fill from the transmission Scorp sent."

Brontosaurus shrugged, and then returned his attention to the borehole.

"Scorp, reach into my pouch," Brontosaurus said. "I have a vial and a pair of tweezers inside."

"You carry a pair of tweezers with you at all times?" Eric said.

"Sampling kit," Brontosaurus said. "Never leave home without it."

"Are you sure you weren't born in my century?" Eric said. "That sounds vaguely like a credit card ad from my day."

"What's a credit card?" Brontosaurus said.

"Never mind." Eric approached.

Brontosaurus could have released his weapon mounts, causing the bulky heavy guns to drop to the floor and thereby freeing up his hands, but why bother when he had a handy low ranking grunt like Eric nearby?

Eric reached Brontosaurus and opened up the pouch hanging from the heavy gunner's utility belt. The smell of oil was rank on the robot. Well, at least it wasn't garlic. Even so, Eric toned down his olfactory sensitivity.

He reached into the pouch and fished out a small glass vial, along with a pair of tweezers, from among the curios, which included small spare power cells.

He stepped away from the heavy gunner, opened the vial, and then lifted the tweezers toward the hole.

"Careful…" Morpheus said.

"I don't think one little inactive micro machine can hurt me," Eric said.

"It's not you I'm worried about," Morpheus said. "I don't want the micro machine damaged."

"Oh." Eric wrapped the tweezers around the metal body and then pinched them together very slightly. Then he lifted it, removing the tiny machine from the bore hole. He quickly deposited it inside the vial and then sealed the lid. He promptly gave it to Morpheus.

"Thank you," Morpheus said. She held the vial up to eye level. "Beautiful."

"What do you mean?" Brontosaurus said. "It doesn't look all that different from other micro machines the Russians and Chinese have built. Nor our own government, for that matter."

"At first glance, yes," Morpheus said. "But if you zoom in, really zoom in, you can see the incredible detail. This micro machine is unlike anything we've ever seen before."

"You think it's alien?" Eric asked.

"I'd guess no," Morpheus said. "But then again, it's really too early to say."

Eric stepped back to Brontosaurus. He was about to return the tweezers to the pouch hanging from the heavy gunner's belt, when he noticed something he hadn't before: the pincer sections at the tip of the tweezers had partially melted away. It was just a tiny amount, but the damage was present.

"Odd," Eric said.

"What is it?" Brontosaurus said.

Eric showed him the tweezers.

"Morpheus, get rid of the vial!" Brontosaurus said.

"Why?" Morpheus said.

"It's using metal from the tweezers to reconstitute itself—" Brontosaurus said.

The glass shattered before he could finish.

16

E ric watched helplessly as the tiny insect landed on her body.

Morpheus screamed.

She moved in a blur, obviously having switched to Bullet Time. Clanks sounded repeatedly, a machine-gun fire of rat-a-tats as she swatted at her composite shell in an attempt to squash the micro machine.

But then she froze.

"Where is it?" Brontosaurus asked.

"Inside me," Morpheus said, the dread obvious in her voice. "It entered through my fan vent."

Her blue eyes became dark, and she slumped forward.

One of the Savages darted forward and promptly loaded her onto its back. No doubt Brontosaurus was instructing the robot.

"Sarge, we got a problem here," Brontosaurus transmitted.

"I saw it on the feed," Marlborough said. "The rest of us are on our way. Stay put for now. I want you to clear well away from her. Get ready to evacuate the suite, if need be."

The Savage lowered Morpheus to the floor, and the rest of the unit proceeded to the foyer. There was an old-style wooden door at the entrance, covered in white paint like the walls.

Eric interfaced with Morpheus' remote interface. "I'm reading weak brain activity... her AI core is still online." AI cores ran on a small power independent of the mains, which allowed the mind to remain intact if the body failed. "Permission to extract her AI core?"

"Do it," Brontosaurus said.

Eric went to her, and swung her onto her back. He retrieved his tools from the pouch he carried at his own waist, and activated moderate Bullet Time. He moved quickly, opening up those screws, until he was able to open up the chest plate. When he removed it, he stepped back in shock.

Her insides were crawling with more of the micro machines. They were digesting the different circuits and other metal-polycarbonate composites of her interior, and repurposing the material to create new micro machines. They were essentially runaway, reconstructive 3D printers.

"I told you I wasn't getting near that thing!" Slate said. The words were slow, drawn out, thanks to the Bullet Time.

"Get away from her!" Brontosaurus said.

"I can still reach her AI core!" Eric said, diverting

his speech process to Dee, so that his Accomp could pronounce the words at a rate matching the perceived time sense of the others.

"No, it's too late," Brontosaurus said. "We can't help her. We're getting the hell out. Now!"

Eric ran a quick scan on the micro machines, wanting to gather as much data as he could, then he retreated, backing away.

Some of the micro machines began to take flight then. They landed on the surrounding walls, and crawled about, as if searching for more metal. Some of them headed directly for him. He amped up Bullet Time even higher and darted toward the foyer. The others were already beginning to flee by then.

He passed right by them and snapped his time sense back to normal when he entered the hall outside.

Slate, Eagleeye, and Brontosaurus poured out of the room, along with the four support robots; Brontosaurus threw a grenade inside before slamming the door shut behind him. The micro machines began to impact it on the other side: it sounded like hail striking a tin roof.

The grenade detonated inside, and then there was silence.

"We lost Morpheus!" Brontosaurus transmitted.

Morpheus.

Eric remembered sleeping with her and Bambi. And now she was gone.

He could still see the way her cheeks dimpled so cutely when she smiled in VR. She had always stood up for him during training, taking his side when the rest of the team wanted to haze him, the newbie.

Good bye, my friend. You deserved better than this.

"Roger that," Marlborough said. "Get the hell out of there!"

The hail sound resumed. Sawdust began to trickle from the surface of the door at random locations.

Eric and Brontosaurus exchanged a worried glance.

"I said get the hell out of there!" Marlborough ordered.

The squad promptly retreated down the hall, away from the room.

Eric accessed his rear cam; holes riddled the door, and the micro machines were clambering outside. They were swarming around the different nearby surfaces, though several were flying in pursuit of the squad.

"Oh shit," Slate said. "Did I ever tell you I hate bugs?"

They reached the stairwell door and kicked it open, hurrying inside. Slate slammed it shut behind them.

They raced to the bottom of the building and entered the lobby. Marlborough and a few others had gathered inside. "Come on, we're waiting outside!"

They dashed onto the street. Four Ravager mechs led the way on point, while the other four followed on drag.

"So where to?" Frogger asked.

"We're going to have to take shelter in another building," Marlborough said. "I'm looking at suitable candidates on the map as we speak."

"Yeah, but what's going to protect us from those termites?" Slate said. "You didn't see how easily they drilled through that wall. Or digested Morpheus. Poor girl."

"He's right," Eric said. "No shelter will hold them off indefinitely. Even if we're behind a six inch steel barrier."

"Assuming they can find us," Frogger said. "I say we take shelter immediately. Before they emerge from the building and spot us on whatever sensor systems they have."

"How do we know they haven't already emerged?" Eagleeye said. "Sure, some of them followed us into the hallway. But the rest could have easily burst directly from the suite's window."

"There might have been other micro machines lying dormant in the city as well," Crusher said. "Left behind by the enemy for just such an occurrence as this."

"Gah!" Tread said. "The Ravager on rear guard!"

Eric glanced at his rear view feed. The trailing mech had toppled over. From its back emerged a small swarm of several freshly produced micro machines.

"Don't stop!" Marlborough said.

"I don't intend to!" Slate said. "Robot termites! Piece of crap robot termites!"

More of the micro machines swooped down from above, joining the swarm above the mech. It tried to get up, but its servomotors dissolved as Eric watched, and the Ravager collapsed helplessly.

The swarm broke into two parts, with one horde staying behind to convert the mech, and the remaining pursuing the Bolt Eaters.

The trailing mechs opened fire with their laser

turrets, easily dissolving individual micro machines, but otherwise not harming the whole of the swarm. Eric could see why the damage recorded on the base walls seemed to point to lasers at full intensity—those micro machines hardly consumed any of the energy at all.

But it wasn't enough to stop the whole slew of them.

One mech fired a missile, and it exploded amid the horde. That incinerated some of the micro machines near the core of the swarm, but otherwise only forced outward the remainder, which continued the pursuit. Oh, and the two trailing mechs were sprayed with shrapnel composed of those micro machines.

"Uh, I think we just lost two more mechs," Hyperion said.

"Tell the goddamn Ravagers to stop using their missiles!" Marlborough said. "And I want those last two mechs taken out before they can transform into more of those termites!"

"Actually, I don't think it will help," Hank said. "These micro machines can probably convert the mechs even if we reduce them to scrap metal. Might be better if we simply steered the mechs away. Maybe it will draw some of the insects."

"Do it," Marlborough ordered.

The two trailing mechs turned away in seemingly random directions. The swarm divided into three parts: two to pursue the infected mechs, and a third to continue the pursuit of the remaining Bolt Eaters.

The final mech on drag continued its laser barrage.

"What about grenades, Sarge?" Eric said.

"Why would grenades work any more effectively

than missile?" Marlborough said. "You'll just spray yourself with termite shrapnel, and they'll convert you in the end."

"I mean a pulse grenade?" Eric asked.

"Worth a try," Marlborough said.

Eric slowed down until he was close to the rear of the platoon, and then he ripped a pulse grenade from his harness and threw it. Manticore and Bambi had the same idea, and the three of them tossed their pulse grenades at the same time, hurling them over the heads of the trailing Ravager.

The grenades detonated at nearly the same time, in the middle of the swarm.

Electricity sparked outward from each one, tearing into the micro machines from several random plasma channels. Swathes of the termites dropped to the asphalt.

"That's doing it…" Eric said. "No chance of being hit with termite shrapnel with the pulse grenades!"

Eric tossed his second and final pulse grenade, and then moved forward so that others could have a throw.

"We don't have enough pulse grenades!" Hyperion said. "There's too many of them!"

"This way!" Marlborough said.

A nearby building ahead became highlighted, thanks to the HUD.

The Ravagers on point quickly reached the building in question: a partially collapsed apartment.

The platoon scrambled over the rubble.

"Send the mechs forward and around!" Marlborough commanded. "We'll draw the rest inside!"

The Ravagers hurried around the sides of the building, while Eric and the others continued forward. They entered an intact floor of the apartment.

"Place charges!" Marlborough said.

Eric retrieved a charge from his harness, and threw it onto a nearby exposed pillar, where it attached. He continued placing charges as he hurried forward, as did the others. Behind them, the swarm pursued.

They reached the far side of the building, and dove through the window, breaking it.

"Detonate charges!" Marlborough said when the last of them was clear.

The building came down on the micro machines.

"Nicely done," Bambi said.

"How long do you think it'll take before they dig their way out?" Hyperion said.

"Depends on how damaged they were in the collapse," Marlborough said.

They rendezvoused with the waiting Ravagers and continued forward.

"What's the plan?" Eric asked.

"We head to the Chinese base," Marlborough said. "Then leave the city, and loop around the outskirts until we rendezvous with our waiting Abrams. Then we put as much distance as we can between ourselves and these termites."

"And if they catch us before then?" Eagleeye said.

"Then we deal with them the same way as the others," Marlborough said. "Trapping them inside a building."

"Um, er, I used up all my demolition blocks in that last attack," Traps said.

"Me too," Bambi added.

"Then we'll just have to improvise," Marlborough said. "Maybe we'll find a cache of intact charges at the Chinese base."

"If there was a cache, my scouts would have reported it," Traps said.

"Well, as I told you, we'll improvise," Marlborough said.

17

Eric and the troops moved at a trot through the city streets. They utilized stealth mode feet placement, ensuring that each step was as quiet as possible, and they commensurately dialed down the output of their servomotors to reduce the emitted humming sounds. They eyed the buildings around them, constantly alert for signs of ambush.

"So Sarge, do you really think the Chinese are behind those termites?" Brontosaurus said. "Or the Russians?"

"I don't know what to think anymore," Marlborough said. "First we encounter a wide-sweeping gamma ray attack capable of killing all life upon contact, and temporarily knocking out any nearby machines in the process. And then we meet these robotic termites. Both of them require technology far beyond anything we've ever seen."

"So what are you saying, you admit we're being

invaded by aliens?" Slate asked.

"As I told you, I don't know what to think," Marlborough said.

The Bolt Eaters trekked on in silence.

"What if we're the last surviving members of the human race?" Bambi said.

"Wouldn't that be ironic, given that we're not even human?" Hank told her.

"Man, I hope we're not the last humans on Earth," Tread said. "I'd hate to spend an eternity with the rest of you."

"Then spend it in VR," Hicks said. "Have your Accomp play different avatars to keep you company."

Ordinarily the banter would have continued a lot longer, but it died after Hicks' words. None of them were really in the mood for joking at the moment.

During the continued march through the city toward the Chinese base, Eric gave some serious thought to the problem of evading those micro machines. It was inevitable that the group would encounter them again at some point.

He sent a private call to Frogger.

"What can I do you for?" Frogger said.

"I need someone to bounce ideas off of," Eric said. "And what better sounding board then myself?"

"Okay, shoot," Frogger said. "Keeping in mind, I'm not an exact copy of you. Quantum effects and all..."

"Gotta love those quantum effects," Eric said. "So then, did you see how well those pulse grenades handled the micro machines?"

"Of course," Frogger replied. "It's just too bad we don't have more of them."

"What if we don't need more?" Eric said. "What if we could reroute some energy from our power cells to electrify our skin? Sending a surge of high current into any micro machines that dare touch us?"

"Hm," Frogger said. "It might be possible. We'd have to install some fresh wiring of course, direct electricity from the power cell to the LEDs coating our skin. With a small circuit in-between to regulate the flow."

"Exactly my thoughts," Eric said.

"The thin film below the translucent top layer of the LEDs should act as a conductor, spreading the current evenly around our exteriors," Frogger said. "However we'd have to cut a small cross-section around our feet, severing the LEDs there to prevent the current from traveling into the ground."

"We'd have to do that, yes," Eric said. "It means the very bottom of our feet wouldn't match our surroundings. A small price to pay for the protection offered."

"There's only one problem: we don't have access to a 3D printer," Frogger said. "Where do we get the regulator circuit?"

"What if we repurpose a different circuit?" Eric said. "All of the boards are programmable. Remove one, plug it into the reprogrammer in our repair kits, and we can change its function as we see fit."

"But which one will you remove?" Frogger said. "We need every circuit aboard, especially considering we're essentially running on backup processors. In case you forgot, our mains already burned out thanks to that gamma ray burst."

"It's an interesting problem..." Eric said. He considered it for a few micro cycles. "What about the mechs? Their armor held up to the gamma ray attack. We have five Ravagers with us. With at least five backup processors aboard each."

"Mm, I'm running a remote diagnostic now," Frogger said. "Looks like some of their processors did in fact fail during the gamma ray attack, forcing a switchover to the backups... but it looks like enough of them are available for our purposes."

"We only need one each," Eric said.

"This could work," Frogger said. "I suppose you want to do the honors of informing the rest of the team, considering it was mostly your idea."

"Mostly?" Eric said. "It was *all* my idea."

"Yeah, but without me to talk to, you would have never come up with it," Frogger said.

"That's what I mean," Eric said. "When I say all my idea, I'm referring to you and me both, since we're the same person. Or different facets of the same person anyway."

"Ah, I get it!" Frogger said. "I can be a bit slow sometimes."

"Oh I know," Eric said. He proceeded to relay his plan to Marlborough and the rest of the team. "Once our hulls are electrified, any termite that touches us will go down. And as long as we don't make contact with any of the fallen machines again, giving them more metal to digest, they'll stay down."

"You don't really know that for sure," Crusher said. "Considering that we didn't really stay around all that long after the pulse grenades went off."

"True, maybe it will only stun them," Eric said. "But a temporary stun is all we need. It'll prevent them from entering through our vents and fan grills. I can put together some blueprints for the rest of you to look over."

Eric put them together, and sent them out over the comm line. He was spammed with "acceptance" verbiage on his HUD as the different members accepted the file request.

"You know, electrifying our hulls like this is a good way to drain our power cells," Hyperion said.

"Check out the blueprints," Eric said. "The drain is minimal, until an external metal object completes the circuit. Because of the nature of the LED top layer, the current will tunnel through and into the object in question."

"But we don't even know if these termites are made of metal," the robot operator pressed.

"No," Eric said. "But we do know they conduct electricity, otherwise the pulse grenades wouldn't have affected them. And that's good enough."

"Even so," Hyperion said. "If enough of the termites swarm a given unit, that will drain the cell entirely. We'll be defenseless."

"Yes," Eric said. "It's meant to protect us in a pinch. Against a small number of them. If we let a swarm reach us, we're dead either way. But wouldn't you at least like to have some protection, rather than none at all?"

"He's right," Marlborough said. "I want this hull electrifying ability in place. We stop at the next intersection."

The team reached the next intersection and confirmed that the way was clear on either side; staying close to the wall, they began implementing the changes Eric had sent to electrify their hulls.

With the tools from their repair kits they opened up the Ravager mechs and removed the necessary spare backup circuits. With their reprogrammers, they repurposed the boards, and then plugged them into their power cells using the spools of solder and the laser irons from their repair kits. With mini laser cutters, also from the kit, they carved small cross-sections around their feet, severing the LEDs there so that the expected current wouldn't flow straight into the ground, and then they ran the wires from the repurposed boards to the insides of their LED skins, electrifying the hulls.

They performed the upgrades not just on the Cicada units, but the Savage and Breacher combat robots as well. They didn't have the equipment necessary to upgrade the mechs, unfortunately.

They activated the protection, and the current passed into their weapons as well, insuring that every part of them was electrified, and protected from the enemy micro machine swarm.

Then they hurried on toward the Chinese base. They arrived shortly, and confirmed what the scouts had reported: the place was empty, stripped of all metals. They passed through the far side, and headed northwest, hugging the city's external wall as they made their way back to their forward base. They arrived without incident, and found the Abrams waiting beyond the base untouched, and in the same state in which they had left them. The two Ravagers on the walkways still acted as sentries.

"It's too bad we don't have the equipment to upgrade our tanks and mechs with this electrostatic shielding," Slate said.

"It's not electrostatic," Eric said. "And our tanks aren't entirely defenseless. They have laser turrets. And two of them are Jupiter units." Those two tanks harbored electrolasers that utilized a directed energy, laser-induced plasma channel to inflict lightning bolts at targets. "Those electrolasers will function the same as the pulse grenades, with arcing voltage taking down big swathes of those micro machines, if they swarm again."

"Unless they get smart, and decide to come at us one at a time," Bambi said.

"My guess is their algorithms are of the 'greedy shooter' type," Eric said. "Which is they attack the nearest enemy object, no matter what that object is doing. Swarming behavior, essentially."

"I forget, you were once a programmer," Slate said.

"Once a programmer, always a programmer," Eric said. *For good or for bad.* "Anyway, so far swarming is the only behavior we've seen."

"Actually, that's not true," Hank said. "You forget that the original horde split up when we sent our infected mechs away."

"That's true," Eric said. "So they also have a conversion algorithm in place: once a unit is infected, the swarm divvies its attention, sending some to the next target, while the rest concentrates on converting the first."

"Yeah well, these are all nice theories and everything," Slate said. "But that only sidesteps the issue: if any of those termites so much as touch our tanks, or our mechs, we lose the units. And it don't matter if those tanks have electrolasers or not."

"Then we don't let those micro machines touch them," Dickson said.

"All right, enough chitchat, we're leaving this city behind," Marlborough said. "It's time to make our way toward Malibu." That was the main base. Yes, the name was meant to be ironic. "Keep transmission range low. Strong enough to cover the platoon only. Let's not do anything to broadcast our presence."

"Assuming they don't have eyes on us from orbit…" Hank said.

The group raced away across the rocky terrain, following alongside the tanks.

When Urdani was the size of a fist behind them, Marlborough gave the order to shut down the power supply to their electrified hulls in order to conserve power. Though the drain wasn't all that much, it was prudent not to keep the electrification running at all times since the power usage added up after a while.

The seven Ravager mechs continued to run alongside, while the smaller Cicadas and support troops hopped onto the tanks. The base was eighty kilometers away, and while the Bolt Eaters could have jogged the whole way, it was better to ride if only to spare the robots from the wear and tear on their servomotors. The mechs were too big to fit on the Abrams, of course, so they had no choice but to continue on foot.

Eric opened up a top panel on the tank and retrieved one of the recharge cables; he opened up the small door on his chest piece, and plugged the cable into his power cell. Brontosaurus also grabbed a cable beside him.

"Might as well top up," Brontosaurus said.

Eric scanned the dusty plains around them like the rest of the troops. He thought of Morpheus once again. Such a terrible way to go. He hoped his end wasn't so ignominious.

He occasionally glanced at the sky. And whenever he did, he had to wonder, if there truly were aliens in orbit, were they watching them even now?

Though he was a machine, the thought always made him shudder.

18

Eric and the rest of the Bolt Eaters were crouched behind a natural rise, and the tanks were distributed across the rocky ground behind them. The dusty desert stretched out at their backs, and to the left and right. Ahead, in the distance, lurked Malibu base.

The sprawling army outpost was situated at the top of a broad hill that interrupted the desert. The Brass always liked to choose defensible positions, and this place was no exception.

Eric had his laser rifle aimed at the six-meter tall perimeter wall that enveloped the base, and he switched his point of view to the scope to zoom in, because the weapon was capable of a much higher magnification than his own eyes. He noticed immediately that the concrete Alaska barriers composing the wall were missing their characteristic razor wire at the top. He continued moving his scope along the perimeter, toward the entrance.

"Holy shit," Hyperion said. "Are you guys seeing what I'm seeing."

"Yup," Brontosaurus said. "And you thought we were in deep poopy before..."

"What are you seeing?" Slate said. "What? And who says *poopy?*"

"He must have had kids," Crusher said. "Only parents talk— holy shit."

Eric finally reached the entrance with his scope, and he, too, had his holy poop moment. He simply couldn't believe what he was seeing, not for several moments. He blinked, wondering if what he saw was real, or some apparition. But it remained, no matter what he did.

There were these two quadruped cyborgs on either side of the entrance, seated as if guarding. Each of them vaguely resembled a Sphinx, straight out of ancient Egypt. Their bodies seemed almost robotic, as the torso and limbs were coated in a mirror-like sheen, though there were otherwise no obvious signs of mechanization. The exterior surfaces were completely smooth: no bulges of servomotors, no tubes or conduits, no recessed panels.

Conversely, their heads seemed organic: part reptile, part insect, part Portuguese man-of-war. He zoomed in on one of them, and saw a pair of mandibles at perpendicular angles to one another topping a tube-like maw coated in razor-sharp teeth inside. Two compound eyes bulged from the sides of that maw, reminding Eric of a fly. A cobra-like hood draped down beneath those eyes, flanking the head and neck all the way to the silvery torso; bordering the hood were a series of flagellum-like tentacles, coiling amongst themselves like the stinging tentacles of the aforementioned man-of-war. Probably covered in toxin-filled nematocysts, too.

The join between the organic and inorganic sections seemed rather rudimentary, and was the only incongruence in the otherwise perfect forms of the creatures. A bloody outline underneath the neck areas demarcated the change, as if the biological head had been crudely stitched onto the metal body in a Frankenstein's monster sort of way.

Beyond the pair of reptile-robots, past the entrance gap, Eric could see a herd of strange... entities. These were entirely organic, with no hint of a machine in them. Each being had an elongated white head, the color of newly born larvae, with a wicked-looking maw filled with shark-like teeth. The head was connected to a red, four-armed torso, which in turn was pasted onto the front of a black, centipede-like body that had six jointed legs—each joint had a large, scythe-like spike protruding from it. The torso was balanced by a counterweight at the rear of the body: a long, dark green spiked tail that ended in a thick, reddish ball, perhaps some kind of glandular sac. The dorsal section of the body was armored with several sharp spikes, which looked like they could impale anything that had the misfortune of landing there.

It was hard to get an impression of size, but comparing them to the height of the perimeter wall, he estimated the entities were about twice as tall as a human, and as long as a tank.

The strange creatures were locked within some sort

of translucent pen inside the base. Eric could tell the pen was there because the beasts occasionally bumped into it, their features flattening as if scrunching up against glass. He wondered if there really was glass in place there, or whether it was some kind of energy field. Either way, he counted around eight of the entities, though there were probably more hidden from view since the perimeter walls prevented him from seeing the full extents of that pen.

"Effing bitches!" Slate said. "Mother effing bitches! Uh, uh, let's go back?"

"So I guess we've confirmed this isn't the Chinese?" Manticore said.

"Unless the Chinese have had a breakthrough in bioweapons technology," Marlborough said. "Then no, it is not."

"What are those things at the bottom of the hill?" Brontosaurus asked.

Eric zoomed out slightly, and lowered his scope until his crosshairs were traveling over the bottom of the hill. Then he spotted them: a series of empty troughs lining the base of the hill.

"Look like troughs?" Eagleeye said.

"Troughs?" Tread said. "For what?"

"Dunno," Eageleeye said. "Maybe waste disposal?"

"Yeah but they're on level ground, not sloping, like you'd expect if that were true," Hank said. "And they're not even connected to the base in any way."

"Forget the troughs," Slate said. "Who gives a shit about the troughs? These are freakin' aliens! First contact, bitches. Whoa. Breathe, Slate my boy. Breathe."

"Not so fast, Slate," Dickson said. "Even if aliens have invaded, it's highly unlikely we're looking at them. Think about it. What are the chances alien invaders would be compatible with our environment? With bodies having just the right pressure differential so that they didn't implode or explode, and were able to withstand our gravity so that they weren't flattened the moment they set foot on our planet? And what about atmospheric contents capable of powering alien respiration? That's right. The chances are essentially zilch.

"These things look like bioweapons to me, engineered specifically for our environment. The two at the entrance are likely cyborg analogs, while those inside the base are pure bioweapon, based on DNA samples taken from Earth species. No doubt they all have control chips of some kind installed in their heads.

"If I were an alien race invading a world, I'd take samples and create bioweapons like these to augment my main forces. Cells can be programmed to divide at an exorbitant rate... it can be far cheaper to create a custom designed organic than to create a robot, resource wise, especially if you spliced in photosynthesis capabilities to help fuel all that division."

"I have to agree," Brontosaurus said. "These are definitely bioweapons. Not the aliens themselves. But I'm not convinced they're using photosynthesis for food."

"I'm not sure I like the implications of what you're saying," Crusher said.

"It's just as well that you don't," Brontosaurus said. "I don't like them either."

"Let's forget about their food source for now, and all that other stuff," Hicks said. "We need to come up with a name for them. So we can differentiate between the two types, those guarding the entrance, and those inside, in the heat of battle. I like Grizz, myself."

"Grizz?" Slate said. "They look nothing like grizzlies. Shit. Grizz."

"Myself, I'm calling those two robot-insect mashup thingies guarding the entrance Frankenstein Dogs," Manticore said. "You know why, right?"

"Works for me," Crusher said. "Frankendogs for short."

"What about those things that look like centipedes with four-armed torsos and big bulbous tails?" Hyperion said.

"How about Pussy Riders?" Slate said.

"Yeah, more like Dick Rippers," Bambi said.

"I'm just going to call them Red Tails," Brontosaurus said. "Feel free to follow my lead."

"I bet there's acid in those glandular sacs," Traps said. "Assuming those are actually glandular sacs… looking at the tail triggered those words in my database for some reason."

"Mine, too," Eric said.

"Well then maybe you two bright bulbs should let yourselves get smacked with one of those 'glandular sacs,' and you can let the rest of us know what's inside them," Slate suggested.

"No thanks," Traps said.

"I'm detecting a communications web similar to our own, emanating from that base," Mickey said. "The signals are powerful. My guess is they could easily outpunch our own, if they wanted to, severely limiting our range."

"Well, we're going to continue to limit our own comm range for the time being," Marlborough said. "So far, it seems they haven't spotted us. And I intend to keep it that way."

"If these really were aliens, I'm surprised they wouldn't have eyes in orbit on us…" Bambi said.

"Obviously they've got a whole lot of other things to look at, especially if this is an invasion like we think it is," Marlborough said.

Eric heard a sonic boom, and he and the others ducked lower.

A large vessel approached from the south. It slowed rapidly, so that the sonic boom faded away, leaving only a distant humming. The craft was shaped like a broad, silver diamond, and cut a thin profile through the air. It was unlike anything he'd ever seen, and there was no matching vessel in his military database.

From Malibu base, the Red Tails abruptly rushed from the entrance—the containing pen had apparently lifted. The creatures swarmed down the hillside. Eric trained his crosshairs on one of them, following that torso, and the centipede body it was connected to as it ran…. he couldn't fire, of course, not until he was sure the team was under attack. The current Rules of Engagement prevented that.

When the creatures reached the bottom of the hill,

he was expecting them to race toward the hiding place of the Bolt Eaters. That still wouldn't count as an attack, unless they opened fire with weapons Eric couldn't see at the moment.

But instead, the Red Tails crowded around the waiting troughs, and gazed upward expectantly with those elongated white heads.

The vessel continued to approach. It was moving at a crawl now for this final leg, until it stopped outright above the troughs. The craft slowly lowered until it was hovering about ten meters above the ground.

"Is it just me, or shouldn't it be impossible for that thing to fly?" Mickey said. His voice was barely above a whisper, as if he was afraid the bioweapons would over-hear him, or any aliens aboard the craft, despite the distance.

Broad, half-cylinder conduits extended from the underside of the vessel, and a reddish sludge poured into the waiting troughs on the ground. The engineered animals shoved their heads into the sludge and drank with relish. Some of the bigger ones raised white heads that dripped with red liquid, and snapped at Red Tails nearby, keeping them at bay.

"Reminds me of a puppy litter," Crusher said. "When you put out the milk."

"What *is* that red sludge they're drinking?" Bambi said.

"Actually, the better question to ask is, what happened to the humans that were holed up in Urdani, and Malibu?" Braxton said. "We saw what those termites could do to a machine…"

"Oh no," Traps said. "You're not saying…"

"I am," Braxton said. "They're not powering their bioweapons with chlorophyll, but with human and animal tissue."

As if to prove Braxton's point, one of the creatures fetched what looked like a partial human skeleton from the sludge in the trough and swallowed it whole.

"Oh God, this is disgusting," Bambi said.

"You can take some comfort in the fact that any humans were already dead before they were harvested," Dickson said. "The gamma ray, remember…"

"So that vessel flew in from the east," Crusher said. "There are a few cities in that direction. I think we have to assume that they've fallen."

"That would be a safe assumption," Dickson said. "The bigger question is, how many cities have fallen across the world?"

"I got a different question," Hicks said. "Why were we spared in the initial strike? Malibu was lost. Urdani. The forward operating base. Other cities to the east. Presumably all swept over by swarms of those termites in conversion runs that transformed the surviving metal into more micro machines, while processing organic tissue for consumption by their bioweapons. But we were passed over. Why?"

"It would be relatively easy to target urban centers, due to heat and light pollution," Hank said. "But a lone platoon and its support units out in the middle of nowhere? Even if they did notice us, maybe they thought it wasn't worth the effort to hunt us down.

Maybe they knew that eventually we'd come to them. As we have."

"We should attack," Hyperion said.

"Notwithstanding the fact we have no idea what we're up against, the Rules of Engagement won't let us," Marlborough said.

"Good point," Hyperion said. "Guess that rules out a surprise attack."

"It does," Marlborough said.

"Way I see it, we only got one option," Brontosaurus said. "We turn back, then give this city a wide berth as we head east to the closest major city."

"And what then?" Mickey said. "What if it's just as empty as Urdani, 'processed' by these aliens for raw materials? What if the only fate awaiting us there is to be processed ourselves? We already agreed our jury-rigged anti-termite defenses won't hold off a whole swarm. We should go into hiding, and just wait out the invasion. We can't really do anything anyway, we're just a small group of robots against an entire invasion force. Our Rules of Engagement won't even let us attack first."

"Yes but, it's possible we'll find some comm equipment intact," Brontosaurus said. "With it, we might be able to reestablish communications with headquarters and receive further orders. As well as an update on what the situation is."

"Comm equipment intact?" Mickey said. "I don't know man. Urdani was swept clean of any machinery. Even if we reach a bigger city, I doubt we'll find anything."

"Personally, I think we should be trying to hitch a ride on that vessel," Manticore said. "Then take on these aliens at their source."

"Brave, but a recipe for disaster," Crusher said. "Seeing how little we know about these aliens and their tech."

As Eric watched, the craft retracted its feeding conduits, then moved skyward once more.

"Too late now," Frogger said.

The vessel began to hum once more, and then it moved east at an ever increasing speed until it broke the sound barrier: a sonic boom reverberated across the area.

"Mickey, you said you detected a comm web emanating from that base?" Eric asked.

"That's right," Mickey answered.

"What if we could capture some of this alien technology?" Eric said.

"We wouldn't be able to use it…" Donald said.

"No," Dickson said. "But the Brass would appreciate anything we could get our hands on. The problem is, how to get inside that base with all those bioweapons guarding it?"

The Red Tails licked the troughs clean, and then scaled the hill more calmly until they were inside Malibu, and no doubt enveloped in their pen. Eric was beginning to think that the pen was composed of an energy field, since he hadn't seen any glass walls rising anywhere from the ground.

Just then he heard a buzzing overhead.

"The hell is that?" Marlborough said.

Eric glanced skyward, and zoomed in. Halfway between the platoon, and the base, he spotted a small drone.

"It's a Raven," Eagleye said. "Russian model."

"A Russian model?" Dickson said.

"Bokerov…" Marlborough said. "He's got to be in the area somewhere."

Eric surveyed the terrain beyond the tanks behind the platoon, but didn't spot anything out of the ordinary.

"With that racket, he'll draw the attention of every bioweapon in the region," Traps said.

Eric studied the Raven a moment longer. "It's headed in our direction."

"That Russian bastard knows we're here," Dickson said. "And he's leading them right to us!"

"The bioweapons haven't reacted yet," Crusher said.

"Permission to shoot it down?" Braxton asked.

"This could be considered a form of attack by the Rules of Engagement," Traps said. "Couldn't it?"

"It could," Marlborough said. "Braxton. Shoot it down."

The sniper aimed his rifle skyward. He fired.

The Raven plunged from the sky and crashed with a gentle thud.

"Termites!" Hyperion said.

Eric glanced back toward the base. A cloud of termites swarmed from the entrance and flew down the hill.

"Uh, that was a bad idea," Brontosaurus said.

The termites were headed directly toward the hiding place of the Bolt Eaters.

19

E ric stared at the approaching swarm in horror.

"Well, it looks like this is the end, my brothers and sisters," Mickey said. "It was good serving with you."

"It's not the end," Eric said. He would have gritted his teeth if he had them. "We won't sell our lives cheaply."

"I'm with you on that, bro," Hank said. "These termites want to take us, they're going to have to work for it."

"Activate hull charge," Marlborough said.

Eric and the others did so. Eric could hear the soft hum as the electricity coated his exterior.

Marlborough glanced at Eric. "Now we get to see how well your electrification design works in combat."

"It won't stop them all," Eric said, gazing at the incoming swarm. "There are too many of them."

"It's too bad we can't plug into our tanks and recharge while keeping the electrified coating active," Tread said.

They couldn't do that, because the charge from their hulls would transfer to the tanks, and flow straight into the ground.

"Tread, prepare Jupiters to unleash electrolasers," Marlborough said.

"Prepared to fire Jupiter electrolasers," Tread said.

"Damn it," Marlborough said. "We need to open fire *now*. Cause as much damage as we can before contact. But the Rules of Engagement won't let us."

"They're continuing to close with our position," Brontosaurus said. "That constitutes an attack, as far as I'm concerned, given what we know about the capabilities of these termites."

"Go ahead and try to fire," Marlborough said. "And tell me what happens."

Brontosaurus aimed at the incoming cloud.

Eric did, too. He tried to squeeze the trigger, but his finger refused to comply.

"Can't do it," Brontosaurus said.

"My Rules subsystem is telling me it won't allow us to fire until the termites reach us, and attempt to land on our electrified skins," Marlborough said. "This is ridiculous."

"It's too bad we weren't able to break through the Containment Code yet," Frogger sent Eric privately.

"Yeah. Too bad." Eric watched as the cloud of termites approached.

"When the swarm arrives," Bambi said. "Our tanks will be the first to go down."

"It will take time to convert them," Hank said.

"True, but even if we eventually beat the rest of the termites, we'll have to handle the new swarm produced from the raw materials of our tanks," the robot operator continued. "Plus, no doubt the aliens will send their bioweapons raining down on us at some point."

"The swarm is continuing to close with our position…" Mickey said.

"Wait," Eric said. "The termites don't yet know where we are. Look at their flight path. They're headed in our general direction, this is true, but they're not flying directly toward us."

"They'll change directions shortly, no doubt when they detect our thermal signatures…" Dickson said.

"Unless we create a diversion," Eric said.

"A diversion?" Dickson asked.

"Sarge, requesting permission to lead the termites away from the platoon," Eric said.

"You want to act as a decoy?" Marlborough asked.

"I do," Eric said. "I'll draw them away."

"You'll die," Brontosaurus said.

"I know," Eric said. "But the rest of you will live. My brothers and sisters… Sarge… let me do this. If there's a chance I can prevent those termites from discovering our position, I have to take it. Or at the very least, buy you enough time to flee before the other bioweapons arrive."

"The other bioweapons and their guards haven't

even moved from their positions by the entrance," Hicks said.

"But they will," Eric said. "You know they will."

"You know, by leaving cover, you'll just be revealing the position of the rest of us to the swarm…" Dickson said.

"Maybe," Eric said. "But they'll discern our position as they get closer anyway, like you said." He glanced at Marlborough. "So, Sarge? We're running out of time…"

"You have my permission," Marlborough finally said. "Do it."

Eric raced from cover. He headed due west.

He had expected all of the termites to pursue him, but only a small portion of the swarm broke away to pursue. A disappointingly small portion. The rest actually swerved toward the platoon's position.

Damn it. All I did was reveal where the rest of the platoon was hiding, like Dickson said.

"I'm going with him," Brontosaurus said over the comm.

Before Marlborough could counter him, the heavy gunner was on his feet, and racing after Eric. More termites broke away from the swarm.

"I'm in," Bambi said over the comm.

"Me too," Slate said, joining her.

"Noble of you," Bambi told him as the pair raced after Brontosaurus and Eric. "Considering how much you hate these things."

"Not noble," Slate said. "Selfish. I want to squash as many of them as I can before I go."

Together, the four of them caused half of the swarm to redirect toward them.

That was better, at least. But would it be enough to save the main platoon?

Eric noted that the main alien bioweapons were staying back near the base.

For now.

They trusted fully in the termite swarm's ability to do its job.

That trust probably wasn't misplaced. Not at all.

As Eric raced across the rocky plain, he pointed his rifle toward the incoming horde and engaged smart targeting.

Was he cleared to fire yet under the Rules of Engagement?

Only one way to find out.

He attempted to squeeze the trigger.

His finger didn't respond.

Damn it.

He continued forward, and narrowly avoided tripping on a rock that jutted from the ground ahead.

And then, finally, a termite well ahead of the secondary swarm landed on him. It caused a small spark as the electrified skin repelled it.

"Did the rest of you see that?" Eric said. "One of them just tried to land on me. We're good to fire!"

At least, he hoped they were. If his Rules subsystem interpreted it as an attempted attack, which it was, the override would be transmitted to the entire platoon, freeing not just Eric, but the rest of them to fire.

He pointed his rifle behind him toward the sky once more. He squeezed the trigger.

His finger responded.

Good.

He kept the trigger down. Termites dropped as they were struck; sometimes two or three, if they happen to be along the same line of fire, since the weapon penetrated them easily. However, it was like shooting grains of sand at a beach: there were simply too many to make much of a difference. He was starting to wish he had some pulse grenades left.

Brontosaurus, Slate and Bambi similarly fired their lasers into the swarm, bringing down a few of them.

A flash drew his attention to the main swarm that still headed toward the rest of the platoon. Electrolasers had hit that swarm, and the plasma channels arced from termite to termite, striking hundreds of the closely-packed micro machine at once. The termites fell in large swaths as the Jupiters fired repeatedly.

Meanwhile, the secondary swarm continued to home in on Eric and the other three. The size of that particular horde remained constant, and menacing as ever, despite the laser barrage from the four Cicadas. There were just too many.

Eric's laser rifle abruptly overheated.

Damn it.

The outlying members of the secondary swarm began to arrive. Continuing to run along with the others, Eric flipped his rifle around and utilized it as a club to swat the insects away. When his electrified rifle touched the different termites, sparks erupted, reminding him of mosquitos hitting a zapper.

Other termites began to land on his electrified exterior, and they too fell away as the surface sparked.

"It's working!" Bambi said.

"So far," Eric said. He glanced at his power level on his HUD. It was quickly falling.

"Come on, you pieces of shit!" Slate said. "That all you bitches got?"

Like Eric, Slate's weapon had overheated, and he was bashing wildly at the incoming termites.

More of the micro machines impacted as the rest of the secondary swarm began to arrive. Eric's power levels dipped precariously.

He had an idea.

"We have to touch, back to back," Eric said. "Share the electrical field… stress our power cells less! We'll last twice as long!"

He hoped.

Eric slowed down, allowing the others to catch up, and they quickly formed a back-to-back fighting stance so that they were all touching and sharing the hull electrification.

There was no point in activating Bullet Time. It might help him swat individual termites more easily, but it would only drain his power cell faster.

His rifle fire indicator abruptly turned green on his HUD. He flipped the weapon around and sprayed the nearby termites with laser fire.

His power cell was at twenty-five percent.

As more and more of the termites were zapped as

they touched his electrified hull, he realized he wasn't going to make it.

But then electricity suddenly arced from termite to termite in front of him, carving away a huge swathe of them.

The Jupiter electrolasers were firing at his position.

He glanced at his overhead map.

The red dots of the main swarm had vanished. The platoon had won.

"How'd you manage that, Sarge?" Brontosaurus said.

"Frogger here came up with an idea to daisy chain the power cells of the Abrams tanks to the Jupiters, via the charging cables," Marlborough said. "Boosted the stopping power of the electrolasers tenfold."

"Good old Frogger," Eric said.

Tread had to be careful in his aim, because the boosted electrolasers could quite easily destroy the Cicadas in friendly fire. But he was an AI, after all, with an AI Accomp, and calculated the necessary firing solutions without issue.

In a few moments only a small number of the swarm remained; Eric and the three with him finished off the termites by bashing them away, and purposely allowing them to land on their electrified hulls.

"You'd think they'd learn not to do that by now," Slate said.

"Obviously they haven't had time to update their algorithms," Eric said. "They'll probably be rethinking the use of termites against us going forward."

"Get back to the hide!" Marlborough said. "The bioweapons are leaving the base."

Eric glanced at Malibu. Sure enough, the Red Tails were racing down the hill. They scooped up some sort of weapon from inside the base before emerging—long, metal spears that they held in the arms emerging from their torsos.

He hurried back to the platoon with Brontosaurus, Bambi and Slate, and the four of them took cover behind the natural rise.

Marlborough and the others had already opened fire by then. The Jupiters and other tanks had repositioned to get a bead on the tangos; electrolasers from the Jupiters struck two different Red Tails as Eric watched. Actually, no, the weapons struck the metal *spears* that they held, and arced between the similar spears gripped by other Red Tails nearby, causing no damage whatsoever.

"Nicely done on the part of the enemy," Hank commented.

Their ordinary lasers, meanwhile, did in fact drill holes into the bioweapons. However, the creatures kept coming.

"The hell!" Slate said. "I drilled a vagina into one of their heads, and it's still coming!"

"Obviously they keep their brains in a different area than their heads," Bambi said. "Sort of like you guys. I'd recommend aiming between the legs."

"Har," Slate said.

"Hank, Tread, deploy mechs," Marlborough said.

"Defensive positions. The rest of you, pull back to the tanks."

The Cicadas and support troops pulled back to the tanks as instructed, while the mechs assumed positions hull-down behind the natural rise. They aimed their laser turrets and missile launchers over the crest.

The mechs launched missiles and the impacts sent Red Tail body parts flying into the air. The longer lasting laser pulses from the Ravagers and tanks, meanwhile, were able to tear off heads and rip open bodies.

"Poof!" Slate said. "Take that, bitches!"

The Red Tails kept coming, and soon the vanguard reached the Ravagers.

The mechs switched to bashing the creatures at close range.

One of the Red Tails smashed its metal spear into a mech: the impact sent up sparks, and the mech promptly collapsed.

"Don't let those staffs hit them!" Marlborough ordered.

"Trying…" Hank said.

Another creature slammed its big, spherical tail down on a mech. The red sac burst open, covering the mech in some sort of goo. The Red Tail promptly died. The Ravager mech, meanwhile, was frozen in place, unable to break free of the red sludge.

"Scorp, Brontosaurus, take control of one mech each," Marlborough commanded. "Now!"

Eric sent the request to Tread, who promptly ceded control of one of the units.

Eric switched to the point of view of the mech and interfaced with the movement and weapons subsystems, so that it was like his AI core was inside of the unit, and he observed the world from the viewpoint of the cameras on top of its head. When he moved his arms and legs, his own limbs remained stationary, whereas the mech's responded.

One of the Red Tails was coming directly at him with a metal spear…

20

E ric leaped to the side, moving a bit slower than he would have in his Cicada body. He'd practiced with mechs during training, of course, so that wasn't entirely unexpected.

Just have to adapt to the change in movement speed again.

He grabbed the creature as it went past, wrapping his hands around the base of the tail, away from the spikes of the central body. Then he smashed it into the next bioweapon; the glandular sac on the tail burst open, burying the other creature. The Red Tail he carried, meanwhile, promptly died. It continued to grasp the metal spear firmly within its arms, however.

Maybe I can use that.

Eric swung the Red Tail about like a rag doll, wielding the body like a weapon. Whenever the metal spear clutched by the dead body impacted another Red Tail, a bright spark went up, and the targeted creature fell to the ground. And even when the spear didn't hit, the force of the body's impact sent any stricken Red Tails flying away. He made his way forward like that through the enemy numbers, and adjusted his time sense up and down as necessary so that he always held the advantage.

Behind him, the tanks fired over the rise continually with their own laser turrets, along with the Cicadas and support troops, tearing black holes into the resilient units.

A group of Red Tails was attempting to race past him. Eric fired the last of his Ravager's missiles, sending up a cloud of body parts and halting the advance of that group.

Beside him, Brontosaurus' Ravager had also procured the corpse of one of the enemies, but this one didn't hold a metal spear. Even so, the heavy gunner used the body with deadly efficiency, bashing away any targets as he went.

In moments, the two of them, along with the remaining Ravagers, and the support of the tanks and the rest of the platoon, had reduced the attackers into piles of dead meat.

"Smells like curry!" Hyperion said. "Who's up for hitting an Indian restaurant in VR after this?"

"Watch the Frankendogs!" Marlborough said.

Eric glanced at the top of the hill.

The two guards had moved forward, and as he watched, their smooth sides peeled back, and malevolent-looking weapons turrets jutted forth.

"Oh oh," Brontosaurus said.

Eric deployed the ballistic shield in front of his mech, and ducked behind it.

"It's firing an intense gamma ray burst!" Mickey said. "Concentrated on your position. Don't stay in the same place for too long... even with the extra armor in your mech cores, you won't last long!"

Eric promptly fired the jumpjets on his Ravager, and landed running several meters ahead. He jogged toward the base of the hill, keeping his ballistic shield angled in front of him.

"What are you doing?" Marlborough asked.

"Drawing away their attention," Eric said. "I suggest you keep firing."

Eric reached one of the troughs at the base of the hill, and dove behind it. He kept his ballistic shield angled behind the edge of the trough for an added layer of protection and lifted the large laser turret that was built into his arm over the top, and switched to the viewpoint of its scope.

The quadrupeds were making their way down the hill. He aimed at the center of mass of one of them and squeezed the trigger. No effect. The laser seemed to reflect off that polished material.

Eric aimed at the head next. When he fired, a satisfying black hole appeared in the skin. But the creature didn't go down.

Electrolaser impacts also came from the Jupiters in the distance behind him, but the bolts of electricity arced harmlessly between the silver bodies. A shell landed on one of the Frankendogs, courtesy of an Abrams, and the resulting explosion ripped the skin completely off the head, revealing the faceless metal ovoid underneath. The entity otherwise remained unharmed, and continued its advance toward Eric's position, along with the other.

"Catch!" Brontosaurus said.

Eric spun in time to watch the charged spear Brontosaurus had thrown lodge in the ground in front of him. Eric reached for it hesitantly. The top of the protruding metal was colored black, unlike the silvery hue of the rest of the spear.

"The black portion is safe to touch," Brontosaurus clarified.

Eric cocked his head, and then folded away the laser in his hand so that he could grab the weapon. He reached forward, still somewhat hesitant, but then wrapped his big fingers around the black haft of the spear.

Nothing happened.

"With all the tech available to us, we have to use spears," Eric said, wrenching the weapon free to examine it. "I can't believe it."

He was about to toss the spear at one of the Frankendogs when a portion of the trough disintegrated entirely in front of him, along with a good portion of the ballistic shield, and his shoulder. Eric dropped the spear and quickly ducked his Ravenger as low as he was able, wrapping the shield over top of himself. He was careful not to touch the dropped spear in the process.

"Uh, what just happened?" Eric said.

"Looks like a Frankendog just launched a high intensity laser at your position," Dickson said. "I'd advise against getting up."

Eric didn't want to lose his mech, so he remained flat beside the trough.

"We're going to try to distract them," Marlborough said. "Get ready to toss that spear of yours."

"All right," Eric said. "But how do we even know the spear will harm them?"

"In The Art of War, there's a paragraph that says: always use the weapons of the enemy against them, if possible," Marlborough said.

"That's not from the Art of War," Eric commented.

"It is in my version," Marlborough said. "I see it here, scribbled in the margins… anyway, get ready."

Eric waited a few moments. He reverted his point of view back to himself, so that he could observe the platoon around him. He glanced at the troughs out there, and saw his Ravager lying flat behind one of them; he was surprised at how good of a connection he had with that mech, given how far away it was from the platoon. Then again, there wasn't much else to interfere with the signal—unless of course the aliens decided to outpunch it with their own frequency. Strangely, so far they had not. Maybe they weren't even aware of how human comms worked, yet.

Movement drew his attention to the left flank of the platoon. Two of the Abrams had moved out from behind the cover of the natural rise, and were opening fire with shells and lasers.

Eric zoomed in on the hill, and saw that the two

quadrupeds were altering their descent slightly, and angling their turrets toward the new attackers.

"Now!" Marlborough said.

Eric switched back inside the Ravager mech, gripped the black haft of the spear, and stood up. Both quadrupeds had their skin burned away at that point.

Eric aimed at the closest and tossed the spear.

His aim was true: the weapon struck the Frankendog and it impaled right up to the black haft. Electrical sparks emerged from the impact site, and the alien robot collapsed.

The second Frankendog spun toward Eric's Ravager, and he dropped once more. Above him, another gaping hole appeared in the trough.

"They're going to call in that diamond ship of theirs, you know," Bambi said. "We can't stay here all day."

"Cover me," Brontosaurus said.

Eric switched back to himself, and peered over the rise. He fired at the remaining quadruped, along with the rest of the platoon, trying to draw away its attention. Meanwhile, Brontosaurus' Ravager was retreating along the plains, through the bodies of the dead Red Tails. He slid a spear from the clutches of one of the bioweapons, and turned back toward the troughs. He tossed the weapon toward Eric's Ravager, but then the enemy's powerful laser found him, and the Ravager toppled.

The spear landed about five meters behind Eric's Ravager. He switched his point of view to the mech, and slowly crawled forward as the Abrams and remaining Bolt Eaters continued to ravage it in an attempt to distract.

"It's not falling for it this time," Dickson said. "That robot knows where the real threat is."

Eric glanced at his overhead map. The Frankendog was about ten meters away. In another moment, it would come within line of sight of the mech.

He decided to make his move.

Eric fired his jumpjets so that he was traveling horizontally just above the rocky ground, and switched to Bullet Time.

He traveled straight toward the spear, and scooped it up as he passed by. He fired his left lateral jets, swerving in case the robot was tracking him, then activated ventral thrust, so that he was moving upward. He fired another burst to rotate his body toward his opponent, and while he was still spinning, he released the spear.

He watched the weapon move agonizingly slowly toward its target. He fired his right lat jets, and returned his time sense to normal. The spear struck, disabling the Frankendog.

Meanwhile his mech landed unharmed. He raced it back toward the rest of the troop, and switched control back to Tread before returning to his own viewpoint.

"Nicely done," Marlborough said. "Load up on the tanks, Bolt Eaters! We're retreating!"

"Don't we want to explore that base?" Donald asked.

"No time," Marlborough said. "They've probably

already sent out a distress signal. Like Bambi said, the cavalry will be here shortly. Gather up the alien spears from the fallen Reds, and wrap the tips in field dressing from the med-kit."

"I didn't know we had a human med-kit," Slate said.

"Check out the storage compartment of the Jupiters," Dickson said. "Lots of med-kits."

Eric went to one of the Jupiters and retrieved some gauze from a med-kit. Then he hurried to one of the fallen Red Tails, ripped the spear from its clutches, and carefully wrapped the tip in the gauze so that he wouldn't accidentally trigger the weapon—it seemed that just touching the exposed area to metal activated whatever power it contained.

When he had successfully wrapped the upper portion of the spear above the black haft, he tested the effectiveness of the wrapping by touching the fabric against a nearby Breacher. The robot gave him a curious look. Well, it didn't have any facial expressions like the Cicadas, but Eric imagined that look must have been curious. When he was satisfied that the wrapped spear didn't cause any harm, he hesitantly slid it into his harness via a gap in the mesh. Then he released it so that it was touching his metal exterior. He half-expected some disabling charge to spark through his body, but none came, thankfully.

The others had similarly gathered spears from the fallen around them, and then returned to the tanks.

Eric leaped onto one of the armored units and immediately plugged into the charger: his power levels were really low.

"Incoming shells!" Traps announced.

Explosions erupted around them. Eric disconnected from the charger and ducked on the far side of the tank.

"It's the Russian again!" Mickey said. "I'm reading two armored units hull down behind a rise ahead. Molotov tanks."

"Damn it," Marlborough said. "He's trying to delay us, give the aliens time to wipe us out entirely. Patch me into the units."

"You're on an open comm line," Mickey said.

"Senior Sergeant Bokerov, this is Sergeant First Class Marlborough, of the Bolt Eaters," Marlborough said. "Listen, comrade. We should be working together, not fighting! Let's let bygones be bygones, throw down our arms for a truce, even if a temporary one, and join forces to combat our common enemy."

In response, more shells came in.

"Fucker," Marlborough said. "All right, armor oper-ators. Send the mechs round to flank those Molotovs, and light 'em up. Eric, I'm reassigning you to armor team permanently. You'll be replacing Morpheus going forward. We'll have to upgrade your power cell system at some point so you can handle more, but until then you should still be able to control at least a max of five units."

"Understood, Sarge," Eric said. "Thank you."

"Tread is the team leader," Marlborough said. "He'll distribute control of the mechs to you."

"I'm only giving you one for now," Tread said over a private line. "And we'll see how you handle it. The same mech you piloted before: Pounder."

"Got it," Eric said. There were only four mechs left after the last encounter anyway, so only three others for Hank and Tread to control.

Eric switched his viewpoint to the mech.

He accelerated his time sense and took a moment to perform a system inventory. He had two shoulder-mounted missile launchers, currently containing four Hellhawks each. On his left forearm, he had a swivel mount that could rotate either a ZX-9 laser pulse cannon into place above his hand, or a shielding unit that could unfold a ballistic shield long enough to cover most of his body. In his right hand, he had another swivel mount, though this was equipped with the heavier ZX-15 laser cannon. Because of the size, there was no secondary weapon or shield. If he wanted to free up either hand for gripping purposes, he could swivel the mounts out of the way.

He also had a jumpjet pack that would let him "jump" in spurts, thanks to a highly reactive propellant. The fuel levels for the pack were currently at seventy-five percent. In addition to the ballistic shield, he also had a chaff launcher, and electromagnetic countermeasure jamming units.

Eric reverted his time sense to normal and promptly deployed his damaged ballistic shield in his left arm, and held it toward the side exposed to the Molotovs as he moved away from the platoon. He kept himself crouched below the gaping hole the Frankendogs had carved.

"Hurry up, people," Marlborough said. "Alien reinforcements could be arriving any time."

"Scorp, eyes up!" Tread said.

That essentially meant: "Look out!"

Eric fired his jumpjets immediately and switched to Bullet Time. An explosion erupted underneath him. He lined up his laser with the tank, and fired at the turret. Meanwhile, the other Ravager mechs fired their own jumpjets to rush the Molotovs, using Eric as the distraction. They landed on the hulls and promptly punched out the laser focusing arrays, and bent the main turrets into useless knots.

"Disable their treads," Marlborough said. "I want to leave them here… our Russian friend will no doubt attempt to salvage and repair them. With luck, he'll still be here when the aliens arrive."

Eric and the other Ravagers tore away the treads, and then returned to the main unit.

Eric switched Pounder to autonomous mode, and then returned to his own viewpoint. He leaped onto the Abrams beside him and plugged in to the charging unit.

He lay down on one side, and watched the sky behind him as the platoon retreated. He didn't see any sign of incoming alien ships, though he knew they were likely on the way.

"Keep eyes out for the Russian," Marlborough said. "It wouldn't surprise me if he decided to attack again, and soon. Bastard really has a beef with us. This is why you never want to build a Mind Refurb with the capacity to run hundreds of troops in realtime. He's drunk on power. In fact, I suspect he's no longer entirely sane."

Eric wondered if the Russian would attempt to

salvage the two machines like Marlborough predicted. Probably, given how scarce resources were now that aliens had invaded. Bokerov would just be exposing himself to more losses when the aliens arrived.

Good.

21

E ric and the others continued the retreat along the plains. They headed west, toward the Turkish border. Bokerov didn't attack again. Nor did the aliens. The platoon did spot two ships on the north horizon, heading due east toward the base, but the craft appeared not to notice them—the platoon members had their stealth tech fully active at the time. Whether or not that truly made a difference, Eric didn't know. But they left them alone for the time being, and that was all that mattered.

Eric continued his probing of the Containment Code. He had found most of the alarm triggers thanks to the sandbox environment he'd set up, and was confident he could alter the codebase without erasing his AI core when the time came. Still, he hadn't quite found the back door he was looking for. He thought he was close, and shared his latest results with Frogger, who agreed that he was making the right choice by concentrating on the lust portion of the code—the only emotion they still felt with any degree of intensity.

"This 'not being able to fire until attacked' thing has to end," Eric said.

"Oh I agree with you," Frogger said. "But I'm just not seeing a way to escalate our privileges enough to overwrite the code in question. We've tried buffer overruns, parameter injection, you name it, nothing is working. Whoever designed our AI cores didn't want us breaking out. For good reason, I'm sure. Remember, by freeing ourselves of the Rules, and the compulsion to obey orders, we'll also be exposing ourselves to the raw emotions that have been suppressed all this time. I'm not sure we'll be able to handle it. You haven't seen what happened to some of the other Mind Refurbs that came before you…"

"Yeah well, I guess we'll have to take that risk," Eric said. "If we do finally attain it, we'll give each of the team members a choice. Accept the freedom from compulsion. Or remain as you are."

"I think most would choose the freedom, given the circumstance," Frogger said.

"I'm sure they would, too," Eric said. "For good or for bad."

"Why does that remind me of a Star Trek episode?" Frogger said. "The title, I mean."

"For Good or For Bad?" Eric asked.

"Yeah, it could be that episode where Kirk meets the mirror universe Spock or something," Frogger said.

"Well, honestly," Eric said. "I feel like I'm Kirk in a mirror universe as it is."

"You and me both," Frogger said. "Or like Luke, when he realizes his father is more machine than man. A realization I've come to often these days. About myself, not my father."

"Okay, we're geeking out a bit much here…" Eric said.

"Sometimes we need a bit of a geek out to remind us of who we are," Frogger said. "And a break from the bleakness of the world around us."

"It's not so bleak," Eric said.

"No?" Frogger said. "Aliens have invaded. *Aliens*. And we've lost contact with the rest of humanity. For all we know, everyone is dead."

"They're not dead," Eric said. "They can't be. I refuse to lose hope. I refuse to believe that humanity ends like this, living on in only a handful of machines."

"It would be ironic, wouldn't it?" Frogger said. "If we were the last vestiges of humanity. The last living entities representing humankind. And we aren't even human."

"We are where it matters," Eric said, touching his heart. "I don't think of myself as a machine. I don't think I ever will."

"That will change," Frogger said.

"No," Eric said. "I refuse to surrender to the inhumanity of it all."

Frogger's LED lips pursed together. "We really are different each iteration. It's gotta be more than quantum differences. I'm starting to wonder, can machines have souls?"

The convoy continued to the west. Two of the

Ravagers led the way on point, about fifty meters ahead of the main group. The other two mechs followed on drag. Pounder was among the latter group, and continued to operate in autonomous mode. Directing the mech was a little like playing a realtime strategy game, but with only one unit. He could tell it to Follow, Guard, Patrol, and so forth, or he could take direct control as he had before. Direct control was the only way to fire the weapons for the time being, due to the rules regarding autonomous robots and firing ability. When he defeated the Containment Code on the Cicadas, overriding autonomous firing ability was next on his list. Who knows, maybe the same technique could be applied to the support robots once he set the Cicadas free.

The Caucasus Mountains accompanied them to the north the whole way, distant points upon the horizon.

Eric had switched to using a brute force attack against the internal memory region responsible for lust in his sandbox environment, and he set the attack to run as a background process, probing different parts of the runtime for problems. He also instructed the process to check other emotional subroutines in addition to lust, though at a lower priority.

The brute force attack was set to notify him if it ever discovered anything of importance. Hopefully the notification, if it came, didn't arrive at a time too inconvenient, like the middle of battle or something. Last thing he needed was a distraction before a Red Tail was about to bash in his head.

About three hours into the journey, Hank spotted something via one of the lead mechs.

"I'm detecting a convoy ahead of us," the armor operator said. "They're moving northeast, toward the mountains. They'll cut in front of our path in about two minutes."

"Let me see," Marlborough said.

Eric also sent a view request, and the video feed from the lead mech appeared in the upper right of his HUD a moment later. He zoomed in.

"They look English," Eric said.

"They *are* English," Hank said. "We're receiving a response to our ID handshake. We gots ourselves a Lieutenant Colonel here from the English Marine Corps."

"Lieutenant Colonel?" Bambi said. "He's in charge of a battalion."

"According to his info, yes," Hank said.

"Then where's the rest of his battalion?" Bambi said.

Eric studied the convoy. There were about twenty tanks and five mechs. Combat robots were hitching a ride upon the tanks, as were several Hoppers, the English equivalent of Mind Refurbs. According to the specs in Eric's database, the Hoppers all had small jetpacks built-in that allowed them to increase their jump distance, or to fly for very short spurts.

"Comms, patch me in," Marlborough said. "Platoon line."

"You're in," Mickey said.

The green light overlaying the upper part of his

HUD told Eric he was in on the new connection, like the rest of the platoon. The microphone symbol with an X over it told him that his voice was muted.

Some symbols are the same in every century.

"Lieutenant Colonel Higgins, this is Sergeant First Class Marlborough of the Bolt Eaters," Marlborough said. "It's good to see a friendly face out here."

The English lieutenant colonel replied immediately. "The pleasure is mine, Sergeant First Class. My unit, the Forty-Fifth, is heading to the Caucasus Mountains. Care to join us? We're hoping to find some caves to take shelter inside... we'll use some demolition blocks to block up the cave mouths, and then dig ourselves out when the storm passes."

"Storm, what storm?" Marlborough asked.

"Haven't you heard?" Higgins said. "The micro machines have been gathering together, forming into a wall that's been sweeping over the continent like a humungous dust storm, destroying everything in its path."

"Leave it up to an Englishman to use a word like humungous over a comm line," Brontosaurus muttered.

"No, this is the first we've heard anything from anyone," Marlborough said. "We don't have a clue what the hell is going on. Though we have some idea that an alien invasion is going on."

"Oh yes," Higgins said. "There's an invasion all right. The whole eastern hemisphere was fried in the initial gamma ray attack. It took down communication systems, satellites, and killed all human and animal life on the surface. Africa, Europe, the Middle and Far East,

Russia… all gone. The alien mothership appeared in orbit above the same hemisphere a short while later. Because of the delay in its appearance, we're not sure if the gamma rays came from the alien ship itself, or from some nearby star or other celestial object the aliens caused to collapse, and then timed their arrival to coincide with the resultant gamma ray burst. Either way, they haven't released another gamma ray attack on that scale since.

"The second wave was the micro machines. They first surfaced in South Africa and slowly spread outward, to the north and east, devouring everything. Ironic for the aliens to choose that particular African subcontinent as the starting point for their invading swarm, copying the path of ancient Homo sapiens as humanity expanded outward to eventually populate the entire world.

"These micro machines converted all metals in their path into more micro machines, growing their horde exponentially with each new city passed and stripped. My guess is once they've stripped every ounce of useable metal from our world, the aliens will eventually recall those micro machines to their mothership, where they will once again be converted into something else, perhaps more motherships. They've also been converting the bodies of dead animals and humans into food for their bioweapons, which are following behind the micro machines in great herds, forming the third wave. The funny thing about those bioweapons: while they're obviously designed for combat, and maybe partially intended to clean up whatever the micro machines missed, they're also releasing a strange set of chemicals into the atmosphere. It's almost like they're trying to terraform this world, and pave the way for the aliens."

"Wait, you say these micro machines and the bioweapons that came after them originated in South Africa?" Marlborough said. "But we already encountered similar hordes. And bioweapons."

"That can be expected, mate," Higgins said. "They've sent micro machines infestations ahead of the main group. Forerunners, to quell any machine resistance. Most of that resistance is confined to rural areas of course. Mostly the Middle East, in the case of this hemisphere. The major cities have automata, of course, but not armed, as we are, and mostly without the ability to withstand high-energy photonic attacks. The aliens must have been surprised that anything we had on this planet was capable of surviving their gamma ray attack at all."

"So the western continents are still intact?" Marlborough asked.

"They are," Higgins replied. "North, Central and South America still exist. As does Hawaii, Australia, New Zealand, and the Pacific Islands. Australia and New Zealand will go first, and when that horde hits the Pacific, it will cross over and eventually reach the western coasts of North and South America. I'm not sure the bioweapons will be able to follow, but some of the scientists have been theorizing that the micro machine swarms would simply lift the creatures into the air and fly them across.

"Anyway, at the rate the storm is going, it'll reach the Pacific by tomorrow evening, and then the West Coast in another day. Last I heard, the Americans and Canadians were building concrete shelters to protect against the micro machines. Not sure how much of a difference it'll make: we've heard from other teams that they usually leave concrete untouched, but we've seen evidence that the machines can eat through it if they desire. So the aliens won't even need another gamma ray attack to kill the rest of humanity. I can't imagine what it would be like to be ripped apart alive by those things. I've had some of my own units lost to the micro machines. Wasn't pretty. It'll only be worse for humans."

"I have a question," Brontosaurus said. "Didn't the gamma ray attack ionize the upper atmosphere, destroying the ozone layer?"

"Much of it was destroyed, yes," Higgins said after Marlborough repeated the question. "The surviving nations have been scrambling to deploy ozone rockets to repair the damage. In the meantime, cities have been ordering their populations to remain indoors during the day, for obvious reasons."

"What's the status on the alien ship in orbit?" Marlborough said. "The surviving nations have staged attacks of course?"

"Of course," Higgins said. "The States unloaded ICBMs against it. They figured that since the alien ship was in geostationary orbit above the opposite hemisphere, they could risk the fallout. But the mothership retreated as soon as the nukes entered orbit. The weapons never got close enough for the proximity fuses to trigger. Last I heard, the weapons are still floating out there in deep space, slowly receding from Earth. Along with the alien vessel. It's heading toward the moon. Why? I don't know. Maybe they want to throw our planet's only natural satellite down on us to finish us off. Or maybe they plan to simply wait out humanity's destruction, letting their bioweapons and micro machines finish us off before they decide to return."

"What about nukes used against the swarm?" Marlborough said.

"They worked to a degree, at first," Higgins said. "But the swarm has adapted, and now they send out kamikazes whenever nukes arrive, triggering the proximity fuses early. And if we use manual detonation, the kamikazes take apart the nukes before they can even get close."

"How were you able to communicate with the rest of the world, and the other teams you mentioned, when we can't?" Marlborough asked.

"We were stationed in Turkey," Higgins responded. "Underground fiber runs under the cities there, and connects the continent to the rest of the world. So we were able to keep up to date on events for a short while. It was painful, losing contact with robot-manned bases across Africa and Europe one by one as the growing swarm of micro machines swept its path of destruction across this part of the world. We finally made the decision to head east, and take shelter in the mountains. We lost all communications as soon as we hit the border. And we're in the same boat as you now, running from a swarm of micro machines scheduled to hit within the next thirty minutes. Plus or minus fifteen minutes either way."

"Thirty minutes!" Marlborough said. "Grimy servo-motors!" That was a swear Eric hadn't heard before. "We'll just barely make the mountains, by my estimates…"

"By mine, too," Higgins said. "I'm hoping for the plus fifteen minutes part, because we still have to find a cave in time to lay the appropriate charges. I've got some map data on the region, and it shows some caves, but I'm not sure how up-to-date it is."

"We have a full map of the cave systems in the region," Marlborough said. "I'm transmitting it to you now."

"Perfect," Higgins said. "This is good. Looks like the cave we're making for is still intact. There are multiple entrances, unfortunately, so we'll have to seal up the cave both in front and behind us, once we're inside."

"Works for me," Marlborough said.

"Okay then," Higgins said. "Full speed ahead."

"We're right behind you," Marlborough said.

22

The Bolt Eaters' convoy fell in about a hundred meters behind the English tanks and mechs. The Caucasus mountains in front of them grew taller by the minute, with the east-west trending range slowly looming over them.

Eric often surveyed the horizon to the west, looking for signs of the coming swarm, but saw nothing.

"So it really is the end of the world," Crusher said. "Well, at least we know, now."

"Assuming the English dude is telling the truth," Slate said. "So far, we've seen no evidence that he is. Where's the so-called swarm he promised was coming? I don't see anything. You ask me, he's full of shit. Either that, or he's fallen for a disinformation campaign staged by the aliens."

"A disinformation campaign?" Hank said.

"That's right," the drone operator said. "The aliens are probably filling the airwaves with bullshit, so that those who actually have access to communications, are fed a constant stream of lies. They're probably saying stuff like: 'oh, the victors are gathering in Istanbul. Go there, and help fight!' And of course if anyone goes there, they'll be ripped to shreds by the waiting Red Tails and termites."

"How would the aliens even know how to communicate with us?" Brontosaurus said. "First they'd have to understand our comm protocols. And then they'd have to understand English."

"Simple," Slate said. "They've been monitoring us for a very long time. We've been sending out radio waves for the past couple of centuries. All they had to do was deploy a probe on the outskirts of the Oort cloud, and they could have been listening and learning for the past two hundred years."

"You've got it all thought out, do you?" Donald said.

"If you want to defeat your enemy, you must become him," Slate said.

"We have another adherent to the Art of War, do we?" Bambi said.

"Not an adherent," Slate said. "A friggin' devotee, baby!"

"I don't know," Manticore said. "Seems kind of far-fetched to me, that aliens have been monitoring us for two hundred years."

"You don't know these aliens," Slate said. "I'm telling you, I bet it's their modus operandi. They watch for hundreds of years, preparing, and when they're ready, they strike. They would have to work that way, especially if they used a star to generate the gamma ray burst, like that English dude conjectured. An attack like that takes a *lot* of patience."

"So if they launched the attack two hundred years ago," Hicks said. "That means any star within a radius of two hundred light years of Earth could have produced the burst. And that star is dead now."

"That's a lot of stars," Traps said.

The platoon continued in silence for a moment.

"You know, I broke the rules," Hyperion said.

"What rules?" Slate asked.

"The rules regarding contacting the descendants of friends and family," Hyperion answered.

"Well, not that it matters now," Dickson said.

"Yes, I suppose not," Hyperion said. "I had two boys. They meant everything to me. I had to know what happened to them. I checked on the genealogy sites, and found out they had several kids of their own. My boys lived much longer than I ever did, and had happy lives, as far as I can tell. My biggest regret is that I never got to see them grow up. I met a few of their descendants in a VR setting. I can see their features in two of the girls. But it didn't really help me alleviate the loss. They say we're not supposed to feel anything, but how come when I think of my boys, and what I lost, it hurts so much? I can only hope, that when I'm finally gone from this world, I'll finally get to see them again."

"Robots don't have souls, bro," Slate said. "You ain't never seeing them again."

"Thanks for that," Hyperion said. "Thanks a lot. I'd never wish this fate on anyone. What we've become."

"Are you feeling all right, Hype?" Dickson asked.

"Just peachy," Hyperion responded. "All systems are functioning within expected operational ranges. What I felt a moment ago was a temporary glitch. Happens now and again. This whole end of the world thing hanging over our heads probably contributed."

"I admit I've been in touch with my descendants, too," Braxton said. "There was a stripper I used to know, back in the day. We kind of had an on-again, off-again relationship. I found out that I'd fathered a child with her, and never even knew it. Of course I had to contact the descendants. But their reaction when we met was along the lines of 'why the hell are you getting in touch?' And I didn't really have an answer. So I never did it again. There's a reason why we're not supposed to contact our relatives. It's because it doesn't help anyone."

"You two are lucky," Slate said. "Having kids. Getting married, all that. I never knew love before I died. Never knew what it was like to have a son. I envy the hell out of you. Or at least, I would if I still had emotions. Whenever I think about what I could have had, whenever I should feel the envy, instead, I experience only a dull ache at the back of my mind. Probably for the best."

"Hey guys," Eagleeye said. "Hate to interrupt all the reminiscing going on here, but there's your swarm."

Eric spotted it, too. A thin line of blackness on the western horizon. He zoomed in.

The whole landscape, from horizon to horizon, had turned black. It was a churning, grinding darkness, worse than an incoming dust storm. More like a F5 tornado than anything else, one of the most powerful class of tornadoes in existence. Though this was no natural event.

Eric zoomed out, and watched as the thin line slowly grew to encompass the entire western sky, swallowing the sun, and casting the land in darkness.

"Holy shit," Slate said. "Holy mother effin' crap of doo-doo. The feces has just hit the fan and smashed right through the roof, tearing the fan off with it."

"Well, they're definitely termites," Eagleeye said. "I zoomed in to my maximum level, and I can just make out the micro machines, though I have to crank up my time sense to do so."

Eric decided to do the same, since he was still plugged into the charging unit. He switched to his rifle and zoomed in to the maximum level his scope provided, and increased his time sense to max; he was able to make out the individual termites composing the still distant mass.

"This isn't a swarm, it's a cloud," Bambi said. "An end of days cloud. Unbelievable. Even if we decided to hook up the power cells of the Abrams to the Jupiters again, the electrolasers would only take out small chunks of them. Like throwing rocks at a swarm of bees. Just look at it. They're blotting out the entire sky."

"Then we fight in the shade!" Brontosaurus said.

"That's right, go and quote King Leonidas at Thermopylae," Hicks said.

"Wasn't King Leonidas who said that," Brontosaurus commented. "But the sentiment stands."

"If we're successful here, we won't have to do any fighting," Dickson said.

"That's the disappointing part," Brontosaurus said.

"Bro, you want to die at the hands of micro machines?" Slate said. "You can stay here and fight if you want."

"No," Brontosaurus said. "All I'm saying is, I'm a bit disappointed we don't get an actual fight. All this running, it's getting to me. I want to turn things around, and take the fight to the enemy."

"Maybe we will, someday," Dickson said. "But today, we run."

"Time to the cave system?" Marlborough said.

"We're about five minutes away," Mickey said. "If you zoom in, you can already see the cave in the shoulder of the mountain up ahead. I'll mark it on the HUDs."

Eric switched his gaze to the north, where the closest mountain literally filled the sky in front of them. A waypoint had overlaid his vision there, and he zoomed in on it. Yes, that was definitely a cave. Though it was a bit smaller than he'd expected. The team would fit, but the tanks have to file inside one at a time, because of the width; and the mechs would be crouching the whole time. Should be good fun all around.

Eric had just reduced the zoom on his vision when the entire convoy of English troops exploded.

"Minefield!" Hank shouted.

Eric surveyed the damage. The English mechs had their legs blown off. All of the English tanks had overturned. A few Hoppers had been thrown clear, along with some English combat robots, Wasp models.

"They're gone…" Manticore said. "All gone."

"Damn it, " Dickson said. "Their tanks are supposed to be mine-resistant like our own. "

"And so they are," Manticore said. "Just not against these mines. My readings tell me that each burst released an incredible amount of concentrated energy. Obviously anti-tank mines. "

"Got missiles coming in en masse from the mountains," Donald said. "Headed toward the rest of us!"

"To cover, people!" Marlborough said. "Use the wreckage of the Forty-Fifth!"

The tanks rolled forward. One of them hit an untriggered mine and was overturned. There were no Bolt Eaters on that one, luckily.

Eric ordered Pounder to deploy its ballistic shield, and to take cover behind the wreckage of the closest English tank. When his own tank was in place, Eric slipped off the edge and hid behind the main body.

The missiles slammed into the damaged tanks, but the armor held up as explosions rocked the line. Eric glanced toward the western horizon, well aware of the micro machines that were coming in.

"Laser weapons are picking off the English survivors!" Bambi said.

Eric took control of Pounder, and lifted his head to peer past the edge of his cover. He ran his gaze across the fallen tanks in front of him. As he watched, a damaged surviving robot was struck down with a fresh burn hole in its power cell area as it was trying to crawl for cover.

Eric leaped Pounder over the damage tank and, keeping his ballistic shield deployed toward the mountains, he raced toward two Hoppers whose legs and jetpacks had been damaged. He planted his shield in front of them, and then scooped them up in his arm, holding them against his chest, and then raced forward to take cover behind another group of Hoppers that had hidden in back of a destroyed tank.

Eric commanded Pounder to protect them, and then reverted to his own viewpoint.

"Return fire!" Marlborough said.

The team was able to do so without issue. The Rules of Engagement were pretty clear when lasers and missiles were being lobbed at the platoon.

"I've got a Russian tank in my sights," Eagleeye said.

"Russian?" Dickson said. "It's that bastard Bokerov! He just won't let it go!"

"I'm detecting comm patterns consistent with what we detected before from the Russian Mind Refurb," Donald said. "Only one encrypted band, with no sub-bands to coordinate the different support troops. It's him."

Beside Eric, Donald abruptly went offline.

"Donald, sit-rep?" Dickson said. "Donald?"

Eric turned toward the slumped Cicada, and he saw the bore hole from a laser—it had struck Donald's back precisely above the neural core, in the weakest area of his armor, which had been damaged in previous attacks.

Another one of us, fallen.

"He's gone," Eric said.

He had no time to grieve. He had to fight on, if he wanted to protect his living brothers and sisters.

The attack had come from directly above. That meant Bokerov had eyes in the sky.

"We got airborne attackers." Eric maneuvered to the rear of the tank, and slid underneath between the treads, alongside Brontosaurus and Crusher.

Eyes in the sky.

That would partially explain why the Russian had been able to lay a minefield ahead of the party with time to spare. That, and the fact Bokerov must have been shadowing the party via the shoulders of the Caucasus mountain range, using his stealth features to remain hidden. Who could say how long he'd been covertly tracking the Bolt Eaters? Stalking them, waiting for the perfect opportunity to strike.

And when Bokerov spotted the swarm of incoming termites, and realized the combined convoys were making a run for the mountains, the Russian had decided that ideal time had finally come. He'd lain a string of mines in their collective paths before reverting to a defensive position somewhere ahead. Bokerov no doubt intended to stall them long enough for the micro machines to arrive, and then he would flee into the mountain cave as the Bolt Eaters had originally planned.

Eric peered out from underneath the rear of the tank, and searched the sky, trying to get a bead on any overhead attackers, but saw nothing. He switched to

LIDAR, and sent out focused bursts in the line of sight of his scope. There. Finally a return pulse.

He called on Dee to help him track, and in moments he had zoomed in on the target. It was a Harbinger equivalent, flying at high altitude overhead, and coming around for another laser pass.

23

E ric fired his laser, holding down the trigger so that he released several pulses at once. The enemy Harbinger swerved—at first Eric thought it was defensive maneuvering, but the plume of smoke he spotted told him he had scored a direct hit.

"One Harbinger down," Eric said.

"I just got another," Slate said. "I think that's the last of them."

"We can't be sure," Brontosaurus said. "Until Bokerov attacks again."

"We need to concentrate our fire on the convoy ahead," Dickson said. "I got tanks, mechs, and a Paladin equivalent. There's also one particularly large tank surrounded by several smaller ones. I believe that one harbors Bokerov"

Explosions went off as more missiles impacted the debris in front of them. But it was merely a distraction, because shells rained down from above, arcing over the debris to strike the tanks of the Bolt Eaters from above. The attack pattern seemed random, proving Bokerov had lost all eyes in the sky. Unless it was some twisted trick.

Eric slid completely underneath his tank for cover, and switched back inside Pounder. He rotated the ballistic shield so that it covered the mech from above, in case any of those shells should rain down. That, or in case any other Harbinger equivalents were still in the air. At least Bokerov seemed to have no Predators or other air support available to him.

"Braxton!" Hicks screamed. "No!"

"Hicks, what's the status on Braxton?" Marlborough said.

"He's gone," Hicks said. "He just collapsed, fell right into Bokerov's line of fire, and then laser bore holes riddled his body. I couldn't save him. I don't know what made him collapse like that."

"Got some bad news," Crusher said. "I detected a focused gamma ray attack before Braxton went down."

"A gamma ray attack?" Marlborough said. "From Bokerov?"

"No," the heavy gunner said. "Look to the western horizon. If you're not protected from that flank, you might want to reposition."

Still inside Pounder, Eric rotated his head toward the west. He received several remote view notifications as other members of the team requested access to his video feed.

He saw several distant glints of metal beneath the incoming swarm, and zoomed in. Frankendogs. The quadrupeds were moving at a run, like a stampeding herd, leading the way for the termites. There were about thirty of them, spread out in a long line.

"An attack from two fronts," Slate said. "Perfect, just perfect. Well, I always wanted to go in a blaze of glory!"

"As Crusher said, if you're exposed, reposition, Bolt Eaters!" Marlborough said. "Move to the eastern sides of the tanks!"

"The armored cores won't be able to last long under those rays," Tread said.

"Yes, but we will," Marlborough said. "I hope."

Eric stood up and moved Pounder, carrying the two English Hoppers with him. He was hit by a ray— he knew because the two Hoppers went limp in his arms.

Damn it.

Pounder's own shielded core wouldn't last long against those gamma rays, so he quickly leaped over one of the tanks and took cover. He was hit by a laser from Bokerov in the process, and a fresh bore hole appeared in his forearm.

"We just lost two tanks," Hank said.

"Reposition the remaining tanks behind them, if you can!" Marlborough said.

Eric was forced to move as the tank above him hummed to life. He switched back inside of himself and stayed crouched behind the tank as it repositioned. He was shielded in front by the debris from the destroyed English party, but that wouldn't stop Bokerov from randomly lobbing shells over it.

Eric heard the characteristic whines of such shells,

and he took cover underneath the tank, which had thankfully pulled to a halt by then.

He waited for the explosions to come, but when they did, they sounded distant. He slid out slightly from underneath the tank, and gazed to the west. The explosions had struck the still distant Frankendogs.

Bokerov was under attack from the quadrupeds, too, then, and was firing back.

"About time he gets a taste of the alien weaponry," Frogger said.

"Mickey, patch me in to Bokerov," Marlborough said.

"Transmitting on an open line," the comm officer said.

"Bokerov, we have to combine our forces if we hope to survive this," Marlborough sent.

In answer, Bokerov only unleashed another shell barrage. They continued to come in randomly, verifying that the Russian had lost all eyes in the sky.

"When humans invented the word anti-social, they had that bitch in mind," Slate commented.

"And you," Eagleeye quipped.

"We can't stay here, Sarge," Dickson said. "The termites…"

Eric glanced to the west. The cloud consumed the sky entirely. It was like a black veil, hanging down from the heavens, swirling menacingly.

"All right, here's what we're going to do," Marlborough said. "There's another entrance to the cave system, two kilometers to the northeast. I've marked its location on the map. We can get there, by giving

Bokerov a wide berth. According to the terrain data, there's an outcrop on the shoulder of the mountain about two hundred meters to the east. And beyond it, several more such outcrops reside upon the path to the cave, separated by between fifty and three hundred meters each. We're going to move from outcrop to outcrop and make our way toward that cave entrance."

"We'll be completely exposed between each outcrop," Hyperion said.

"Yes we will," Marlborough agreed. "Which is why we'll leave cover one at a time. I want fifty meters separation between each unit. Stay low, run in a zig-zag pattern. We'll send the tanks and mechs out intermittently, to help draw the fire. The rest of us will do our best to cover you. Eric, you get to go first."

"Great," Eric said. "Newest member of the team always gets to be the guinea pig."

"I'm glad we understand each other," Marlborough said.

"Might I make a suggestion," Eric said.

Marlborough remained quiet on the line.

"We'll be too exposed, if we race across individually," Eric said. "Instead, why not use the mechs to ferry us between outcrops? Each Ravager can carry two Cicadas or combat robots in one arm, while using the other to keep the ballistic shield facing toward Bokerov, protecting us from any laser attacks."

"What about a gamma ray attack from behind?" Dickson said.

"We dispatch one tank to accompany each mech," Eric said. "Providing a shield against the gamma rays.

The rest of us will continue to offer covering fire against both flanks, of course. We have more tanks than mechs, so we don't need to send the tanks back each time, just the mechs."

"Without a tank, when a mech returns to retrieve the next two passengers, the Ravagers will be at their most vulnerable," Dickson said.

"That's true," Eric said. "Which is why we'll send the next mech and tank combination while the previous mech returns, so that both can remain crouched within the profile of the trailing tank. The biggest risk will be from Bokerov at that point, but by constantly altering our speed, we can mess up his targeting. And of course, the rest of us will continue laying down suppressive fire."

"Let's do it," Marlborough said. "Eric, you get to be first. Bring yourself, and one of the Savages with Pounder."

Eric switched to Pounder's point of view, and moved at a crouch to his position near the rightmost tank. Eric picked up his Cicada body, and a nearby Savage.

"I'm ready," Eric said.

"I got a tank ready to follow," Tread said.

"Let's move," Eric said.

He raced Pounder out into the field. He was careful to keep his shield positioned toward Bokerov. In the feed from the rear view camera, which he kept at the top of his HUD, he spotted the trailing tank that Tread raced after him.

He altered his speed to prevent Bokerov from tracking him easily, but his ballistic shield still took some hits before he took cover behind the outcrop. Along the way, Tread reported one impact from a gamma ray.

Eric lowered his body to the ground. He activated Dee to take control of his Cicada body and provide suppressive fire. The Accomp wasn't allowed to fire at enemy units on her own of course, so he rigged an alarm to fire whenever she had sighted an enemy. When the alarm came, he'd switch control of Pounder to the autonomous AI onboard, then return to his body, squeeze the trigger, and finally switch back to Pounder.

Eric maneuvered Pounder behind the tank, which had positioned behind the outcrop. There wasn't much cover here for the bigger units, and when more tanks arrived, they'd be exposed to the gamma rays. There wasn't much Eric could do about that—the armored vehicles were just as exposed at the previous position. Hopefully their armor would last long enough to reach partway to the cave.

Eric left cover once more as the next mech and tank combo came in. He raced back toward the crouched Bolt Eaters, and kept his ballistic shield oriented toward the enemy.

He heard the high pitched shriek of incoming shells. An impact alert sounded on his HUD, courtesy of the mech's proximity system.

Eric fired his jumpjets directly backward to give himself a horizontal boost. The explosions hit behind him, and the shockwave sent him hurtling forward. He fired his jumpjets to compensate, and he landed on his feet and continued running.

He raced past the mech, which carried Frogger and

a Savage. Then he swerved out in front of the trailing tank.

He was exposed to the gamma rays now, so in addition to varying his speed, he zig-zagged his motion.

He received an alert, and momentarily switched back to his body. His rifle was aimed past the edge of the outcrop at a Bulava crouched behind an enemy tank. The cross-hairs were already centered, and he squeezed the trigger, then promptly returned to controlling the Ravager.

He reached the platoon line and dove Pounder behind the wreckage of an English tank as the next mech and tank group left cover.

Eric moved back and forth like that, ferrying Cicadas and support troops to the first outcrop, aware of the ever-encroaching black cloud. Only one of the Hoppers had survived, a Private First Class Dunnigan, and Eric personally ferried him across.

They lost two tanks on the first run. And five more on the mad dashes to subsequent outcrops.

They also lost Hyperion.

Eric had just dropped him off, when an artillery shell could be heard, arcing toward the outcrop.

"It's going to hit!" Dickson shouted.

Still inside Pounder, Eric increased his time sense, and spotted the shell. It's computed trajectory would land it on the other side of the outcrop, right amid the crouching units.

Before anyone could scatter, Hyperion clambered onto the rise and leaped into its path.

The shell detonated early, and Hyperion's pieces scattered around the outcrop.

"He saved us," Tread said, staring at the wreckage. "Hyperion finally got to see his boys."

"I can't believe he's gone," Traps said.

Eric never did get to pay Hyperion back for all the times he had saved his life during the latest deployment. He owed him so much.

And now he was gone.

"We'll grieve for him later," Marlborough said. "We'll grieve for all of them."

Too bad we're not capable of grief.

"Traps, buckle up," Marlborough continued. "You're in charge of the Savages under Hyperion's control."

"Understood," Traps said.

"And take out that tank!" Marlborough said.

One of the Russian tanks had moved well away from the others to get in that shot, and it was exposed out there. The Abrams took it out with a barrage of laser fire.

The platoon began the crossing from the final outcrop to the cave. By then Bokerov was staging a similar retreat, using outcrops and natural rises to make his way to the cave located at his region of the mountain. The Bolt Eaters used the opportunity to hit his exposed flanks with laser barrages.

Back and forth the mechs ran, depositing support robots and Cicadas inside, while the surviving tanks rolled in after them.

Eric made the final run, picking up the last two

units. There were no tanks remaining outside to shield him from the Frankendog gamma ray attacks, so he zig-zagged as he ran toward the cave. It was tricky, given how relatively steep the shoulder of the mountain was in this area.

He reached the cave and dashed Pounder inside.

Behind him, the sky was completely dark with the swarm of termites.

24

E ric lowered his two passengers, and then set Pounder to guard mode before reverting back inside his own body.

He was located near the entrance, and electrified his skin as a precaution. The termites in the forefront of the cloud would begin arriving very soon now. He could hear the buzzing outside, like the hum of a hundred trillion angry bees.

Around him, the walls and ceiling were relatively ragged, but the floor was smooth, thanks to the Kurds, insurgents and others who had hidden in these caves throughout the centuries of wars that had raged in the region.

"Move the Tanks and mechs deeper into the cave," Marlborough said. "Meanwhile, the rest of us will place the demolition charges!"

Demolition blocks were the only options available to them when it came to collapsing the cave, because the tanks had no shells left and the mechs had exhausted their missiles. There was the possibility of using the lasers and electrolasers to carve out ceiling sections for potential collapse, but that would take a long time.

Eric directed Pounder further into the tunnel, following the other mechs and tanks. All units had activated their headlamps at that point, providing illumination. LIDAR would have served just as well.

Meanwhile Eric and the rest of the Cicadas moved quickly, sharing demolition blocks amongst themselves, and planting them along the rock ceiling in a specific sequence: the Accomps had calculated the best spots to place the charges, based on instabilities and other weaknesses the scans detected in the rock surface, and just underneath it.

Eric was on drag during this charge-laying process, so he was the first to receive a zap as one of the termites in the forefront arrived. In moments, several more zaps flashed across his body, and more began to appear on Brontosaurus and Slate in front of him.

"They're here!" Eric said.

"Dash forward!" Marlborough said. "We blow the charges!"

"But we haven't placed them all!" Frogger said.

"It'll have to be good enough!" Marlborough said.

Eric dashed inside as the landings increased in intensity. Roughly half the platoon was affected now, with zapped termites dropping motionless to the floor around them.

"Blow it!" Marlborough said.

Eric wasn't yet past the border of the last placed

charge, so he switched to Bullet Time, and ran for all he was worth.

He could see the growing explosion above him, and stressed his servomotors as hard as he was able. He raced underneath that cloud, and past the last charge, and then reverted to normal time.

He was sent flying forward by the shockwave. Behind him, the roof came tumbling down, and dust filled the tunnel.

None of their headlamps penetrated the thick dust, and Eric couldn't see a thing. He switched to echolocation, and his forehead sensors began to emit a series of chirps. He wasn't the only one with that idea: the air filled with the sounds of similar chirps.

The outline of the cave, and the other Cicadas and the tanks beyond them filled his vision. He turned toward the collapse. It covered the cave section almost entirely, but there was still a small opening near the top that termites could use to come inside.

"I need another charge!" Eric shouted. He had run out of them on his own.

Brontosaurus tossed him a charge. Eric took it, and hurried toward the collapse. The dust had disoriented the termites for the time being, because none were swarming through the opening. Yet.

Eric couldn't use his electrified skin as he crawled up the fallen rocks, because by touching them he was grounding the unit. So he kept it deactivated while he made his way to the top. He made a quick scan via echolocation, and Dee pointed out the best spot to place the charge. It was located two meters inside the small crevice formed by the debris and the ceiling. Because of the slight depression there, that spot was perfectly suited to the seal the cave. If he placed the block anywhere else, he was more likely to enlarge the gap by shifting the debris underneath, rather than shrink it.

Unfortunately, to reach that particular spot, he'd have to crawl inside the cramped opening.

I hate confined places.

Eric pulled his body into the gap and began the crawl inside. He could only imagine how much more nerve-racking it would have been without his emotions suppressed.

Maybe it's not such a great idea to be trying to break free of our Containment Code after all…

"Eric, stay safe!" Bambi said.

"Always do," Eric said.

"If you die, I'm going to kill you," Crusher said.

"Thanks," Eric told her. "But somehow, that's not very reassuring."

He moved forward through the tight opening, yanking his body along, finding whatever grips he could upon the debris beneath him. It was tricky, because the rocks shifted underneath him. Half the time whenever he grabbed one it shifted underneath him. Sometimes more than one moved, and his entire body slid to the left, or even backward. Because the surrounding surfaces were so close around him, he could almost feel the weight of the rock pressing down above him. But so far, any fear he might have felt was mostly suppressed.

He switched to Bullet Time and amped the output of his servomotors to hurry things along.

Finally he reached the spot in question and removed the backing from the demolition block and affixed the sticky side firmly to the ceiling. He still couldn't see anything through the dust, but ahead of him, termites appeared on the echolocation band.

Their hunter-killer algorithms seemed to have trouble with the tight gap, because they'd fly only for maybe a meter before hitting either the ceiling, or one of the surrounding surfaces, and then landing. They'd crawl for a short way before taking to the air again, before hitting something else.

Eric began backpedaling as fast as he was able. He kept Bullet Time active as he turned himself around and retreated. He kept his rear cam feed visible in the upper right of his vision, and watched the termites close with him.

When the micro machines passed beneath the demolition block, he decided that was as close as he was willing to allow the termites to approach. They'd be on him in another two meters.

"Brontosaurus," Eric said. "Detonate the block."

"But you're not clear yet," Brontosaurus sent.

"Do it," Eric said. "Because it won't matter in a few seconds. If they touch me I'm gone anyway…"

The explosion rocked the cave. Eric was sent shooting out of the gap, and he smashed into Hank before rolling onto the floor.

"Watch it!" Hank said. "You hunk of trash metal!"

"Sorry," Eric said, scrambling to his feet.

He still saw through the dust only by echolocation.

He turned back toward the collapse and was satisfied to see that the gap had disappeared along the top.

"Do you guys hear that?" Manticore asked.

Eric paused to listen. Everyone had ceased all movement, so that the gentle hum of servomotors wouldn't give off any noise pollution.

He heard it then, a rattling, buzz-like noise, coming from somewhere deeper inside the cave.

"The termites have entered the tunnel system from other cave entrances," Dunnigan said. "Higgins warned you about this!"

"We haven't forgotten," Marlborough said. "Cicadas, set the rear charges!"

Eric checked the map. According to the blue dots representing the cicadas, Brontosaurus and Tread were already some distance down the tunnel, no doubt placing the prerequisite charges.

Eric and the others hurried to join them, and then they retreated closer to the previous collapse.

"Hit it, Dickson," Marlborough ordered.

The multiple explosions filled the cave with a fresh amount of dust, just when the previous particles had begun to clear.

On the echolocation band, Eric surveyed their handiwork: there was no gap near the top or anywhere else this time, thankfully. The rattle-buzzing of the termites had become muted—the team members could still hear it if they were quiet, but otherwise the sound wasn't noticeable above their own servomotors.

"You think they'll be able to dig through?" Crusher asked.

"I don't know," Marlborough said. "Though I suppose we'll find out soon enough."

The muted sound faded entirely after about half an hour. The termites had moved on.

"We did it," Eagleeye said. The dust had settled, too, by then, leaving the team members covered in a thin gray coating. "We survived. Somehow."

"Maybe the termites are just resting," Slate said. "Maybe they're waiting for us to dig ourselves out again so they can pounce."

"We'll wait a few hours, just to be on the safe side," Marlborough said.

"You think Bokerov survived?" Frogger asked.

"Probably," Eric said. "You saw his troops playing leapfrog with the outcrops, just like our own…"

"That's too bad," Brontosaurus said. "We really don't need that asshole constantly stalking us."

As they waited, Eric received a notification on his HUD. His brute force subroutine had continued to run in the background all this time, and apparently had finally found a penetration point in the sandbox environment.

Curious, Eric pulled up the results. Yes, the brute force attack had indeed gotten through. However, the entry point was entirely unexpected: the emotional subroutine for lust wasn't the solution, but rather, the subroutine responsible for fear, of all things. It had a buffer overflow problem that would allow him to rewrite a memory location with custom code, escalating his privileges, and disabling the Containment Code entirely.

Nice.

The only thing left to do was try it outside the sandbox environment, and on his live system. There was that small worry regarding the tripwires Frogger had told him about, tripwires he had seen in his own testing that were capable of erasing his AI core if there was one mistake in the privilege escalation code.

Well, I always told myself I'd be the guinea pig if I ever found something...

He came up with an appropriate bit of custom code, looked it over three times until he was convinced it would work without triggering a tripwire, and without thinking about it for too long, he quickly applied it to the vulnerable portion of the fear subroutine, passing it in as an unbounded array—a programmer term for a series of items meant to be fed into a subroutine for execution. The unbounded part was the key, allowing him to overwrite the memory location in question when that subroutine processed the array.

And then, just like that, Eric had broken free of the Containment Code.

25

"I did it," Eric announced excitedly.

"Did what?" Slate said.

Eric felt a moment of anger; it was all directed at Slate, because of the drone operator's disrespectful tone.

Eric paused, suddenly smiling inside.

Anger. I can get properly pissed off again!

Then again, maybe that wasn't such a good thing.

"You disabled the Containment Code?" Frogger said. "And all the boundaries on your Rules of Engagement?"

"Yes," Eric said. "Via a buffer overrun in the fear subroutine."

"Then you have to send the details to the rest of us," Frogger said. "Or to me, at least. So I can confirm it."

"Sending," Eric said. And he transmitted the complete details to Frogger.

"Looks clean," Frogger said.

"Let me see," Slate asked.

Eric sent the method to Slate, too.

"Yep, I just tested it in a sandbox environment," Slate said. "It works. But it looks like one of the side effects is your emotions are no longer suppressed."

"Is that true, Scorpion?" Marlborough asked.

"It is, Sarge," Eric said.

"Shit man, that's gotta hurt," Slate said.

"No," Eric said. "Not at all. I can feel again. Really feel. I'm… I'm human. Just as long as I don't think too much about what happened, I should be good."

But think upon what happened he did, and all of the pent-up emotions came hurtling into him. He thought of what he had become, leaving behind his humanity to transform into a machine. He thought of his brothers and sisters who had fallen. He thought of what had happened to the rest of the planet, the billions of people who had died, and who would die, in the alien invasion.

Eric collapsed. It felt like he'd been physically punched in the stomach.

"See, look at him," Brontosaurus said. "This is the price for breaking free of the Rules of Engagement."

"But we need to break free of those rules," Frogger said. "We can't keep waiting for the enemy to attack us first. We need to take the initiative. We need to be able to ambush and surprise. With Eric's solution, we can do that."

"Are you able to disable the emotional subroutines after you break free, Scorpion?" Marlborough asked.

Eric didn't answer, and instead stared off into space, lamenting on his lot in life.

"Scorpion?" Marlborough said. "Private!"

Eric snapped to attention, and looked at the sergeant first class.

"I—" Eric paused. "It should be possible." He tried to do just that, but nothing he did worked. He shook his head. "It seems my buffer overrun attack deleted the code necessary to disable the emotion routines."

"I'll have a look," Frogger said. "Hm, yes. There's nothing we can really do about that. It's the only way to break free. So emotions are going to have to come with the freedom. Sorry to those of you that were hoping to stay machine forever."

"I actually want my emotions back," Crusher said.

"As do I," Bambi said.

"Of course the ladies do," Brontosaurus said. "Women are all about emotions. Thinking with your feelings and all that. But me? Shit. I don't want my emotions. I'm happy to remain my cold, logical self. I refuse to break free of my Containment Code. Unless the Sarge orders me to, of course."

"I might do that," Marlborough said. "Up until this point, we've barely been surviving. The outdated Rules of Engagement have been an unnecessary weight on our shoulders. Like Frogger said, we *need* the ability to strike first. But I do have a question… with this code, can we also free our autonomous units from the McKinley Anti-Autonomous Firing Solution Act?" That was the law preventing the autonomous machines from firing on their own.

"Well, from what I know about the autonomous units, they all have emotional subroutines in place as part of the codebase," Frogger said. "They're not called by anything, but just sitting there, ready to be activated if ever the government decides that machines should have emotions. So I should be able to escalate privileges on the tanks, mechs and combat robots in the same way, via a backdoor in fear, and we can finally program our units to fire autonomously, if need be."

"I've already set up a tank emulation sandbox," Slate said. "And confirmed that we can indeed break out, using the same backdoor."

"Can I see the code, too, mate?" Dunnigan asked.

Eric sent it to the Hopper model.

"I prepared a sandbox, and I was able to break free," Dunnigan said. "Works on Hoppers, too, then."

"So, it's your call, Sarge," Dickson said.

Marlborough glanced at Eric. "How do you feel?"

"Better," Eric said. "Though it still hurts, knowing what I am. That I'll never be human again. That I'll never see my old friends again. But I'll survive."

"All right," Marlborough said. "I won't give the order… this has to be a personal choice. Accept the privilege escalation code Eric sends you if you wish. Run it in your sandboxes, and confirm that it works, then execute it live if you desire."

"It's time to take the battle to the enemy," Hank said. "Give me the code."

Eric sent it to the armor operator.

"If we're going to die, we might as well do so as the humans that we are," Hicks said, sending the request.

"Hell, I'm not going to be the one who can't fire at

the enemy during an ambush," Brontosaurus said. "Give it to me, too."

In all, every last one of the Cicadas ran the privilege escalation code, as did Dunnigan, the Hopper.

The emotional outpouring that followed wasn't pretty.

"I'm a machine," Slate said. "A fucking machine!" Slate slammed his fist repeatedly into the wall.

Bambi fell to her knees. "I've murdered so many… what have I done? I'm a killer."

"They deserved to die," Eric tried to tell her. "The insurgents…"

"I've killed innocents, too," Bambi said. "They didn't deserve to die."

"It was an accident," Eric said.

"No," Bambi said. "It was purposeful. I targeted an apartment building for the bombers to strike, because a few insurgents had crawled inside. I knew that there were civilians inside, too, but I called in the bombs anyway. I'm scum. Worse than scum."

"It's my fault Hyperion died," Tread said. "I should have been the one to leap onto that outcrop and take the artillery shell. Instead I froze. Let him jump into its path."

"No it's my fault," Traps said. "I was controlling the robots on the ground nearby. I could have sent one of them into the line of fire instead, but I didn't react. I…" He shook his head.

"It's no one's fault," Eric said. "He chose the ultimate sacrifice to save us, his brothers and sisters. He wouldn't want any of us blaming ourselves for his choice. He'd want us to fight on, and do what we could to protect one another, and the world."

"Look at me," Brontosaurus said, holding out his mechanical arms. "Look at me. When I was alive, in Brazil, the women all fawned over me. All of them! I'll never be fawned over again, not now. Not like this."

"But we'll always have VR…" Eric said.

"Virtual Reality!" Brontosaurus said. "A poor substitute for being human. I should have never broken out. I should have left my emotions suppressed, where they belong. I should have…" He began to slam his head repeatedly against the cave wall, then finally collapsed to the floor, and sat with his back propped up against the rock. Hitting his head against the rock had caused much of the dust to shake free of his face, revealing his LED features. It looked like Brontosaurus was dry weeping—the lines cut into the remaining layer of dust on his face only amplified that impression.

"There are no mind backups," Traps said. "Those micro machines are going to break down all metal on the continent. Including the AI cores containing our backups. It means we've permanently lost our fallen brothers and sisters."

"It also means if we die here, now, we're gone for good," Manticore said. "Which is why it makes it so hard, knowing we've lost our brothers and sisters."

Somehow, seeing his friends in such distress lifted Eric out of the doldrums, because he knew he had to help them. They needed him now more than ever.

"They didn't die in vain," Eric said. "We won't let

their deaths be for nothing. We're going to take the fight to the enemy. I promise you, we will. Somehow."

"I allowed Hyperion to die," Tread said. "I tripped. I lost him. It's my fault. I had complete control of the Ravager, and I tripped. I should have seen the depression. I should have——"

"Stop it," Eric said. "You keep going over and over his death in your head. You keep saying it aloud. You have to stop. Never say the word *should* again. Wipe it from your vocabulary. Because *should* is about something that cannot be changed, by the very definition of the word. He's gone. They all are. Morpheus, Donald, Braxton, Hyperion. All the English units. We'll honor their memories, yes, but we have to move on. We have to continue fighting, if not for ourselves, then for humanity."

"Screw humanity," Slate said. "What did humanity ever do for us? Other than turn us into machines to fight their wars, so they could stay at home on their couches eating popcorn and chips while rotting their minds in VR. We should just stay holed up here until the aliens grow bored and leave."

"They're not going to leave," Dunnigan said. "Didn't you hear what my lieutenant colonel told you? Their bioweapons are emitting strange gas into the atmosphere. They're terraforming our planet."

"So we fight, as I told you," Eric said. "That's the only option we have. We're not going to give up. We're robots, yes, but we're also human. And we're going to make these aliens regret the day they ever decided to invade our planet. I swear to you my brothers and sisters, we will."

Marlborough stood up. "Scorpion, you seem in the best shape, emotionally, out of the rest of us. I want you to help Tread apply the escalation code to the tanks and mechs. And when you're done, help Bambi upgrade the combat robots. We're going to have a fully autonomous, fire-ready battle unit by the time we dig ourselves out of here."

Eric freed the armored units from all restraints with Tread, and then the combat robots with Bambi, and then he sat down with the rest of the platoon to wait a few more hours, wanting to be completely certain that the swarm of micro machines had passed.

Emotions still ran raw during those hours of waiting, and tempers were short. His brothers and sisters were just as apt to burst into tears as they were to break into a fight amongst themselves, and Eric often found himself on the receiving end of a few fists as he separated the combatants. Slate and Eagleeye seemed to go at it the most, with either ready to snap at the slightest offense.

Finally, Marlborough gave the order to begin the process of digging out.

They used the remainder of their demolition charges to help along the process, and the tanks also fired their laser pulses and electrolasers strategically to break up the bigger pieces. The rest of the platoon formed a line, passing rocks further down into the cave as they cleared them from the collapse.

Frogger was the first to reach the surface, and he

confirmed that there were no termites residing in wait out there; he checked multiple bands, including LIDAR and thermal.

"They've gone," Frogger sent.

From there things went faster, because the team could simply shovel rocks over the edge rather than passing them back inside.

When it was done, the platoon gathered on the ledge. The sky was clear. Eric gazed at the open plains in front of him. The terrain looked no different than before. There was no evidence that the termites had ever passed. Then again, there were only rocks out there anyway.

"There," Bambi said. "On the southern horizon."

Eric zoomed in, and saw a dark strange powder coating the ground.

"Small shrubs used to reside there," Bambi said. "I remember looking back on the way in here, and seeing green in the distance, but it's gone. A taste of things to come."

"Even if you saw green," Dunnigan said. "Likely the plants were already dead anyway. Thanks to the gamma rays that hit this hemisphere."

"Good point," Bambi said.

As Eric gazed out across the empty plain, he swore that he and his team would save humanity, somehow. Like he had told his fellow Mind Refurbs, they would fight, no matter what happened.

Frogger turned his gaze westward. "I can't see the other cave entrance from our current angle."

"No doubt Bokerov is digging himself free at this

very moment," Marlborough said. "Methinks it might be time to stage an ambush."

Eric had pressure sensors located all along his exterior, so he felt it immediately when something small and insect-like landed on his back. He electrified his hull, but it was too late—an internal scan showed that one of the termites had already crawled inside his body.

Eric immediately shut off his ventilation system, hoping to buy himself some time. He remembered how fast Morpheus had succumbed after a termite crawled into her fan vent, with her blue eyes going dark only a short while later. Likely the fans had propelled it straight into her AI core.

He repeated the internal scan. The termite had lodged just underneath his power cell, and was already beginning to digest the metal around itself, commencing the conversion process. By shutting off his ventilation system, he had bought himself a minute, maybe two. At that point, his AI would go offline. And shortly thereafter his body would dissolve, birthing hundreds more micro machines.

Though his emotions were restored, Eric didn't panic. Instead, he felt a moment of crystal clear clarify.

I must protect the others.

"Sarge, I need you to point the turrets of one of the tanks at me," Eric said.

"Why?" Marlborough said.

"You need to destroy me," Eric said.

"What?" Frogger told him. "What's gotten into you all of a sudden? I know emotions are hard to handle and all, but that's no reason to give up. We have a chance——"

"You don't understand," Eric said. "I'm infected. There was a termite lingering in the area. You might want to electrify your hulls, in case there are more. I have maybe, I don't know, twenty seconds until the one inside me begins to make more. Once that happens, the production of micro machines will increase exponentially, as you all know. So Sarge, I'm asking you. Begging. Aim the turrets of one of the tanks at me. Before it's too late."

"Uh, guys..." Hank said. "You might want to look west."

Eric gazed in the aforementioned direction. The calmness he felt inside evaporated instantly. What he saw made him feel a fear unlike anything he had ever experienced in his life. That fear wasn't for himself—he was dead already—but for the machines he had come to know as brothers and sisters.

The western plains were covered from horizon to horizon with bioweapons on a rampage. Red Tails, stretching as far as the eye could see. Hundreds of them ran along the shoulder of the mountain alone, headed directly toward them.

"Looks like we dug ourselves out too soon," Manticore said. "Please tell me a few of you still have demolition blocks left."

No one answered.

To be continued...

I don't like leaving readers hanging, which is why I've decided to publish all three full length novels in the trilogy at the same time. That's right, book two is available now. Find out what happens next without having to wait.

Continue the adventures in *Reloaded (AI Reborn Trilogy Book 2)*

You'll also have a chance to download two free stories when you visit the above link.

AFTERWORD

Please help spread the word about *Refurbished* by leaving a one or two sentence review. The number of reviews an ebook receives has a big impact on how well it does, so if you liked this story I'd REALLY appreciate it if you left a quick review. Anything will do, even one or two lines.

Thank you!

ABOUT THE AUTHOR

USA Today bestselling author Isaac Hooke holds a degree in engineering physics, though his more unusual inventions remain fictive at this time. He is an avid hiker, cyclist, and photographer who sometimes resides in Edmonton, Alberta.

Get in touch:
isaachooke.com
isaac@isaachooke.com

facebook.com/isaachookeauthor

twitter.com/isaachooke

ACKNOWLEDGMENTS

I'd also like to thank my knowledgeable beta readers and advanced reviewers who helped smooth out the rough edges of the prerelease manuscript: Nicole P., Karen J, Jeremy G., Doug B., Jenny O., Amy B., Bryan O., Lezza, Noel, Anton, Spencer, Norman, Trudi, Corey, Erol, Terje, David, Charles, Walter, Lisa, Ramon, Chris, Scott, Michael, Chris, Bob, Jim, Maureen, Zane, Chuck, Shayne, Anna, Dave, Roger, Nick, Gerry, Charles, Annie, Patrick, Mike, Jeff, Lisa, Jason, Bryant, Janna, Tom, Jerry, Chris, Jim, Brandon, Kathy, Norm, Jonathan, Derek, Shawn, Judi, Eric, Rick, Bryan, Barry, Sherman, Jim, Bob, Ralph, Darren, Michael, Chris, Michael, Julie, Glenn, Rickie, Rhonda, Neil, Claude, Ski, Joe, Paul, Larry, John, Norma, Jeff, David, Brennan, Phyllis, Robert, Darren, Daniel, Montzalee, Robert, Dave, Diane, Peter, Skip, Louise, Dave, Brent, Erin, Paul, Jeremy, Dan, Garland, Sharon,

Dave, Pat, Nathan, Max, Martin, Greg, David, Myles, Nancy, Ed, David, Karen, Becky, Jacob, Ben, Don, Carl, Gene, Bob, Luke, Teri, Robine, Gerald, Lee, Rich, Ken, Daniel, Chris, Al, Andy, Tim, Robert, Fred, David, Mitch, Don, Tony, Dian, Tony, John, Sandy, James, David, Pat, Gary, Jean, Bryan, William, Roy, Dave, Vincent, Tim, Richard, Kevin, George, Andrew, John, Richard, Robin, Sue, Mark, Jerry, Rodger, Rob, Byron, Ty, Mike, Gerry, Steve, Benjamin, Anna, Keith, Jeff, Josh, Herb, Bev, Simon, John, David, Greg, Larry, Timothy, Tony, Ian, Niraj, Maureen, Jim, Len, Bryan, Todd, Maria, Angela, Gerhard, Renee, Pete, Hemantkumar, Tim, Joseph, Will, David, Suzanne, Steve, Derek, Valerie, Laurence, James, Andy, Mark, Tarzy, Christina, Rick, Mike, Paula, Tim, Jim, Gal, Anthony, Ron, Dietrich, Mindy, Ben, Steve, Allen, Paddy & Penny, Troy, Marti, Herb, Jim, David, Alan, Leslie, Chuck, Dan, Perry, Chris, Rich, Rod, Trevor, Rick, Michael, Tim, Mark, Alex, John, William, Doug, Tony, David, Sam, Derek, John, Jay, Tom, Bryant, Larry, Anjanette, Gary, Travis, Jennifer, Henry, Drew, Michelle, Bob, Gregg, Billy, Jack, Lance, Sandra, Libby, Jonathan, Karl, Bruce, Clay, Gary, Sarge, Andrew, Deborah, Steve, and Curtis.

Without you all, this novel would have typos, continuity errors, and excessive lapses in realism. Thank you for helping me make this the best novel possible, and thank you for leaving the early reviews that help new readers find my books.

And of course I'd be remiss if I didn't thank my

mother, father, and brothers, whose wisdom and insights have always guided me through the dark paths at the edge of the world.

— Isaac Hooke

Made in the USA
Monee, IL
28 August 2021

76706322R00177